TIME IS OF THE ESSENCE

Gail Logan

iUniverse, Inc.
New York   Bloomington

TIME IS OF THE ESSENCE

Copyright © 2009 Gail Logan

iUniverse books may be ordered through booksellers or by contacting:

iUniverse
1663 Liberty Drive
Bloomington, IN 47403
www.iuniverse.com
1-800-Authors (1-800-288-4677)

ISBN: 978-1-4401-7037-9 (pbk)
ISBN: 978-1-4401-7041-6 (ebk)

Printed in the United States of America

iUniverse rev. date: 9/16/2009

Introduction

Whether their introduction comes in undiluted book form or animated film, legends, folklore, myths and fairy tales touch the lives of people. The ancient classical myths are sources from which TIME IS OF THE ESSENCE draw inspiration. TIME IS OF THE ESSENCE's main source of inspiration though springs from James Churchward's writings depicting the existence of a mysterious lost civilization known as Mu. The book's intent is not to focus on a subject Churchward developed fully in his non-fiction books.

TIME IS OF THE ESSENCE'S intent is to draw the reader into a fantastic realm where adventure is combined with everyday problems that confront an ancient modern Martian Society of 16,000 years ago and a present day 21st C. Earth Society. If such a situation seems implausible from a scientific point of view: The sole purpose OF TIME IS OF THE ESSENCE is to entertain.

What is life? T'is but a madness.
What is life? A mere illusion,
Fleeting pleasure, fond delusion,
Short-lived joy, that ends in sadness,
Where most constant substance seems:
The dream of other dreams.

Pedro Calderon de la Barca

CHAPTER ONE

▼

Harry Worthy Jr. inattentively sat at his office desk. He restlessly gazed down at the floor's oriental carpet where early morning light cast fleeting patterns across the carpet's intricate design. The mesmerizing movement of light and shadow played havoc with the task he struggled to complete. He wearily closed his eyes then opened them. His attention shifted. His thoughts strayed far from the reality of the room's surroundings. He got up from where he sat on the 93rd floor of the Global Trade Mart. He crossed the room and hesitantly glanced at a landscape painting hanging upon the wall. Harry Jr. wasn't sure. He thought he'd recognized a scene in the painting other than the reality of the one depicted there. The Forgotten Island, the world his father had once glimpsed, the one Harry Jr., had longed to find, had never seemed so distant yet so near.

A discontented young man in his early thirties, Harry Jr. turned from studying the painting and returned to his desk. He picked up the report he'd planned to present later that day to Worthy International Enterprise executive board members. Bored by the task confronting him, he placed the report aside. He rose from his desk. He yawned and stretched. He reached for a mug of coffee atop his desk, and walked toward a window where he gazed at a flawlessly beautiful fall morning.

It was 8:00 am, November 13, 2003. The room was still. For a moment, even the street noises far below his window, seemed muffled and silent. Harry Jr. placed his empty coffee cup aside. Deciding to take a break, he walked toward the open door, and left his office suite. His footsteps echoed eerily as he moved along the hallway toward an adjacent office where a door had been left ajar. Harry Jr. wasn't sure what it was. Something compelled him to enter the room. He curiously gazed at the room before encountering the image of a slightly bent over gray haired old man who smilingly invited him to sit down.

"Allow me to introduce myself," said the man sitting opposite the comfortable chair where Harry Jr. now sat. "I'm Dr. Arthur Whitfield. I divide the time I spend here with my work at the Primary Institute for Advanced Study."

"And I'm Harry Worthy, Jr.", said the young man leaning forward and extending his hand so he could shake Whitfield's. He watched the old man get up and walk over to a strange looking contraption positioned in the center of the office room's floor.

"This is an example of the sort of paraphernalia I build here within this building and at the Institute too."

"What is that thing?" asked Harry Jr. getting up and crossing the room so he could get a closer look at the bright red two-seater vehicle.

The professor didn't answer the question. Instead, he continued to gaze longingly at the contraption."Oh, I do wish I could take it for a test drive" he said evasively.

"Where would you take it?" asked Harry Jr., pointing to four very solid walls surrounding them.

"Well, certainly not down the hall quipped the professor a little flippantly. That would be no journey at all. You see, Mr.Worthy----

"Oh, please call me Hal", interrupted Harry Jr. trying to compensate for a feeling of alienation. "All my friends call me that." Then Hal remembered that like most people, he had many acquaintances but few friends.

"Well then, Hal. Allow me to explain. In my string theory study at the institute, I've discovered dimensions where minute objects may slip and disappear into obscurity without being missed. You see, in their raw state, the strings that make up the cosmic fabric of everything, defy the realization of time and space before they change shape and encounter one another. In that cosmic world, there is no notion of before. It's only when these infinitesimally small strings undergo sympathetic vibrations that they encounter space and time."

"What do you mean by sympathetic vibrations?" asked Hal.

"Call it acknowledgement of a sort". One particle meets another and they encounter space and time."

Hal ran his hand over the strange contraption. "May I sit in it?"

"Of course" replied the professor, drawing a hankerchief from his pocket so he could dust off the time machine. "Oh, I do wish I could take it for a whirl. If only I could slip into obscurity without being missed. I'm afraid I lack the daring. Everything I've ever learned or studied has indicated to me that to go beyond the speed of light is to disintegrate entirely. An object's speed through space is a reflection of how much an object's motion through time is diverted,"

"Diverted where?" asked Hal a little impatiently.

"I've been trying to figure that out", replied the professor thoughtfully. "So

I've devised this machine. You see, my boy, within string theory there are more than the usual four dimensions (three space and one time). Once one has crashed the four dimensional barriers, one is set free and goes soaring into other dimensions, other worlds, and outside the limits of time and space."

"Really?" replied Hal skeptically. He thought the likelihood of exploring another dimension improbable especially since he knew the professor's string theory approach had never been tested.

"An object's speed through space is cancelled when one crashes the light barrier. There is no passage of time at light speed", said the professor sitting down beside Hal in the contraption and gazing at the time machine's control panel.

"A photon that emerged from the big bang is the same age as it was then", he said aloud to himself as if Hal wasn't listening or was no longer there. "If only one could simulate the big bang", he said morosely. The professor, who had seemed oblivious to everything but his sense of personal inadequacy was suddenly startled by a deafening noise and shadowy darkness. He had hardly finished speaking when, Hal grabbed him by the shoulder and cried, "Look out!" A passenger airplane struck the north tower of the Global Trade Mart. The building swayed, and the two men were hurled to the floor with the crash impact. At first they lay on the floor stunned. Then having realized what had happened to them they sat upright and gazed in horror at the enormous gaping hole in the building. A portion of the ceiling above had collapsed into the office. Heat and flames from beneath them seared the room where they were now trapped. Screams and cries from terrified people were heard coming from floors above and beneath them. The sickening smell of burning human flesh and airplane fuel made both men want to vomit. The heat surrounding them was almost overwhelming. Whitfield, covered his mouth and nose with a hankerchief, and wept at the terrifying images of burning tables and chairs and melting office supplies.

Hal crawled around the room and desperately looked for an escape from the building's encroaching flames. His clothes and those worn by the professor were torn and burned from the sudden devastating crash. "We're doomed", he cried.

"Perhaps not yet", said Whitfield, valiantly responding to Hal's remark. Still sitting upon the floor, he managed to crawl toward the time machine. He struggled to his feet, and told Hal to be seated next to him in it.

"Fasten your seat belt", he shouted and handed Hal a crash helmet. "I've never touched the computerized emergency switch before", he said with trembling hand. We've nothing to lose from the consequences of journeying into the unknown now". Whitfield then pushed a lever forward to sustain maximum power from the machine.

"Let's go for it", said Hal.

Humming, like the music of the spheres at the dawn of creation, the time machine seemed to be moving yet at the same time appeared to be going no where. The building's fire beneath them was gone. There was no gaping hole, no smell of burning flesh or airplane fuel.

"My boy", the time machine has diverted a catastrophe by erasing it from the pages of history".

"You mean we haven't died?" asked Hal.

"Of course not. My machine has removed us from harm's way. The catastrophic event has been frozen and sent back in time. Nothing has happened in the conscious realm you and I acknowledge as reality. Our universe is intact. The destructive event we thought we witnessed has been pushed into oblivion, away from a universe where there is only one perfect equation, one perfect reality."

After he spoke, the professor pressed a few more buttons on the time machine's control panel and began singing a classic old children's song. "'Row, row, row, your boat gently down the stream, merrily, merrily, merrily, merrily, life is but a dream.'"

Hal closed his eyes. He'd remembered his mother Jaime singing that song to him when he was a child and couldn't fall asleep at night. His parents would be relieved to know he hadn't died in the Global Trade Mart. "Thank God, I'm still alive" he thought pinching his arm.

"Well, I guess I'd better get back to the business at hand," said Hal feeling foolish for reacting to what he now thought must have been a terrible hallucination. "We've both had a bad dream this morning", he said starting to unfasten his seat belt.

"Ah, yes, my boy. But what a dream awaits us. You mustn't leave now. If I remember correctly, your father made a most extraordinary journey to an island many years ago in search of an old friend of mine, John Pelletier."

"You know Pelletier?" asked Hal.

"Yes. He stumbled upon an extraordinary civilization quite by accident."

"I know", said Hal, "I tried to rediscover the lost island several years ago but failed".

"You mustn't give up so easily". Whitfield instructed Hal to sit down again in the time machine. Hal hesitantly fastened his seat belt and placed the crash helmet on his head.

Whitfield pushed the time machine's throttle forward to warp speed. Again, the humming noise like the music of the spheres filled the room. Hal felt a strange sensation sweep over him. The light in the room changed. He felt himself being transported, drawn upward from the Global Trade Mart until the time machine now had taken the shape of a space capsule, and the men within it were soaring above New York City. The confusion of busy streets had disappeared. "We've left the city behind", said Whitfield, who gazed downward. He knew they were leaving the planet behind too. The Earth had become an infinitesimally small atom until it had disappeared entirely and was absorbed by the infinite grasp of outer space. Hal gazed at the scene in front of him. He suddenly became aware of his personal absorption into an infinite universe. "Size must be of little consequence here. There must be something much larger underlying the reality of all this" he thought.

"Oh for heaven's sake" cried the professor. "I'm afraid I've entirely overshot the mark. We must somehow find our way through this cosmic maze and re-enter the solar system. We don't want to be swept away by a time warp and end up on some God forsaken planet."

Hal gazed downward from a small capsule window. The planet they orbited was reddish in hue. "Steady we go" said Hal, thinking the planet they orbited couldn't be Earth. "I hope we've found our way back to the right solar system."

"Allow me to show you another time and place", said Whitfield. "You wouldn't want to visit Earth right now: In some places, it's quite inhospitable. Large beasts of prey are everywhere. Only the continents of Earth's Mu or Atlantis, originally settled by Martian and Venusian settlers, and now both colonies of Mars and Venus, are as civilized as their mother planets."

"But Mars is desert" contradicted Harry. "Its temperatures are unbearable".

"Nonsense" replied the professor. "The temperatures on Mars are far more hospitable than temperatures were earlier at the Global Trade Mart. It's all a matter of timing. We are approaching Mars as it once was not as men in the time and place where you come from perceive it to be." Hal was skeptical. His desire for adventure into the beyond had momentarily left him. He longed for familiar landscapes but he knew he had to trust the professor if ever he was to find his way home again through time and space.

The time capsule gently entered Mars' gravitational field. It easily slipped into orbit as if it were defying matter itself. There was no friction, no violent entry. The music of the spheres was heard again. Then the time machine, no longer a space capsule but an odd looking contraption, slowly landed upon Martian soil.

Hal cautiously stepped from the time machine. The momentous journey, full of wonder and tinged with anxiety, had made him feel weak and dizzy. He gazed into the distance where huge snow capped volcanic mountains loomed, and where a strange seemingly fathomless canyon appeared.

Whitfield, who stood alongside Hal said, "The canyon's river, according to the machine's computerized report", stretches for 8,000 miles before it empties into a sea."

"Where are we?" asked Hal sounding bewildered.

"With an insouciant air Whitfield said, "where we are depends on when we are. According to the time machine's calculations, we've traveled 16,000 years ago back in time when Mars was a flourishing empire within the solar system."

Hal listened to the professor with a mixture of dazed attention and disbelief. "I guess we won't need breathing apparatus to survive here", he said gazing at an exotic green, orange and red landscape composed of gnarled primeval looking trees. "Why is it that I didn't notice that city when we first landed?" he asked pointing in awe at all the fascinating things emerging before his eyes.

"It's because the city you see in the distance had not yet fully materialized to your concept of it in time and space. You're adjusting to the time zone into which you've now entered. It's as if you've had to reset your watch but you've made the quantum leap. You won't need a space helmet. From a human's standpoint, Mars is a very habitable planet."

"You sound as if you've visited this place before" said Hal.

"No, I haven't "replied Whitfield, who with a mysterious air said, "My friend, John Pelletier, who many refer to as late and elusive, has visited the Martian landscape as we encounter it today, and informed me of its hospitable climate. I didn't believe the report until now. Pelletier makes it a practice, since his return to Earth's immortal lost city, of traveling back through time to cities of the legendary golden lost age."

"Will we meet Pelletier today?" asked Hal

"Probably not. He spends most of his time these days with Ramira and Vorelis in the lost city on the legendary Forgotten Isle."

"Have you any way of contacting him today?" asked Hal, who was anxious about finding their way around the new environment.

"I'm not usually a name dropper. Mention of Pelletier's name, once we encounter some Martian inhabitants might be sufficient for obtaining the red carpet treatment".

Hal was skeptical. His parents, who'd never met Pelletier, knew him by reputation only, and that reputation wasn't especially glowing.

"What if the Martians don't really like Pelletier? What if he's done something to offend them?" he asked.

"I can assure you that Pelletier has done nothing to offend his Martian friends. I'm sure they respect him."

Hal realized he and Whitfield were very much on their own. He advised his friend that it might be unwise to stray too far from the time machine. "Nonsense" said Whitfield, who now wearing a jacket offered a spare one to his friend: You might need this. The wind seems a little brisk today."

Hal put on the jacket the professor had handed him. He then gazed upward, and basked in the sun's welcoming warmth as light streamed down through the branches of trees.

"Listen", said Whitfield who raised his hand and pointed ahead. A great song was coming from a golden structure resembling a temple laden with precious alloys. A chorus of welcoming voices, lyrical and sublime, echoed and reverberated around the men before suddenly becoming silent.

"Are you sure we haven't died and gone to heaven?" asked Hal thinking the setting in which they'd found themselves was too surreal to be actual. The sound of faint music resumed. Enticed by its beauty, the men continued in pursuit of it.

"We've entered another world. I assure you, we haven't set foot in heaven", Whitfield reached for his hankerchief so he could blow his nose.

Lying on the outskirts of the city, the temple appeared to be about a quarter mile from where they stood. As they approached it, the music first increased in volume then became almost inaudible. The intricately carved temple doors, laden with gold and silver, were open as Hal followed the professor into the edifice.

"I believe the building is empty", said Hal who having looked around could find no sign of habitation. The professor didn't answer him. Instead he continued to listen to the singing that now seemed to be coming from every corner of the temple.

The men continued to wander through the huge edifice, seeming to lead nowhere. They were about to give up their search for temple occupants and return to the time machine: Then, from behind a pillar, a furry creature, the size of a man stepped forward and greeted them with a huge extended paw. Startled by the sight of the unusual looking creature, Hal wanted to run from it. Whitfield caught his arm preventing him from doing so.

Whitfield shook the creature's paw that wasn't a paw at all but resembled a human hand with five perfect fingerlike appendages.

"Hello", said the huge mole in a polite but rather a reserved tone of voice.

"My name is Murdock. I act as intermediary between the human population and other beings of this planet", he said extending a paw to Hal so he could shake it too. I've been told that I resemble certain species of your earthly animal population. I'm much larger than most moles. Unlike them, I have excellent eyesight but like them I have a beautiful fur coat which is welcome in this sometimes cool Martian climate."

Light from a strange but beautiful stained glass window streamed down upon the mole as he displayed the deep gray color of his fur's rich texture. Murdock then took two steps forward, bowed and said proudly. "I'm also special emissary to Her Majesty the Queen."

"Which queen is that?" asked Hal.

"Why, Queen Myaca," replied Murdock. "She witnessed your progress today as your time machine made its way through time and space. She has instructed me to help you acclimate yourself to your new surroundings. I shall act as your host for a few days. Eventually, you shall be granted a private audience with the queen, who is eager to hear of your journey through time and space."

"Don't you people--I mean beings, travel through time and space all the time?" asked Hal.

"Yes", replied Murdock. "Her Majesty knows that the humans from your time and place don't. She admires your courage for venturing into the unknown today. You have pulled off a wonderfully rare feat for the beings of your era."

"We had to do it", interrupted Professor Whitfield. "Hal and I had to save not only ourselves but the moment too."

Hal noticed that the singing they'd heard earlier had stopped.

"The voices," he stammered, "were sublime."

"Ah yes" replied Murdock, "You were listening to the interplanetary choral competition. I had the competition beamed down so that I could listen to it while I worked. It seems Venus has won the competition, with representatives from Jupiter's moons placing second and third."

"Did Mars place?" asked Hal.

"We Martians didn't place this time", replied Murdock who pointed to ten awards displayed upon a computerized screen.

"The voices sounded as if we were standing in the same room with them," said Hal.

"Yes, the transmission of sound was excellent. The competition took place on Venus this time."

"I see", said Hal, noticing mathematical equations displayed upon a computerized screen. "What are you working on?" he asked.

Murdock was thoughtful before answering the question. He chose his words carefully. Then taking Whitfield's arm in his furry one, and followed by Hal, Murdock led them to a room adjacent to the one where they'd been standing.

"There is more than one reason for your visit to our planet today. After you evaded destruction, our paths might never have crossed had you not also realized that you could defy the events of history by denying their reality in time and space. What I have in my possession, what I was about to show you, Professor Whitfield, is a formula for the perfect equation. Whether or not you ever solve the equation depends totally upon your civilization's support and initiative in helping you to do so."

"What do you mean?" asked Whitfield.

"You shall learn more about what I've just said to you when you meet with representatives from our solar system and nearby galaxy planets. Until then, please relax after your perilously long journey. I will show you to your accommodations later. First allow me to show you my burrow."

Murdock led his guests down huge white marbles steps winding deep beneath the temple's foundation."My burrow may seem elaborate by most mole's standards: I assure you that it should meet with your human expectations of comfort."

The burrow, encompassed by unseen lighting, was spotlessly clean, and sumptuously furnished with Martian antiques. Displayed upon the burrow's walls, were portraits of Murdock's ancestors.

"My father, grandfather and great-grandfather, were all scientific advisors to the Imperial Family. They divided their time as I do with periodic visits to the planet Venus, one of the seats of Chucaran Imperial Power. Queen Myaca of our Martian planet and King Menelus of Venus, rule the solar system—but of course Saturn is the undisputed ruler and ultimate authority within that hierarchy."2

Amazed at Murdock's flawless English, Whitfield and Hal asked him where he'd learned to speak so fluently.

"I had a microchip implanted enabling me to speak not only all the languages of the solar system and some of the galaxy but languages of the past and of the future such as English. In all, I'm able to speak over 50,000 languages, an inbuilt accomplishment I find to be useful since I often come in contact with time travelers from distant eras such as yours. I must say I do enjoy reading some of your great works of literature—the plays of Shakespeare, the writings of Milton, not to mention the Greek tragedies in the original Greek. I also enjoy reading modern works of your era, some of which have been made into Hollywood films. Your planet has been beset by much violence and such turmoil is reflected in your art and literature. I do wish I had time for more reading but I'm devoted to my duties as Scientific Advisor and Emissary to Her Majesty.

"In contrast to your art and literature," said Murdock inviting his friends to sit down in chairs opposite him, "you will find our art and literature to reflect the peace and tranquility of our age, the Golden Age." 1

"Murdock pointed to paintings upon his burrow's walls of landscapes and seascapes attesting to the planet's great natural beauty. "They were done by my cousin", he said proudly.

Hal and Whitfield, who seemed impressed by the beautiful paintings, were hesitant to ask Murdock where were Mars' human inhabitants? As if anticipating the question, he led his guests down a hall where they stood before a portrait of a very beautiful young woman. Turning from his guests, Murdock poured himself a glass of sherry from a flask resting on a nearby table, and toasted the image of Queen Myaca. Then reaching for two other glasses, he poured his guests a glass of sherry too. After replenishing his own glass, Murdock invited Hal and the professor to be seated in chairs opposite him.

The sherry, sweet and nutty in flavor, was from Murdock's own vineyard.

"I must remember to bring a bottle with me when the Queen receives us", he said. "This particular wine is one of her favorites."

Later, after they had drunk a toast to their arrival, Murdock introduced a robot butler to them. "Rufus will show you to your accommodations", he said. "Just let him know should you need anything. Later I will take you on a tour of the Sun Temple".

*   *   *   *

Gold and marble stairs leading to an ancient door wound precipitously from Murdock's burrow to the edifice above. Following Murdock, who led the way, Hal and Whitfield stepped from a spiral gold staircase and gazed at a portion of the Sun temple they hadn't seen earlier.

"You've perhaps seen chairs such as these in the tombs of Earth's Egyptian pharaohs," said Murdock proudly sitting down in one. "All the chairs and most of the furnishings in the Sun Temple are similar to some discovered in Earth's major sun temples.

This temple's objects and furnishings are revered symbols of the sun. Without the sun's radiance we would be lost in space without any concept of time. The ever-present sun magnifies life within human and non-human recorded history.2 Left is the illuminated corridor leading to past eras. The one to the right leads to the future."

"Are predictions regarding the future kept in the temple as well?" asked Hal.

"Some replied Murdock, pointing to a large bookshelf:

"The news of the future isn't good," he said nervously turning his back to his guests. "Right now, there is peace and prosperity. We can't ignore the mounting tensions with our nearest neighbor Venus. Menelus is becoming a threat. He is ignoring the importance of maintaining a peaceful solar system. He wants power and he doesn't want to share it with Mars or the less powerful moons within the solar system.

"We Martian ministers have come to the unanimous conclusion that the past is far more important than the future. If the future of the solar system is to be saved, it must be saved by those courageous enough to return to the past and cancel the errors that have occurred there. History holds the record of too many atrocities. The destruction of Earth's Mu and Atlantis could have been avoided if men had been forewarned of impending tragedy. Mars and Venus wouldn't be desolate in your time if beings in our time had thought to cherish what peace they had by imparting good will throughout the solar system and beyond.

"Even nearest neighbors on planets in closest solar systems warned us of our downward spiral toward self-destruction. The powers that be of this solar system ignored the warnings. Our friends in distant galaxy solar systems, not wanting to take sides or to become involved in a solar system war, turned from us. We were alone in our misery. Heavenly war broke out", said Murdock sadly. "That is the future confronting our solar system. That is why your visit to us today is so important. That is why the Queen demands an audience with you. I'm sure she won't allow you to leave this planet and return to your time and place on Earth until you help us save this time and age from self-destruction."

"You are asking the impossible of us", replied Whitfield.

"No, we're not asking you to do the impossible", said Murdock. "Your own future salvation depends upon ours as well."

"I don't see how", replied Hal stubbornly.

Unmoved by Hal's response, Murdock continued to elaborate.

"When your father visited the lost city on Earth's Forgotten Island, he realized he had to go home and change the way he did business. Now that he has done so and his business has become an example to Earth of good industrial environmental management, you and the professor must carry on the work he started but on a larger scale. Your mission is to impart solar system peace and prosperity. That mission begins here by devising a strategy to bring it about."

"I don't think either of us understands what you mean" interrupted Whitfield.

"Please, let me explain", said Murdock. "When you were at the Global Trade Mart, you entered a second dimension: You denied the existence of the one you were in and left in your time machine for a neighboring higher dimension."

"That dimension was your time and space", interrupted Whitfield.

"Not entirely" replied Murdock. "The dimension you entered was your concept of our dimension in time and space. You didn't enter it until you had taken care of business in your own time by first cleaning up the mess at the Global Trade Mart. You have entered our peaceful realm because your individual consciences were ready for the encounter. We need peaceful allies such as you. Unfortunately, there are negative forces in neighboring dimensions trying to erode the Golden Age by dragging it into a dark hole. We mustn't allow those forces to gain momentum within our world or future worlds.

The perfect equation must be solved. That is where your expertise and ours come together", said Murdock.

Hal felt his heart sink. "My father and grandfather never attempted to revisit the forgotten island. They felt as though they'd been expelled from paradise."

"And they were expelled from it" agreed Murdock. "The situation on Mars is different. We are extending a welcome to you and Whitfield. Vorelis, Pelletier and I have come to the unanimous conclusion that the future shouldn't depend upon a few who gaze at impending doom from the safety of their Golden Era. Valiant men must reach out in all directions. They must penetrate neighboring dimensions and heal the ills confronting us. You will learn more of how this problem is to be dealt with when in a few days we meet with the Queen.

"Until then, I hope you'll allow me to show you something of Mars as it is now over 16,000 years ago." Hal turned from Murdock. He started to walk down the corridor leading to the future. He halted when Murdock warned him that few were permitted to go into the future. "It's much too dangerous right now."

"What do you mean?" asked Hal.

"You'll discover the reason soon enough."

Hal turned from the corridor. He gazed uneasily at the Sun Temple's stained glass windows as sunlight from above streamed down upon them. A peaceful silence pervaded the temple as Murdock mentioned to his friends that he knew the hour of the earthling's customary mealtime was approaching.

"An array of dishes is being prepared. It is my hope they shall meet with your approval. Following lunch, I'll take you sightseeing in the nearby Martian city. You saw it materialize earlier today when you first set foot on our planet".

Following lunch, Hal and the professor stepped from the Sun Temple into Murdock's touring vehicle. The craft hovered twenty feet or so above ground before alighting in the center of a busy metropolis where Martians, some human, humanoid or animal like individuals went about their daily routine.

"Our diversity is one of our strengths," commented Murdock. "City residents come from all over the solar system. Some even come from planets within the galaxy. You'll find most of the beings here to be not only amiable but peace loving as well. This community is the essence of what the Golden Age symbolizes."

Murdock stopped to purchase some fresh fruit from a Martian street vendor."I prefer doing my shopping here rather than in our enormous greenhouses where fruits and vegetables are genetically altered." He then selected some huge red pomegranates.

Placing them in a shopping bag he'd brought with him that day, he said, "They're beautiful and red just like the Martian planet". Murdock then reached into a valise and paid a hairy creature resembling a rabbit. The vendor's whiskers twitched with pleasure in payment for the goods. "Rupert owns several farms", said Murdock introducing the rabbit vendor to his friends.

"I have a farm on Venus as well as one here where I spend half of my time", said Rupert. "When Martian fruits are ripe, and in season I like to visit this planet."

"Rupert and I have some jolly good times together when he's in town", said Murdock.

"Yes,"agreed Rupert. "I only wish the Martian growing season were longer. I hate to return home to Venus where I find myself working much too hard in a rather warm disagreeable climate."

After leaving Rupert, Murdock explained that ever since Rupert's mate had died, he'd been very downcast and spent too many hours by himself. "When he's in town, he sometimes needs a bit of cheering up so I always invite him to my burrow for dinner and a few laughs. The Venusians love to laugh. If they seem a bit tipsy at times it's probably due to the fact that their planet turns in a counter clock wise direction."

As Murdock talked, he also pointed out several different species from neighboring planets and galaxies. "Those waxy looking little men with the huge football shaped eyes are the ones who've been the subject of so much controversy during your era. They come and go in their flying saucers, and are great time travelers and explorers of the universe. They call no galaxy or solar system home. They are what you might refer to as rolling stones. I can assure you, they aren't as frightening as they appear. Once you get to know them, you'll be fascinated to hear of their adventures throughout time and space. Although they owe no allegiance to any government, Queen Myaca has made them welcome in her realm. In return, they are loyal to her. No doubt they would help protect her Martian domain should it ever come under attack."

Hal and the professor, who'd been staring at the waxy looking little humanoids, had heard of earthly abduction tales.

"They're galactic pirates" said Hal.

"Not really" replied Murdock. "Human imagination plays a large role in the close encounters to which you refer."

"Just the same" said Hal, "I think neither the professor nor I wish to be introduced to your humanoid friends."

"Perhaps you should schedule a meeting for us with them at another time," said Whitfield, who unlike Hal was curious and really wanted to meet the strange alien visitors.

"As you wish", said Murdock who led his guests to his hovercraft parked mid air about ten feet off the ground. Murdock then pulled a remote from his valise, and pointed it at the vehicle. In an instant, the vehicle was upon the ground. A door swung open and the passengers stepped inside the craft.

Murdock adjusted the hovercraft's visor controlling the amount of sun glare allowed to enter the vehicle's encompassing cabin window. He then released the air anchor keeping the craft from moving off into space, and adjusted his seat belt for maximum comfort.

Seated in the rear of the craft, Hal and the professor, gazed down at Martian city streets where beings lived and worked. Those on business stepped into sleekly designed Martian buildings, others on daily errands, made their way toward shops and markets.

On the outskirts of the Martian city were public parks and gardens. Huge flowers, some as tall as trees, bent slightly in the breeze. "I've never seen such large tulips", remarked Hal who looked on with fascination when a huge petal from one fell nearly grazing the hovercraft.

"Martian tulips require much care and attention", said Murdock. "Their beauty makes the effort entirely worthwhile," he said with a sneeze, and pointed to a field of wild roses intertwined with an exotic variety of honey suckle and pink and purple wisteria. Murdock allowed the craft to glide over the spectacular garden just long enough for the men to smell the perfume.

"The flowers' aroma is overwhelming when the garden blooms are at their peak. It's best to view these flowers from the air. Such a vantage point offers visitors to this paradise a fast exit from it". Murdock then released the air anchor demonstrating such an exit, and the craft flew off to another Martian destination.

In the distance, snow capped peaks surrounded a sapphire sea, and pink waves close to shore, beat upon multi-colored rocks of different shapes and sizes.

"Why are the waves pink?" asked Hal who distinctly remembered seeing only a very blue ocean,

"To the casual observer the ocean is a bright sapphire color. When the water near shore becomes shallow the waves reflect the color of the Martian pink sand", said Murdock, who with the aid of the craft's landing system, deftly maneuvered the vehicle between two monstrously huge volcanic peaks. Within seconds, the craft sat on a very inaccessible beach, and the craft's occupants alighted from it. The cool Martian sea breeze at times gusted heavily. Hal finally put on the jacket he'd carried under his arm.

"Look" said Whitfield, pointing to an enormous species swimming parallel to the shoreline

"What you see is a species of reptile similar to ones that used to thrive in your Earthly seas but is now extinct."

"Is the sea serpent friend or foe?" asked Hal who thought the creature resembled something from earth's Jurassic era

"He is neither", replied Murdock. "He's just a shy creature who enjoys his own privacy and anonymity too much to have any time for land animals like ourselves who find him so fascinating."

"Too bad" said Hal watching the creature plunge first his huge pink scaly head, followed by a pink scaly tail, beneath the water's surface before disappearing into the depths below. "I must say, that creature creates something of a splash", he said stepping back from an enormous oncoming wave crashing along the pink sand beach. He then bent, picked up a fluted pink seashell that had washed ashore with the wave and placed the souvenir in his pocket. Murdock then suggested to the professor, who was studying the pink seaweed, that it was time to return to the Sun Temple.

Once the hovercraft was airborne and flying over an area where the time machine had been left, the Professor asked Murdock if they could check on his time machine. Murdock, who seemed embarrassed to think that Whitfield needed to keep an eye on his precious time machine, responded a bit huffily.

"I assure you professor, nobody around here would steal your time machine. Time travel is no curiosity to us Martians. We've been doing it for centuries. If you'd feel more secure about the matter, we'll whisk over that mountain where the machine is parked, attach it to the hover craft's electro magnetic tether, and take it with us."

Within minutes, the time machine had been towed inside the Sun Temple's main entranceway. Murdock then draped a huge gold cloth over the contraption and said. "Here, this should keep your machine out of harm's way. Don't you have a disguise mode on the remote you carry with you? I really believe this cloth, since it's spun from gold, is more valuable than your time machine."

"Please don't concern yourself with the problem", replied Whitfield. "Your assurance that the machine is safe from theft, is good enough for me—after all, this is the Golden Age and people— beings just don't do that sort of thing", he said with a bit of a smirk.

Murdock, who'd stuck his pointed furry nose into the air as if he hadn't heard a word Whitfield had said, didn't bother to comment.

Later, following evening refreshments when the pomegranate tea had made both Hal and the professor a bit drowsy, Murdock again reminded his guests, rather casually, that travel into the future during Mars' Golden Age was forbidden. Since at that time, both men seemed a bit incapacitated, neither was about to argue the matter but the point had been made.

When Murdock left Hal and the professor to themselves, it wasn't long before Hal knocked upon the door of Whitfield's room. After opening the door, the professor told Hal to be seated, in a chair opposite him. Hal began the conversation with a worried expression on his face. "If we are forbidden to traverse the temple corridor leading to the future, might we also be denied access to the time machine? Both lead to the future."

"I've been thinking the same thing", said Whitfield. "I'm sure that Murdock and his Martian friends have the means to block our access to the time machine if they so desire. Let's not jump to conclusions though. Murdock seems hospitable enough. We must wait until we've had the audience with Queen Myaca before we take matters into our own hands." Whitfield then took a computerized key from his vest pocket. After pressing a few buttons on the key's remote panel, he announced that the time machine's lock was reprogrammed and inaccessible to anyone who might tamper with the controls.

"Don't overtax yourself with worry. Put your mind at ease and try to get a good night's sleep. Murdock has told me that tomorrow he wants to show us more of the wonders of the Martian landscape", he said as Hal got up to leave. Whitfield then patted Hal, on the back, led him toward the door, opened it for him, and said "good night".

Hal didn't return directly to his rooms. Instead, he walked down a long corridor before spotting a strange pathway leading to an exit. As he approached the exit he climbed steep stairs winding in a circular pattern toward a door. The door swung open and Hal stepped outside where he gazed up at the

Martian evening sky ablaze with a spectacular aurora borealis. Earlier in the day, he'd listened as Murdock told him that unlike Earth, Mars had not just two magnetic poles but four, produced by low levels of magnetic radiation emitted by the planet's diminishing magnetic field. "In your time, Mars has no magnetic core but in ours, there still exists a weak core which shields this planet from powerful solar and galactic radiation" he had said.

Hal continued to gaze at a brilliant sky now strewn with stars and galaxies. In the distance, he saw a small but brilliantly luminous sphere he knew to be Earth. He tried to imagine what life must be like on Earth 16,000 years ago. He longed to travel back to his own time there. He knew that unless he and Whitfield were finally granted access to the time machine, they were marooned, virtual prisoners of the lush exotic Martian landscape.

Placing his hands in his pockets, Hal wearily yawned as he walked amidst the sweet fragrance of a primeval garden. The fragrance soon became overwhelming. Hal's knees started to buckle beneath him. Then feeling a tap on his shoulder, he strained to see who was there as Murdock lifted him to his feet and said: "You really should return to your lodgings. It's quite late. I have planned a long day for us tomorrow."

Still overcome by the weakness he felt from breathing the fragrant night air, Hal allowed Murdock to take his arm and lead him back to the Sun Temple.

"I'm used to the Martian evening air but for strangers from alien environments, the evening air here can be quite overwhelming. I'll have a special tea sent to your room. It should serve as an antidote to the effect the night air might have had upon you. Once you are used to our Martian environment, you'll discover that the effects you now suffer from will entirely disappear", said Murdock starting to leave.

Thanking Murdock for his kind attention, Hal slumped into a large chair. When the tea was brought to him only minutes later, Hal slowly sipped the delicious warm liquid. Then placing the cup in its saucer, he fell asleep in the chair where he dreamed of home and familiar faces-- his mother and father, his grandparents and, of course his little son.

"They must think I'm dead", he thought when in the morning he finally awoke. The memory of Earth's dear friends and landscape stayed with him and haunted him-- so did the stress of being in a strange new environment. At breakfast he almost begged off joining the Professor and Murdock on the planned visit to the Martian Scientific Palace until Whitfield suggested to Hal that rejection of such an invitation would be looked upon as rude among new found Martian friends. "I guess I'll have to go", said Hal who hated to have his morning and free time so well planned by Murdock.

*   *   *   *

Murdock parked his hovercraft in an area reserved for distinguished visitors. Once his guests had alighted from the craft, he began leading them toward a huge imposing building that appeared at first to be triangular in shape but with closer observation, was actually rectangular.

"Why the building appears to be open on all sides", said Hal quickly withdrawing his hand from trying to penetrate a very solid transparent substance. He then watched as Murdock nodded to a friendly robot guard.

"Welcome" said Sarius, who'd recognized Murdock "You may proceed through the building's entranceway."

"The entranceway remains blocked by a small force field for those denied access," remarked Murdock who chatted amiably as they made their way toward the building's main auditorium. As they traversed a huge corridor they gazed upward and noticed the building's magnificent ceiling. The images of stars and galaxies surrounded them within the focus of a huge unseen ceiling telescope. Murdock made a slight gesture with his paw and the field of stars and galaxies disappeared. In an instant, the room was transformed to a pleasant sun-filled environment where lush exotic plants grew around them from behind a protective transparent screen.

Without noticing that they had instantly changed from one floor to another level, Hal and Whitfield were surprised to find themselves seated inside an auditorium, where several hundred beings from other planets and galaxy solar systems waited to be addressed by today's speaker.

Murdock nodded his head in recognition. Hal and Whitfield looked on in amazement: A lizard headed creature gently extended a five-fingered claw in greeting to him. Then, turning to his friends, Murdock said to Thetis, "Allow me to introduce our new found time travelers. Hal and Professor Whitfield dropped in on us rather recently. I've been busy showing them around."

"Really? I'm afraid today's meeting is about to begin. Perhaps later I'll have the pleasure of getting to know your guests and learning more about the nature of their visit."

Murdock then invited Thetis to share the honor of introducing the guest speaker, and gestured for him to mount the stage with him.

"Beings and Friends on behalf of Her Majesty Queen Myaca, the planet Mars welcomes you and our distinguished speaker, Medusaurus, who visits us today from the outer reaches of our galaxy." Murdock then stepped aside so Thetis could say a few introductory words too.

During his introduction, Medusaurus, a green horny reptile sat centerstage in a chair fashioned entirely from reeds taken from his favorite habitat. He adjusted an invisible microphone and hearing device affixed to the top of his scaly head. Then standing up and with a whisk of his long leathery tail, he dimmed the room's lighting. Taking immense pleasure in being in the spotlight, Medusaurus was in no hurry, to deliver a lecture. He turned to Murdock and Thetis so he could have a word with them as species, representing various rungs of the evolutionary scale, waited patiently for him to begin his lecture.

After he'd told a few galactic jokes, the lecture began and its serious tone became apparent: "We are aware that the Martians and Venusians, who appear to be living in peace are on the brink of war unless they unite in a common effort to solve the perfect equation. Failure to comply with galactic treaties designed to boost progress and peace within our solar systems, will not be tolerated. One small tear within the fabric of space might bring us all to annihilation if ensuing tensions among Martians and Venusians aren't appeased."

After the guest speaker had left the podium, Murdock introduced Hal and Whitfield to several Martian dignitaries. Sylvanius and Proteus nodded their heads politely."I trust you both will be present at the upcoming meeting with Queen Myaca."

"I'm afraid neither of us will be attending the meeting", said Sylvanius.

"Menelus has invited us to a symposium he is hosting on Venus."

Surprised to think that a meeting with Menelus should be more important to them than one with Myaca, Murdock said nothing but quickly left their presence.

When the Martians were out of earshot, Hal asked Murdock why Queen Myaca hadn't been at today's scientific galactic assembly of distinguished visitors?

"The Queen rarely ventures into public these days. She is embarrassed that Mars and Venus have become the focus of such anxious attention by galactic neighbors. Those who made us the focus of their critical ultimatum today, who more or less told us to shape up or ship out, ought to mind their own galactic business. I really can't speak for Her Majesty. Frankly, I regard such long distant light years away meddling into Martian and Venusian affairs annoying. I wouldn't have attended today's meeting if the Queen hadn't insisted that I go on her behalf."

"I hope you took good notes".

"I always do", said Murdock defensively. "I never would let the Queen down in that regard. I keep her well informed and up-to-date on all matters of state. You see, the Queen understands my heart better than I do. I am here today because my species was saved from annihilation quite by accident nearly a thousand years ago. At one time my species was considered to be a step down from yours on the evolutionary scale. We were saved from extinction when men, who'd originally settled the Martian and Venusian landscapes, abandoned their planets. They thought they'd found more hospitable homes on Earth. You and all earthly beings are merely descendants of alien early settlers who found it inconvenient to return to planets they'd once called home. Earth became their permanent home-- they were pioneers there and established the great civilizations of Mu and Atlantis. Unfortunately, those Martian and Venusian pioneers weren't prepared for the problems that faced them in their new homes. Travel between Mars and distant planets became unhealthy. Human diseases were introduced to the old Martian landscape where many Martians still lived. Mars' human population declined sharply. As a result, animals such as myself, with the aid of Martian humans who had survived an epidemic, were able to evolve into higher beings. We worked alongside a declining human population in a desperate effort to hold onto what civilization remained here. Finally health was restored to Mars. The ruling human family, The House of Chucara, is revered by all species for the leadership they provided in the face of planetary catastrophe.

"As a result, there has always been a strong bond between my family and the House of Chacura. We have served it for centuries and will continue to carry on the tradition of loyalty that exists between our species and theirs. Queen Myaca, like her father and grandfather, has enormous respect for all living things, great and small. Mars today thrives as a healthy ecosystem because the delicate balance between plant and animal life is respected. All species are allowed to thrive, grow and evolve within this Martian setting because the potential for greatness is understood within creation's cosmos. One reason you saw such diversity of species at today's meeting is because Mars established an alliance with other species within the galaxy when it was most needed. Yet history's final note in this epoch drama has yet to be played."

"I don't understand, how such a drama is to be played or how we are to help you?" said Whitfield. "Your Martian civilization seems so much more advanced than ours."

"The Golden Age needs assistance from other times and dimensions. We must work together. In that way, the Golden Age will be sustained throughout all time and history."

Hal heaved a big sigh and started to ask another question but Murdock quickly directed his guests to an exit within the building. Once again, they passed Sarius the robot security guard, who nodded politely as they started to leave. Acknowledging the robot's presence, Murdock turned to Whitfield and told him, "Sarius has a wonderful personality. He is really quite brilliant. He must find his job as security guard here to be rather tedious. I sometimes forget he is a robot and that he has feelings just as you or I do."

Overhearing the comment, Sarius said, "You're right, I don't have feelings exactly like yours. I'm not like you. I don't mind being a guard. My job is important. I can tell you who passed through the building today. I can tell you exactly what business each individual carried out within the building at any given time."

Startled that Sarius had overheard his comment, Murdock tried to apologize but Sarius was quick to respond. "The only drawback to being me is that I get lonely. I was created and raised by beings. I miss the companionship of beings such as yourself."

"Well then" responded Murdock, who had a big heart, "there's no need for you to be lonely. When you get off work today, before you return to your quarters at the scientific programming lab, why don't you visit us? We would be delighted if you'd join us this evening. These earthly time travelers no doubt would like to make the acquaintance of a robot such as you. I'll send my hovercraft to pick you up at precisely 7:00 pm."

Later that evening, as Murdock and his guests were preparing to be served the evening meal, a furry marsupial butler directed Sarius into a room and seated him next to Murdock.

In embarrassment, Murdock quickly looked down at the table when he realized that Sarius, being a robot, wouldn't require anything to eat. Sarius stared down at his empty plate. Then looking up, he told Murdock that he was programmed to enjoy most Martian fruits and vegetables. Murdock placed aside the wine glass he was holding. Then turning to the furry butler whose nose was held high in the air, he directed him to serve Sarius a plate of Martian fruits and vegetables.

Following the evening meal, Murdock and his guests retired to his sitting room. Midway through the evening conversation, refreshment was served in the form of a frothy after dinner drink similar to coffee and topped with a deliciously rich sweet cream.

"The drink is made from a plant that grows at the base of a Martian extinct volcano the size of your state of Arizona." Murdock watched his guests enjoyed the frothy substance. He then suggested to them that it might be time to play a Martian version of euchre.

Seeming slightly embarrassed, Sarius gazed at the floor self-consciously. He thought he might be overextending his welcome. Sarius had been programmed to beat most beings at almost any game. He didn't want to draw attention to his excellence in that regard.

"It's getting late. I really should be going", he said politely. "My friends at the programming lab will be looking for me. Sarius placed the unfinished cup of coffee on an intricately carved table. He got up to leave but hesitated. In a burst of unexpected emotion he said to Murdock: "I've been programmed for more than the usual tasks one might expect of a robot. I don't mean to boast. I think I know more than you do about the clandestine political undercurrents involving certain ambitious individuals who attended today's scientific meeting. I've been programmed to read character. Unlike most robots, I've developed a mind of my own. I regard you as a friend, Murdock. You respect my artificial intelligence. You don't look down upon me as a mere machine. I'd like to offer my services to you when you meet with Queen Myaca and her other representatives. The Queen's interests and that of all law abiding individuals within the solar system must be protected. I can serve as your guide through dangerous political waters."

Murdock's whiskers twitched nervously. He wondered what Sarius knew regarding the strained political environment surrounding him that he didn't know. Murdock liked Sarius. He felt instinctively that he could trust the robot but he was hesitant.

Murdock stared at him as Sarius said almost humbly, "I know the hearts and minds of your political enemies far better than you do."

"I see", said Murdock who didn't want to appear too eager to accept Sarius's offer to spy for him.

"I know what you're thinking. You're wondering if you can trust a robot. We'll, I can assure you that I'm loyal and I can be trusted. You'll need all the help you can get if we or rather you are to pull off the momentous feet of solving the perfect equation."

"How did you know about that?" asked Murdock.

"I know far more than you think I do". "I assure you that I'm a friend."

With that said, Sarius turned to leave followed by Murdock who walked alongside his guest to the burrow's exit.

"I'll send a hover craft to pick you up for the meeting with Queen Myaca the second day of the Martian month next week. Until then, be careful. Trust no one, confide in no one and tell absolutely no one of your inclusion in the scheduled meeting."

"You needn't warn me of a thing. I can tune into a hostile environment before hostilities become apparent. Your alliance with me will bring you the protection your mission justifiably deserves."

"I'm glad to have you with us", said Murdock holding open the door for him. He then watched as Sarius stepped into the hovercraft and was whisked away toward his quarters at the scientific programming lab.

"Murdock watched the lights of the hovercraft disappear. Later after he'd told his guests good night, Murdock wandered alone along the corridors of his burrow. He climbed the winding carved pink granite stairway leading to the outside, and gazed up at the Martian evening sky where light from the evening borealis faintly enveloped flowering vines clinging to enormous trees resembling Earth's Gingko species. Murdock listened to the wind gently rustle the trees' leaves as he turned and walked down winding carved stone steps leading to a temple courtyard. It was very late—almost time to offer prayers to the sun. The night was fast fading. The sun would rise in less than a Martian hour. After contemplating the conversation he'd had with Sarius, Murdock felt unsure of himself. Should he trust Sarius? Murdock was no fool. He'd always been able to spot insincerity in others. Yet Sarius, that poor lonely robot, seemed to be genuinely honest. Murdock yawned. He walked along the path leading to his burrow beneath the sun temple. He opened a door to his apartments, curled up on a golden straw mattress, and slept.

CHAPTER TWO

▼

A flock of white birds resembling doves circled the palace where the meeting with Queen Myaca was to be held. A hovercraft carrying Murdock and his party flew just beneath the flock before it alighted in an enclosure resembling an Earth-like Florentine garden. A tall guard attired in plain Martian clothes equivalent to an earthly suit and tie, saluted the visitors as they stepped from the craft. Sarius accompanied a confident Murdock as Hal and Whitfield walked behind them

Queen Myaca, who wasn't one to be concerned with formality, was gathering flowers from her Martian garden when the guard ushered the visitors into her presence. Wearing a simple dress trimmed in silver thread, and embroidered with colorful floral images from her garden, Myaca extended her hand in greeting to Murdock and his companions.

Murdock, who'd always basked in the presence of Myaca, gazed at the lovely Queen with her long soft brown hair wound in a chignon atop her head. She smiled at her visitors as her green eyes, matching the garden's lush greenery, searched their faces.

Setting aside the flower basket she'd carried with her, she placed it near a fountain where water spilled over the fountain's edge onto exotic plants. Hal watched in mild horror: The gentle Myaca picked up a nearby watering can and began watering a Venus Flytrap busy devouring an insect that had alighted upon it. He gazed at her lovely face and started to say something to her but she turned and faced Whitfield who was standing alongside Sarius and Murdock.

"This plant reminds me of my power within the solar system, and how easy it is for me to devour my enemies sometimes without a thought," She then placed aside the watering can. Whitfield said nothing in response to the remark but Hal boldly asked a question, "Do you think of yourself as ruthless?"

"Not really" she said a little sadly. "As some might tell you, I've been made what you might term as ruthless by circumstances. My husband was lost to me when he was abducted and unwillingly drawn into another dimension at the hands of my cousin, King Menelus of Venus. For the time being, my cousin has superior power and knowledge of the solar system. I dare not accuse him of any wrongdoing. He supposes that I believe my husband's disappearance was quite by accident. I'm afraid that I or one of my loyal advisors, might suffer the same fate as my husband Prince Sentius."

"Is that why we've been invited into your presence today?" asked Hal trying not to appear too inquisitive but at the same time eager for an answer. Ignoring the question, Myaca cast her eyes in the direction of Sarius, who muttered a little nervously, "I'm Murdock's friend, Your Majesty. He trusts me. He's accepted me as an ally. In serving him, I serve you as well" he said humbly bowing.

Myaca, who'd understood Sarius was an android/robot, was touched by his sincerity. Smiling, she invited Murdock and his companions to follow her into the palace's reception area.

A huge door swung open for her as Myaca led her guests along a splendid corridor surrounded by mirrors. Garden views, magnified by mirrors, brought the sense of the outdoors into a sophisticated interior. Hal and Whitfield seemed bewildered and disoriented by the huge corridor's interior décor. Martian mountainous scenery now encompassed them and diverted their attention from everything else.

"Your planet is truly a remarkable place", said Hal. Coughing nervously, Whitfield wondered if this Martian show of scenic excellence within Myaca's imperial residence wasn't just a bit ostentatious. Myaca continued walking ahead of her guests, totally unconcerned with what they might be thinking of the interior decor.

"Your love for your planet is certainly manifested in the manner in which you have introduced its beauty into your surroundings. I've never seen anything quite like it before," said Hal.

Myaca momentarily turned her head then smiled. She made a slight gesture with her hand as she and her companions entered another level of the palace. They were now inside a room where two individuals, who'd been sitting in elaborate gilt chairs immediately stood as Myaca entered the reception area. "I believe you gentlemen may know one another. Perhaps there is no need for me to make any introductions."

Whitfield was the first to step forward and extend a hand in greeting.

"What an unexpected pleasure, John. I'd hoped but never expected that you would be present here today."

"You underestimate me as a time traveler then," said the elusive John Pelletier extending a hand in greeting to Murdock and then one to Hal and Sarius. John then turned and introduced his friend Vorelis, as not just a time traveler but as a master of the universe.

"We all know dear Vorelis by reputation" said Queen Myaca, who invited her guests to be seated so that they could discuss the day's sensitive business. Turning to Vorelis, Myaca asked a little hesitantly. "Shall I begin the discussion or do you have something you'd like to say first?"

Vorelis' reply was diplomatic and under the circumstances appropriate as well.

"As our beloved sovereign, we all look to you to begin today's discussion."

"Very well, I'll get to the point. As you know, the galactic community has made our affairs theirs. They criticize us unmercifully for what they perceive to be our inability to bring about peace within our solar system. We are rapidly becoming the pariahs of the galaxy and it's because my cousin Menelus is thirsting for power within the solar system. He'll stop at nothing to achieve his goals. He will draw us into his black hole of corruption and chaos if we don't act immediately."

"Well said Your Majesty", said Murdock who stood up and applauded with his furry paws.

"The Queen continued to talk. "Menelus is dangerously ambitious. He uses his son Mars as a spy, and is informed of my every activity through his son's clandestine network of espionage. I have no way of stopping them but something must be done to bring a halt to their activities. Our Golden Age is gradually being swallowed up by their desire for power and wealth. My cousin plans to invade the peace of domains distant and near, including the Earth colonies of Mu and Atlantis. We must stop him now"

"And how are we to do that?" asked Whitfield, who'd suspected his services would be required soon enough.

Myaca gazed at Whitfield with a benevolent, almost angelic expression before saying, "Menelus thinks he has superior ability to invade time and space but we know you can foil his destructive plans. We saw what you did at Earth's Global Trade Mart. Now you must turn back the clock again."

"Row, row, row, your boat gently down the stream." Whitfield was singing silently."Merrily, merrily, merrily, merilly, life is but a dream."

"Empires can be built and when they fall they can be put back together again as if nothing ever happened isn't that so professor?" said Myaca

Whitfield swallowed. He modestly bowed his head before he looked the queen directly in the eye. "It is my humble belief, indeed, a belief that is part of my research, and remains unproven: There is one dimension upon which all others are subordinate. To enter that dimension is to attain supreme power within the cosmos. To step into that dimension is to hold the very grail in one's hand—to have the potential to shape or to reshape history within subordinate dimensions."

Myaca rose from the chair where she sat. She faced Whitfield then took his hand in her own. "There is an equation to be solved—the perfect equation. Only then will our partners within the galaxy who call upon us to solve that equation respect us."

Hal swallowed as he listened to Queen Myaca's words. Whitfield mopped his brow with a handkerchief. He lowered his gaze and stared down at the floor. Myaca's words had moved her guests. Everyone was speechless. Even Pelletier, who wasn't easily impressed by remarks, appeared rather shocked by the Queen's ultimatum. "You are serious then in having us partake in this mathematical conquest of the solar system,"

"You and Vorelis may at times be called upon to render services for me. You're not indispensable. Since you both are time travelers of the highest order, I shall expect you to perform missions."

"Are you asking us to challenge your cousin's power?" asked Pelletier.

"Only indirectly," replied the Queen. "I"ll not ask you to endanger your lives. The best way to repel my cousin's evil actions is not to confront him at all. You must work from behind the scenes. Professor Whitfield will unravel the mysteries surrounding the perfect equation. The rest of you will apply the practical knowledge of that equation and foil Menelus with it." The expression on Whitfield's face was one of mild horror.

"I see," replied Pelletier. "Everything depends upon our friend Professor Whitfield then."

Myaca smiled a look of self-satisfaction. "We all must work together for the betterment of the solar system," she said softly.

Then turning to Murdock, and taking his furry arm in her own, she decisively said. "Today's meeting is concluded. If you'll all join me for the midday Martian meal, I would be honored to have you as my guests."

Immediately Murdock proudly produced a bottle of the Queen's favorite sherry he'd been hiding under his imitation moleskin jacket.

"How kind of you Murdock" she said handing the bottle to a servant. "You've always been so thoughtful of me. If you'll follow me into the dining area, your favorite fruits and vegetables are waiting to be served to you."

"During the meal, Myaca was flanked on either side by Murdock and Sarius.

When everyone had dined, and it was time to get up from the huge finely carved Martian wooden table, Myaca turned to Murdock: "It is much too dangerous for Sarius to return to his work as security guard at the Scientific Palace. He is a member of my security force now. As such, he demands special attention. Sarius is to stay with you at your burrow. If he requires additional programming or repairs, I'll have a technician see to his needs. Mr. Worthy and Professor Whitfield shall continue to have the protection of Murdock's burrow. Professor Pelletier and Vorelis shall remain here at the Palace. "Now if you'll excuse me, she said smiling, there are other matters awaiting my attention."

Later, after he knew the Queen was well out of earshot, Hal turned to Whitfield. "I must admit I wasn't expecting to meet such a determined young woman."

Responding to the remark, Murdock said, "Myaca has taken the loss of her husband rather hard. He's just the latest member of her immediate family, who while traveling from one dimension to another, suddenly vanished into the nothingness of space. Her father, King Aurelius suffered the same fate. Myaca was beside herself with grief at the loss of her father."

Hal started to say, "we all suffer from life's trying moments" but Whitfield quietly interrupted him.

"Hush, be careful what you say." Both men were feeling hemmed in by present circumstances. Murdock had hidden Whitfield's time machine. He had evaded any questions as to its whereabouts when Whitfield asked him. Exhausted from the day's meeting with Myaca, Whitfield was relieved to have it concluded. He followed his companions as they slowly made their way toward the hovercraft tethered in the palace garden. Being the last to board the craft, Whitfield wearily took a rear seat.

After arrival at the Sun Temple, the professor quickly escaped to the sanctuary of his room where he sat in silence until he decided to leave his room so he could take an early evening walk.

On his way to a familiar temple exit, glare from the late afternoon sun penetrating a transparent temple window nearly had blinded him as he climbed stairs and took a wrong turn. He turned down a wrong passageway and looked for an exit. Instead of finding an exit, he found himself facing the forbidden corridor of the future. He took a step toward it but he felt Murdock's paw upon his shoulder.

"You look tired, Professor" said Murdock suggesting that Whitfield should return to his room.

"I'm fine. I can assure you", he said ignoring Murdock's suggestion.

Following his exit from the hovercraft, Hal too had wandered alone outside the Sun Temple. Hoping to find a means of escape from his present circumstances, he instead had found himself face to face with Sarius.

"I've just been shown my accommodations. I understand my room is next to yours. Murdock wants us in close proximity to one another in case of an emergency."

"I don't expect they'll be any emergencies", said Hal. "Since my arrival at the Sun Temple, things have been pretty quiet."

"Nevertheless" said Sarius casually." We're supposed to look out for one another."

"How convenient" said Hal who thought Sarius was being used to spy on him.

"I'm sure we'll become good friends", called Sarius as Hal turned and walked from him.

Later, as Hal was returning to his room, a light immediately switched on as he entered his room but dimmed after he prepared to rest. When he was half-asleep, he found himself enveloped in cocoon like semi darkness. When he gazed across the semi-darkened room, a wall suddenly gave way to a strange subterranean garden. Artificial light, streaming down into the garden, revealed a path to an inaccessible world. Suddenly Hal felt overwhelmingly homesick. He thought he was hallucinating. He rose to his feet and walked toward the garden. He was prevented from entering the scene by an invisible impenetrable wall. Resigned to his surroundings, and completely overcome by weariness, he fell across his comfortable bed and drifted off to sleep.

When he awoke the following morning, the garden and semi darkness were gone. Only the room's all pervasive artificial lighting encompassed him as he stepped from bed and walked toward something resembling a shower where he bathed then changed into new clothes laid out for him to wear.

Hal opened the door and stepped from his room. Closing the door behind him, he was pleased to run into Professor Whitfield. Having risen earlier than his friend, the professor had been doing some investigating.

In a cheerful mood and looking refreshed, Whitfield remarked, "There's a magnificent library tucked upstairs just to the left of the corridor to the future. Stacks of ancient manuscripts piled high to the ceiling along seemingly endless shelves appear to be the record of this strange Martian civilization. The writing within the manuscripts, although unique in some ways, is similar to hieroglyphic inscriptions I've seen in some of Earth's ancient scrolls."

Since childhood, Hal's father Harry had trained him to translate ancient hieroglyphic inscriptions. "If Murdock doesn't have anything scheduled for us to do after breakfast, do you suppose you could show me the library manuscripts?"

"Of course" replied Whitfield.

Unbeknown to Hal and Whitfield, the ubiquitous Sarius had overheard the pre-breakfast discussion between Hal and Whitfield. He'd told Murdock about Whitfield's secret visit to the library. Although the subject wasn't mentioned at breakfast, Murdock decided that if Hal was to have a look at the library's manuscripts it would be he who would show him around and not Whitfield.

Following breakfast, Murdock rose from the table and said he wished to show them a room of great knowledge and mystery. His guests then followed Murdock along a corridor where an intricately carved door, swung open for them revealing a room's treasures. "Please follow me", he said showing his guest's the library's stacks of endless volumes.

"Since most of these volumes are valued for their rarity and antiquity, only a few privileged scholars are permitted to view them. The volumes are irreplaceable and must never leave the library."

"Why shouldn't the volumes leave the library?" asked Hal.

With a forbidding almost stony expression, Murdock gazed at Hal and replied, "To remove one of the highly prized volumes might mean a small piece of Martian/Solar System history might, for the worst, end up on the cutting room floor: The volume could fall into the wrong hands."

Desiring to examine a volume, Whitfield asked, "might I have a look?"

Pointing to a comfortable study area replete with intricately woven rugs, wall paintings and cushioned chairs, Murdock replied "of course."

"Thank you" replied Whitfield, who having glanced through its pages, struggled to return the heavy mathematics volume to its proper shelf.

"Here, let me help you", said Hal taking the volume from Whitfield's hands then stepping upon a ladder so he could put the volume back in place. As he did so, he noticed the corner of an envelope protruding from the volume's pages. Hal quickly glanced across the room where he saw the ever-observant Sarius with back to him, studying the contents of another volume.

Hal pulled the envelope from the corner of the volume he'd replaced. He then slipped the envelope inside the vest he wore over his new shirt.

Whitfield, who'd seen what Hal had done, took a deep breath as he watched hm descend the ladder. Then turning his head away, he glanced upward at the library's stained glass ceiling dome. Solar light penetrated the glass dome, and enveloped the entire room in colorful brilliance.

"This library has become the very cornerstone of our Martian civilization. The beauty and revered contents of these rooms, attest to the greatest recorded thoughts of Mars and of the solar system", droned Murdock

Hal felt guilty for pilfering the letter. After reading it, he would return the letter to its hiding place.

He was relieved when Murdock, turned on one furry heel and announced, "Gentlemen, it's impossible for me to show you the complete library today. The library's contents require an infinite amount of time and space. The inquiring mind must be patient. May I suggest we conclude today's visit. If you wish, I'll show you more of the library tomorrow." Accompanied by Sarius, Murdock then led his guests from the library and left them. Before he returned to his room, Hal whispered toWhitfield to meet him later in a sanctuary outside the Sun Temple.

The two men met in a place pleasantly shaded by exotic shrubs and trees where they could chat unnoticed. Sitting in carved wooden chairs overlooking a small lake, they watched as huge frogs, peeked from behind lotus blossoms and loquaciously comversed with one another. The frogs jumped from one lily pad to the next and played a game of carefree leapfrog as Hal and Whitfield became caught up in a different sort of game.

"I've been studying the letter I took from the library. "Its contents are entirely decipherable. The hieroglyphics are similar to what I've seen in Earth's ancient texts.

"Years ago, my mother discovered a sundisk lying in a field near our family farm. The deciphered hieroglyphics on the sundisk, led to my father and grandfather's discovery of the Forgotten Island."

"Do you suppose there's a connection between the sundisk and the letter?" asked Whitfield.

"Yes", replied Hal. "The letter's opening phrase, 'the serpent coils in the sun where mother earth opens to the sea,' is the same as the initial translated line deciphered from the sundisk.

"Are there other similarities?" he asked.

"There have to be more. Let's return to the library when Murdock's not around. The library may hold other surprises for us. We'll wait until tonight when Sarius and Murdock are resting. I believe Sarius is programmed for sleep. We'll slip into the library and look for the things Murdock either didn't show us or he didn't want for us to see."

"Such as?" asked Whitfield tensely.

"Perhaps there is another helpful letter hidden in another mathematics volume." Lowering his voice and gazing around them, he whispered a little desperately: "I have a feeling that Murdock may have hidden the time machine in the library. The library has nooks and cranies. It's a perfect place to hide something. Somehow we've got to find the time machine and get out of here. If we don't get out of this place and soon, we may end up like Myaca's father and husband."

*   *   *   *

The corridors were silent and empty, when late that night, Hal and Professor Whitfield approached the strange Sun Temple Library. A constant solar powered light enveloped the corridor as they pushed against the library door. The ornately carved heavy wooden door creaked then opened for them. "Let's leave the door open just a crack. We don't want it to lock behind us."

Despite Whitfield's warning, Hal unwittingly allowed the heavy library door to close behind them. He quickly made his way through the library and found the stack where earlier he'd discovered the letter. "There's got to be something else here", he said pulling volumes from their shelves,

Hal had hardly gotten his words out when Whitfield, who was leaning against the bookcase, noticed it moving. Hal quickly stepped down from the ladder and saw that the bookcase revolved in a semi-circle revealing a corridor.

"Let's follow that corridor and see where it leads, suggested Hal glancing at fully illuminated elaborately painted ceilings and walls surrounding them. "The wall and ceiling paintings are depicting something about the Egyptian god Horus the son of Osiris and Isis", said Hal.

"Yes, agreed Whitfield, biting upon his pipe's stem. We've found the right passage. Apparently Horus was a time traveler. According to the ancients, Horus supposedly lived 22,000 years ago and maintained his health and vigor until about 5,000 years ago. He lived to be the ripe old age of 17,000 years. 1

The corridor narrowed and darkened until it ended in front of a closed door.

"Perhaps the door is locked", said Hal nervously standing in front of it

"Turn the door's handle", said Whitfield.

The men gasped in relief when what they saw before them was the red time machine. Quickly they stepped into the machine. Whitfield passed Hal a crash helmet before placing one upon his own head. He pressed a few computerized keys activating the time machine, and was relieved to hear the machine's familiar humming. He'd been afraid that Murdock, who'd tampered with the device enabling him to locate the hidden time machine through time and space, might have disabled the machine itself. Whitfield pushed the machine's throttle forward for maximum velocity through time and space. "If my calculations are correct, I should be delivering you to your home in almost no time at all. Your family must be anxious about your recent disappearance".

The time machine hummed and vibrated as it first orbited Earth then made entry into its atmosphere. Whitfield gently set the time machine down in a pasture adjacent to Hal's family farm. He then flipped on a control panel switch and disguised the time machine as a small farm tractor.

Gazing at the tractor in amazement, Hal asked. "How did you know where I live?"

"Any journey through time results in acquistion of data. When applied properly, such information reaps desired results" said Whitfield gazing at the lovely bucolic setting where cows in a pasture grazed peacefully.

Hal and Whitfield walked toward the old family farmhouse. Jaime, Hal's mother was sitting on a porch swing when she saw her son and Whitfield approach her. Hal stepped onto the porch and embraced his mother who wept tears of relief as she asked, "Where have you been? We've been so worried. When you failed to show up for the New York board meeting last month, we thought something something terrible had happened to you."

Hal winced. "Something terrible almost did happen. It's over with now. I'll tell you about it someday."

"Where's dad?" asked Hal after introducing Whitfield to his mother.

"He's in New York doing the job you should have been doing for the past month", she said a little brusquely. Jaime opened the farmhouse door and invited Hal and Whitfield inside. "Excuse me professor, my husband should be here to greet you. The rest of the family is in the living room."

"Sit down" said Jaime to Hal and Whitfield. "You have a lot of explaining to do."

"I guess I do", agreed Hal who knew he somehow had to find a way to explain the circumstances surrounding his recent time travel to the people sitting before him.

Hal hadn't realized his family didn't know the distinguished Professor Whitfield. He seemed embarrassed when Jeannie asked the elderly guest if he was retired.

"Of course not," said Hal answering for his friend. "Professor Whitfield divides his time with work he does at the Global Trade Mart with his physics research at the Primary Institute for Advanced Study."

"I've heard about the work you've been doing in physics", said Tom now recognizing the distinguished guest. "It's an honor to have you in our home. We hope you'll accept the invitation to stay with us for a few days."

"Why, thank you" he graciously replied. "We have much to discuss". He then motioned for Hal to show his grandfather the letter smuggled from the Martian Library.

Hal proudly handed the letter to Tom: "I realize your experiences on the Forgotten Island have often been doubted by people who've searched for the island but have never found it. Now I'm going to ask mother, and Jeannie to believe that Professor Whitfield and I have returned from visiting a place that you might say exists only in our imaginations."

"Please open the letter", interrupted Whitfield. "When you've finished reading it, we want you to ask us where we found it."

Tom removed his reading spectacles from his pocket. He placed them on his nose and noticed the letter's thin paper that was like none he'd seen before. Familiar cara maya script of which he'd spent a lifetime studying was beautifully transcribed in gold symbols. Glancing up from studying the letter, he asked Hal, "Where did you find this?"

Hal answered thoughtfully. "If you believe that your visit so many years ago to the Forgotten Island was real, then you must believe me when I tell you that Professor Whitfield and I have not only visited a remarkable place too, we've defied history."

Puzzled by what Hal had said, Tom didn't ask him to elaborate.

Instead, he continued to study the letter's contents. He glanced up from the letter only when Hal said, "The letter's contents haven't been fully deciphered. Your expertise is required, grandfather."

"The letter appears to be an important document. It bears the royal escutcheon of Mu. Are you asking me to believe that this letter originated from the lost continent?"

"If you'll study its cara maya inscription, the letter refers to the history surrounding ancient Earth settlements. Close to a million years ago Venusian and Martians became Earth's early settlers. They left their planets when Mars rapidly was being reduced to desert, and Venus, was undergoing an ecological disaster similar to global warming. To make matters worse, warfare between Mars, Venus and the moons of the solar system later broke out on an unprecedented level. Those who had settled Earth's Mu and Atlantis were drawn into the conflict: Asteroid/ missiles directed at them by the Venusians for siding with Martian leaders who'd advocated peace and planetary ecological protection caused earthquakes."

"Total annihilation was the tragic outcome for all warring planets except for planet Earth," said Tom grimly finishing Hal's narrative of the letter's contents. "Are you expecting me to accept what this letter says without offering me any proof of the letter's authenticity?"

"Ancient Greek records allude to the connection the ancient city of Athens had with early civilizations and with the city of Sais." said Hal.2

"Yes, Churchward alludes to such a connection", replied Tom. "He found many temple records stating that Asia Minor, the lower Balkans and Egypt were first colonized through Mayax and Atlantis. According to the Greek historian Solon, a city existed on the spot which Athens occupied 11,500 years ago and was built 17,000 years ago—a thousand years before the history of Lower Egypt commenced. After the defeat of Atlantis by the Athenians, violent earthquakes occurred and both civilizations were flooded and submerged. Atlantis never rose again and remains the stuff of legend. The ancient city of Athens rose anew: It exists to this day." 3

"The letter's information seems to reaffirm the truth surrounding the story", said Hal. At one time there was great conflict in the ancient world that resulted in widespread destruction. That conflict extended not just to Atlantis but to Mu and certain warring planets within the solar system."

"Hal is right said Jaime.

"Don't you remember when Ramira showed us through the Sun Temple on the Forgotten Island? She told us about the ancestors and the land from whence we came."

"I remember".

Jeannie reached out and grasped Tom's hand in hers. She'd never accepted the strange experience of visiting the Forgotten Island as real. "Tell me Hal, where did you go?"

"Professor Whitfield has fashioned a machine enabling men to travel back and forth through time. I accompanied him on such an adventure. We visited Mars."

Stunned by Hal's remark, Jaime said: "When you were a little boy you pretended you'd visited places you'd never been to before. Surely you're re-enacting that childhood game."

"I'm serious. We were testing Professor Whitfield's time machine out at the Global Trade Mart in an office adjacent to the Worthy Enterprises' suite. The Professor happened to thrust the machine's emergency throttle forward. We went catapulting into space and backward in time."

"It was an exhilarating experience" interrupted Whitfield, who knew by the looks on their faces, that he and Hal hadn't convinced Hal's relatives of their story's truth. "Actually I'd never dreamed the machine would carry us so far back in time or so far into the solar system."

Whitfield then suggested that perhaps Hal's family would like to have a look at the time machine but Hal interrupted him. "Let grandfather have another look at the letter borrowed from the Martian Library."

Tom once more reached into his pocket for his reading glasses. Placing the glasses upon his nose, he began reading the letter aloud.

"'He who begins anew the passage to Mu will lift time's curtain, marking the hour for few.' The letter says more but the meaning is cryptic. I need more time to study it," he said handing the letter back to Hal. Tom then removed the pipe from his pocket and filled it with tobacco. "The Forgotten Island obviously had a connection with Mu. I doubt if either your father or I would wish to retrace our steps back to the Island even if we could find our way there again."

Jaime listened to what her father had said. She'd remembered it had been she who'd begged Harry to lead an expedition to the "Forgotten Island. "You'll never know what Pelletier might have stumbled upon unless you go. It's everything you've ever hoped for".

Jeannie's memories weren't as rosy. "If only I hadn't shown you John's last letter to me. Perhaps we might never have embarked upon that wild goose chase"

"The expedition was no wild goose chase", argued Jaime. "Harry and Dad- - if you'll remember, were sure that Pelletier had stumbled upon something of great importance on the Island."

"And so he had" agreed Tom. "It's just too bad it dissolved before our eyes."

"Dissolved? Perhaps not entirely", said Whitfield, who having been returned the letter had recognized a formula for an equation at the letter's base. "I too recognize familiar symbols within the letter's content. Perhaps the information I need to solve the equation might be found upon The Forgotten Island", he said thoughtfully.

Hal began to ask his friend why he thought the Forgotten Island held the key to solving the perfect equation. He was interrupted. Whitfield rose from his chair, and crossed to a window. He gazed at the time machine disguised as a tractor and said, "We must find Pelletier. Perhaps it was something he said at the meeting with Queen Myaca. He didn't elaborate on anything during our discussion. Specific answers to most questions raised that day seemed to go unanswered. I'm convinced that Pelletier is harboring a secret. He may be able to help us unravel a deep mystery of the solar system."

"Surely you're joking" replied Jeannie.

"You mean you've really met Pelletier?" asked Tom who knew they'd all believed him to be dead.

"It seems", said Hal, interrupting the discussion, "John Pelletier is alive, well and has become the quintessential time traveler. In fact, Professor Whitfield and Pelletier are old friends."

"Yes, that's right", said Whitfield who was glad Hal had mentioned it. "My friend Pelletier is a time traveler of the highest order. He's told me that while he resided on the Forgotten Island, Vorelis and Ramira taught him how to travel through time within the solar system. I didn't believe his time traveling tales until Hal and I tested out my time machine at the Global Trade Mart. I discovered that what Pelletier had been telling me was true."

"You really don't expect us to believe what you're telling us, do you?" asked Tom

Jaime was sure that Hal and Whitfield had made a quick visit to a still before dropping in on them for a visit. "I bet you two would like a good strong cup of coffee", she said, starting toward the kitchen.

"We don't need sobering up. The professor and I would enjoy some of your cooking though. It's been quite a while since we had our last meal."

Jaime stopped and looked at Hal. With a mild look of amusement upon her face, she said, "How can you think of food at a time when you are planning to embark upon a journey that will help Professor Whitfield to unravel a great secret of the universe?"

"You must know me by this time, Mother. I think best on a full stomach, I'm sure the professor does too."

"All right", sighed Jaime, moving again toward the kitchen. "Supper will be ready soon".

Jeannie, who'd been assisting her with the evening meal by setting the table, still thought Hal had been hallucinating. She placed a large pot of coffee in the center of the dining room table. Then, rejoining Jaime in the kitchen Jeannie said,"I hope John doesn't pay us a visit. He may be a great time traveler but I'm not sure what I might do to him if he decided to show up."

Jaime sliced a few tomatoes and placed them on a platter, "You and Dad are happily married. John will know that when he sees you together. Besides, Dad and the renowned John Pelletier are old friends. Don't you think John could answer those unanswered questions we've had for years about the Island?"

"He probably could", said Jeannie sighing then wiping her hands on her apron.

"Let's join the others in the dining room" said Jaime leading the way then sitting down between Hal and Whitfield. Tom sat at the head of the table and said the blessing. Then helping himself to the main entrée, he passed the platter to Whitfield.

As everyone was busy eating, Whitfield placed his fork down and said, "After supper, we'll show your grandfather how to email from the time machine. If we send a message drawing our friend here we might persuade him to accompany us to the Forgotten Island."

For a moment there was silence in the room. Everyone who'd heard Whitfield's remark tried to make the connection between visiting an island and solving the perfect equation.

"Myaca should have made John more accessible to us", said Whitfield.

"Myaca? Who is she? asked Jaime, placing her fork down then looking at Hal.

"It's Queen Myaca. You really should meet her", said Hal. "Perhaps if we locate Pelletier you'll have the opportunity of being introduced to her."

It was after supper when Hal and Whitfield led everyone outside to have a look at the strange time machine disguised as a small farm tractor. Whitfield touched a key on the tractor's control panel and the startling metamorphoses took place: On display before the spectators was the red time machine that Hal had first glimpsed in Whitfield's office. Just how long ago that meeting had taken place was unclear. The two time travelers had traveled thousands of years since then.

"What day is it?" asked Hal turning to his mother Jaime, who in disbelief stared at the machine.

"Why it's December 13, 2003."

"We've been gone a month then."

"There's no telling how long we've been gone", said Whitfield proceeding to contact his friend Pelletier.

"Queen Myaca has made it clear. We must work together", said Hal

"Will you please stop alluding to people we've never met or know nothing about."

Hal apologized for not telling his mother more about the mysterious Queen Myaca.

"Myaca may be someone we wouldn't want to meet", said Jaime.

"If you'd ever met Myaca you wouldn't say that. She is one of the most real and sensible people I've ever known", said Hal. "She's a very beautiful, and powerful Martian ruler. Unfortunately, she is at odds with her equally if not more powerful evil cousin Menelus who rules Venus."

"Myaca and her trusted scientific advisor, Murdock believe that in solving the perfect equation, order may be restored to the solar system and war and bloodshed cancelled for all time," said Whitfield.

"That's a tall order", said Tom, passing off what had been said to them with a grain of salt.

"It is my humble belief: Once one has solved the perfect equation one virtually may hold the key to controlling hidden dimensions within the past, present and future of the universe" said Whitfield.

"How utterly terrifying" said Jaime.

"No it isn't" said Hal. "Only those with the desire to help other beings should be able to solve the equation. One must align his thinking with the highest ideals of universal peace and unity."

"Well then," said Jaime. "It looks as if Myaca's cousin, King Menelus is in for a big disappointment."

"Theoretically power should belong to the few willing to take responsibility for it" said Whitfield suddenly feeling humble. He wondered if he or anyone else he knew was worthy enough to solve the equation.

Seeing that Whitfield was struggling with his personal inadequacies, Jaime looked at him and said. "You are correct. Theoretically power should belong only to the few willing to take responsibility for it, and in a most unselfish and humane manner too."

Whitfield began sending Pelletier a message through the time machine's intricate system.

"One can't have too many friends willing to abet a worthy cause", he said to Tom who stood behind him.

"I don't really think we need Pelletier's assistance", insisted Tom. He was still furious with the way Pelletier had avoided him during his family's visit to the Forgotten Island. "As for Pelletier's friend, Vorelis the magician, he kept interfering with our attempt to discover the island's lost city."

"From what you've told me though", said Whitfield, "you eventually accessed the city."

"Yes, they finally pulled aside the curtain and let us see how well they played the game of pretend." Tom, who'd continued to go on about the miserable treatment they'd had while on the island, was interrupted.

"I believe our friend Pelletier has received my message. He's in the process of sending us a reply."

* * * *

Pelletier, Queen Myaca and Vorelis were standing next to one another along a spacious palace corridor when the message was received and displayed on a large screen.

When Myaca realized who'd sent the message and what he wanted, she swept past Vorelis and Pelletier and left them to study the screen.

Realizing she was gone, Pelletier followed Myaca downstairs to the Palace gardens where she always went when she was trying to regain her composure. After he found her, she said to him, "Tell your friends that it's impossible for you to leave us right now. Your protection against my cousin's efforts to overthrow my power is needed here."

"That's exactly what I was about to tell my friends on Earth."

John didn't want to tell Myaca that he was afraid to face his former wife and the people who'd accompanied Jeannie to the Forgottten Island so many years earlier. He didn't want Myaca to think he was a coward.

Later Myaca watched as Pelletier replied to the message: "My services here are indispensable."

Bowing slightly, Pelletier left Myaca standing alone with an amused expression on her face.

Later when Pelletier met with Vorelis, he told him about the message he'd sent replying to Whitfield's request. Vorelis knew there was more than one reason for Pelletier wanting to remain on Mars. "I can't blame you for not wanting to face the people you've been running so hard from all these years", he said smirking. "I'll, let Myaca know she has our undying loyalty."

Leaving Pelletier standing by himself Vorelis then made his way to palace gardens where he was sure he would find Myaca. Light from a magnificent transparent solar tower refracted the sun's rays and created rainbow multicoloredhues as Vorelis descended stairs and stepped into a garden. When he found the Queen gazing at some exotic blooms, she seemed lost in thought.

"Have no fear my dear. John and I have no intention of abandoning you to your cousin's plan to usurp your power—although I'm sure you are well able to defend your domain without our help."

Unmoved by the remark, Myaca responded by saying, "I really expected you as well as Pelletier to rush off to help your friend Whitfield solve the equation."

"Nonsense" replied Vorelis, "I've always had a dreadful time solving math problems. Whitfield would find me of no use to him at all."

"Isn't it true though, that you know where to look for the information that would help Professor Whitfield solve the equation?"

Vorelis felt uncomfortable answering that question. He knew how to find the information Whitfield would need. He didn't want Whitfield to take center stage, by solving the equation and upstaging him. "I've always been the only ruler of my modest domain. That's why Pelletier and I will do everything in our power to defend your territory. Trust me, you mustn'be alone. You need your friends. John and I are ready to serve you faithfully."

"I'm no fool", said Myaca. "I think neither you nor John relish the idea of having to face the same people you expelled from Earth's Forgotten Island years ago. I appreciate your loyalty though. I'll accept your invitation to remain with me here. With your superior knowledge of the solar system, our alliance should inevitably foil Menelus' plan to overthrow me", she said leaving a slightly embarrassed Vorelis standing by himself.

Myaca walked alone along a path leading from her palace garden.

She gazed at a grotto extending to a subterranean Martian Sea as Vorelis gazed after her. He was humiliated to think that she had seen right through him. For the first time in his career as a supreme master of the universe, Vorelis felt ashamed and sorry for himself.

Later, after Myaca returned from the sea grotto, Vorelis enviously watched Myaca take Murdock's furry arm as he accompanied her up huge stonecarved steps leading to a magnificent sitting room where she daily held audience with her most trusted advisors.

"Forgive me", said Murdock "for allowing our Earth visitors to escape undetected". Perhaps Sarius and I were programmed too heavily for sleep that night. Neither of us noticed our friends were missing until later that morning when neither Hal nor Whitfield showed up for breakfast in the dining room."

Knowing that she had the power to draw Hal or Whitfield back to her domain should she so desire it, Myaca replied, "That's quite all right."

With the matter settled, Myaca invited Murdock to tea, an invitation he accepted with the utmost grace and enthusiasm. "I had the chef prepare some of those delicious almond and fruit nut cookies which you so enjoy", she said leading Murdock into the sitting room where he graciously accepted a cup of tea and took a bite from a cookie served to him from a golden tray.

Following tea, Myaca bid her friend and advisor good bye. She made her way to an adjoining room where there was a mound of state papers awaiting her perusal. "Oh, I do wish Prince Sentius was here so he could assist me with all this work", she thought.

Chapter Three

▼

As Myaca, deep in study, began her work, elsewhere in time and space, Whitfield, Hal and his relatives, were about to embark on an adventure:

"I think my family needs to experience a ride in the time machine before we ascribe to the truth concerning your recent journey", said Tom.

"I'd be delighted to demonstrate my machine's ability to transfer us to another time and place" replied Whitfield."

"How are we all to fit in the time machine?" asked Jaime, who, noticed that it was much too small to accommodate everyone. Considering the problem, Whitfield put on his glasses and scratched his head.

"It has occurred to me that I may have to make some adjustments to the machine. I also may have to fine tune it if we are to set a direct course first to Mu."

"Why aren't we going directly to The Forgotten Island?" asked Hal seeming puzzled.

"Mu is the motherland. The Forgotten Island is merely an extension of Mu. If Mu's central library is any bit as fine as the one we saw in the Martian Sun Temple, I think it deserves our attention."

Seeming hesitant about embarking into the unknown, Jaime said, "You must be tired. I know I could use a good night's rest before we undertake this adventure."

"Very well" replied Whitfield, We'll leave for Mu first thing in the morning."

*   *   *   *

After accepting a pile of towels, a pair of pajamas and a toothbrush from them, Whitfield said good night to his hosts. He then wearily made his way upstairs toward the guestroom. It was while he was turning down the covers to the guest room bed, that he began considering one of the great theories of the universe:

The continuous creation theory associated with the names of scientists such as Jordan, Bondi, Gold and Hoyle, had long been a favorite of his. He vowed it would be the focus of his research as he worked to solve the problem surrounding a proof for the perfect equation. "The primeval atom that contained everything is illusory. The past is just as infinite as the future he mumbled to himself as he drifted off to sleep". 1

The following morning, Whitfield felt relaxed and confident. He'd always regarded the world as changeable and surreal. Now he would put his belief once more to the test. The time machine had defied the laws of matter. It had made the world and the things surrounding it seem hardly more real than the images of a motion picture. Whitfield was lost in thought when he heard a knock on his door, and a voice calling, "time for breakfast".

"There's no sense in leaving in an empty stomach", said Jaime setting a platter of scrambled eggs and bacon in the center of the dining room table.

"Do Bill and Lillie know where we're going?" asked Jeannie, terrified by the thought of embarking into the unknown.

"Of course not" said Tom. "I simply told Bill we'd be out of town for a few days. I've paid him to care for the farm animals while we're gone."

Following breakfast, everyone made their way toward the field where the time machine, no longer disguised as a tractor, was ready for boarding.

"I believe you'll find there's a seat for everyone", said Whitfield passing crash helmets around before putting one on his own head. He was about to push forward the throttle sending them careening through time and space when Jaime exclaimed, "Wait! Harry would never forgive me if I didn't call him and tell him we're going out of town. We'll have to figure out some way to get him to join us once we've reached Mu."

"Well, then", said Whitfield. "Perhaps you'd rather stay behind this time and wait for your husband to embark with you on the next journey to Mu."

Jaime hesitated before answering Whitfield. She was remembering the summer when she'd fallen in love with Harry and he'd gone off to C. America without her. At the time, she'd thought it was all over between them. As things turned out it wasn't. She still found it hard to forgive Harry for leaving her behind. "I'm coming with you", she said decisively.

"Dad should be here with us", insisted Hal. "The most efficient vehicle ever built for travel is here in our cow pasture and Dad hasn't even had a glimpse of it."

"Never fear", said Jaime, "I'll see that your father isn't left out of anything, which is something he always didn't do for me. We'll get your father to Mu through time and space—somehow. Right now, someone has to mind the family store."

Seeing Hal wince at the remark, Whitfield said, "Don't worry, my boy. With the time machine's superb communication system it may be possible for you to be two places at once."

"Let's not invite your father to join us until we are comfortably settled on Mu" said Tom, who'd always been rather resentful that Harry had made most of the major decisions on their first journey through time and space.

Jeannie placed her hand in Tom's and wistfully gazed at the pasture that appeared so tranquil and beautiful in the early morning light. "I really hate to leave this place", she said.

At last Whitfield pushed forward the time machine's throttle. The pasture and familiar farm scenery suddenly disappeared. There was a hum as the machine, encompassed by rainbow clouds appeared to be disintegrating. Whitfield hastily readjusted the machine's thrust forward mechanism until Hal shouted to him: "Stop, or we may never get out of this no man's land."

Perhaps it was Hal's remark, not to be taken seriously but for a moment the time machine seemed to falter.

"Hang on", said Whitfield as the machine, succumbed to gravity and started to fall. "We'll have to ride this one out. It's just a little turbulence, nothing to be concerned about." The rainbow hues came into view again.

"I think we're floating now", said Hal who saw nothing but empty space surrounding them.

Whitfield glanced down at the time machine's special barometer and sophisticated radar indicator revealing that they were nearing their destination.

"Don't hold your breath. I think we're almost there". No sooner had Whitfield gotten his words out than the machine began to drop like a dead weight. Replaced by lightning shafts, the rainbow clouds evaporated.

"I must have done something wrong" said Whitfield who felt he was losing control of the machine. "Perhaps a little on the spot finetuning would help", he said pressing the emergency control dial guiding the time machine. There was a hum followed by a loud sonic boom as the time machine hit the ground, bounced a few times then came to rest in a ditch.

"Welcome to the lost continent of Mu", said Whitfield. "I expect that momentarily we'll be met by a distinguished welcoming committee."

No sooner had Whitfield gotten his words out than in the distance the familiar image of the lovely Atira, daughter of Vorelis could be seen walking toward them.

"I sent Atira a message telling her and Vorelis to expect a visit from us. It looks as though she's received it"

The mid afternoon sun bathed a white sandy pathway near Mu's shoreline as Atira made her way toward the new arrivals. Upon meeting them, she extended a welcoming hand and gestured for them to follow her.

"My father has a castle here that overlooks the sea. You can rest there and acclimate yourselves to this time zone."

As they approached the magnificent castle fashioned in gray and white marble, a gate swung open for them, and the visitors followed a path leading to a transparent looking door.

"I expect you must be hungry right now", said Atira leading her guests toward an airy balcony where a table laden with fruits, delicious looking breads and cakes had been laid out for their consumption.

Sitting down in a beautifully carved wooden chair, she gestured for her guests to join her at the table. Then biting into a plump mango, she passed a fruit basket to her guests.

Tom selected some figs and grapes from the basket and wondered where Vorelis was. Before he had a chance to ask, Atira volunteered the information.

Father is unable to meet with you today. He is busy helping someone else. He sends his regrets and promises he will meet with you as soon as possible."

Hal started to ask her who else besides them needed Vorelis' help right now but he was interrupted by Jaime. "You mustn't pry", she whispered. "Atira and Vorelis are very secretive. It's best just to play along with them and see where the game leads you."

Embarassed at having his manners corrected, Hal nearly choked on the delicious rum punch he'd been enjoying.

"I wasn't trying to pry mother. I was just interested," he whispered.

"When you've rested and you feel like having a tour, I'll be glad to show you around Vorelis' palace. This home is one of his favorites. He definitely prefers it to his dark damp castle overlooking the Forgotten Island's lost city of gold. Father would like to spend more time here but his busy schedule, with so many appointments within the solar system, makes it quite impossible for him to be in two places at once."

"Oh, we do understand", said Jaime speaking politely.

Whitfield, who seemed impatient with the polite conversation going on between Atira and Jaime said: "We came here for a purpose. I am here to undertake important research."

Surprised at Whitfield's remark, Atira smiled uncomfortably. She wanted to remind her guests that they'd invited themselves to the Forgotten Island. Instead she said, "After you're rested I'll show you some of Mu's most interesting landmarks. For the time being though, if you'll excuse me, there is something I must do."

Getting up from the table where she had been sitting. Atira disappeared around a palace corner, and entered an empty room. With a sweeping gesture of her arm, she drew aside a curtain revealing a large screen enabling her to transmit and receive messages through time and space.

Gently touching the screen, Atira received a video transmitted message from her father, Vorelis. "In my absence please entertain our guests but inform them as little as possible regarding my present affairs elsewhere."

Atira sighed. She started to draw the curtain across the screen but hesitated. The screen was revealing another message. This time the message was from Queen Myaca.

"Vorelis has been monitoring a situation here on Mars which has become increasingly grave. He will remain with us while we assess it. Have no fear, your father is well and Menelus' power is inferior to that possessed by Vorelis. We are certain that you and your friends will meet him shortly."

Atira thoughtfully considered Myaca's message. Then touching the screen she, watched the message disappeared, and hoped that Menelus hadn't intercepted it.

Smiling, Atira returned to her guests. "You must be feeling rather bored just sitting here in the dining area. There are other parts of the palace, connected to the outdoors you might find more interesting."

Atira's visitors obligingly followed her as she led the way across a very solid but transparent bridge forming a link to the ocean several miles away.

"I feel as though I'm suspended in space", said Jaime who saw waves rush in and around her but could feel nothing.

"The walkway was built in this manner so it would seem as if you were standing in the water without actually being in it. Actually, the walkway is just a huge magnifying device that makes objects at a distance seem as though you're almost part of them."

"Well, to tell you the truth" said Hal, "for a moment, even though I didn't feel wet, I thought we were all going to be swept out to sea."

"The walkway is just one of the illusions my father is so adept at creating. Some of Father's other designs are so baffling even I couldn't explain how he managed them."

Atira pointed ahead to some palm trees blowing in the breeze. Behind the palms was a waterfall flanked by colorful orchids, and a grotto where a fresh water stream flowed from a subterannean source. Atira approached the grotto and was met by a handmaiden who placed a sacred crystal skull in her hands. 2 She then raised the skull to the sunlight. The landscape surrounding her and her companions changed: They stood in another time. Atira turned the skull away from the light: The scene was the one they'd left behind.

"Please don't tell me this is an illusion too" said Jaime who marveled at the hidden grotto's beauty. Atira didn't answer her.

"Perhaps you've seen enough." Atira began leading her guests toward Vorelis' palace. They crossed a garden bridge spanning a brook and listened to the soothing sound of rushing water as dragonflies and humingbirds hovered around them.

Once they had crossed the bridge and came to a transparent staircase that appeared to be nothing more than a climbing vine, Atira said: "If you find yourselves becoming at one with this garden environment, you'll desire nothing more. You'll be satisfied to stay here through time and eternity", she said turning a corner and disappearing.

"Surely she isn't planning on leaving us here indefinitely" said Jeannie

Tom removed the pipe from his pocket and placed it in his mouth. "Perhaps Atira has left us here for a purpose. Until we discover what that purpose is, we'll remain here", he said gazing at the stairway fashioned from vines.

"Look" said Jaime who spied a shrub and garden maze. "Let's follow the maze and see where it leads. The maze wound and turned in every conceivable direction. As its design became more intricate, so did its size. The maze narrowed until the shrubbery was up against them and there was hardly any room for them to move.

"I don't know what purpose this ordeal could possibly have", said Hal removing a few unwanted leaves from his mouth.

"The ordeal, as you call it, might be trying to teach us something", said Jaime, nearly stepping on a small turtle before seeing it and stooping to pick it up. The turtle quickly withdrew into his shell. With only his head barely peeking out, he stared at her with frightened eyes.

"I believe the turtle is as lost as we are. I imagine he was looking for the garden pond but he couldn't find it. Somehow he got entangled in this maze", said Jaime spying an opening in the tangled shrubbery directing her to a path. "Let's follow that path."

Within minutes, Atira's guests had found their way out of the maze and were standing on the opposite side of the pond. With the turtle still in hand, Jaime walked to the pond's edge, placed the turtle in the pond, and watched him swim away.

"I think we've passed the test", said Tom who knew they'd found their place within the garden community.

*   *   *   *

The following morning, as Atira made her way along the garden path and prepared to meet her visitors, she was surprised to see an old friend. The deer's curled antlers similar to those of a mountain goat's attested to his unusual pedigree

"Good morning, Atrius" said Atira, immediately recognizing the deer she had taught to speak so he could communicate with her.

"Excuse me. I'm afraid I was so busy enjoying the delicious salt lick you had placed upon the ground for me that I hardly noticed your approach."

"I apologize for startling you."

"You should have startled me. I should be wary of the hunters' arrow. Even though I'm not the sort that makes for good venison, I'm still served for dinner. It really gives me an inferiority complex to have to run for my life. People forget this is the Golden Age. We animals should be safe from predators. 'Does nothing please except to chew and mangle the flesh of slaughtered animals? The Cyclops could do no worse! Must you destroy another to satiate your greedy gutted cravings?'" 3

Embarrassed by the deer's frank insight Atira said,"You're right Atrius. Father will make certain that Queen Moo is made aware of the poaching problem within her domain. The ' no hunting decree' within her realm will be upheld."

"The sooner the better. If the decree isn't upheld soon there will be no better for my friends. Some of them pass directly within the arrow's aim almost on a daily basis."

"Poor dear Atrius—please tell your friends that the meadow and vegetable garden are safe havens."

"Thank you, madam, I will deliver your message to them" said Atrius bounding away.

*   *   *   *

After Atrius left her, Atira met her guests and led them along a path bordered by enormous fronds and ferns nearly obscuring a huge towering building.

"What is that structure?" asked Hal, who took his machete in hand and cut his way toward the edifice.

"It's best that the building remain hidden from those who seek to penetrate its interior. That's why father allows vines and shrubs to grow around the tower."

"Why doesn't Vorelis just have the building destroyed?"

"I'm afraid that would be impossible. The Dark Tower was a gift to Vorelis from Menelus and those who rule the underworld. The Tower's destruction would incur hostility among them and my father. Vorelis choses simply to keep the Tower entangled in vegetation so that those adventurous enough to enter it won't."

"Surely there can't be any harm in going inside and having a quick look".

"The tower's stairs, mazes and many entrances have hidden exits. To enter the tower is to become entangled in an endless web of chaos and confusion. Such confusion leads to dimensions from which there's no escape."

"I have an excellent sense of direction", said Hal who wanted to put the tower challenge to a test.

"Please don't try", said Jaime trying to reach out to her son and hold him back.

"I've never been afraid of anything."

"Don't do it son", said Tom who watched his grandson approach the tower.

"We must keep an eye on him", said Whitfield slowly approaching the tower too.

"I'm going to see if I can make it to the top" he shouted.

"No" shouted, Jaime.

It was too late. Hal was already inside the tower. He thought he'd heard a faint voice. "Did you hear that?" he asked turning to Atira, who had cautiously followed him into the tower.

"The voice is that of the imprisoned Prince Sentius", she said.

When Hal called in answer to the voice, the face of Menelus appeared on a great screen. "How dare you enter this tower and challenge my supremacy? If you both don't withdraw at once, I'll see that you end up alongside Prince Sentius"

"And how are you to manage that?" asked Hal bravely.

Atira, who'd taken Menelus' remark to be more than just a threat, thought it best to withdraw immediately.

"No" Hal whispered. "Ask Menelus where he's holding Prince Sentius prisoner."

Overhearing the remark Menelus replied. "He is being held within a hidden tower room. Only those armed with an ultimate knowledge of other dimensions will be able to confront him."

Menelus' image then disappeared from the screen. Hal and Atira found themselves staring into utter darkness.

"I dare not challenge Menelus", said Atira. "Only Father is strong enough to do that."

Hal took Atira by the arm and led her toward a dimly lighted passage, away from the place where the image had appeared. Within minutes they were safely outside the tower's confines and secure in the curious company of companions wanting to know what terror and mystery lay behind the dark tower walls. Hal who could still feel his heart pounding and the rush of adrenalin said, "let's steer a course for safer landmarks." Atira then led her guests along a path toward another destination.

"Before we return to the palace for lunch, said Atira still visibly shaken by her encounter with Menelus' image, perhaps you'd like to see one of Mu's great temples of Worship. The Temple of Ra is directly ahead of us along this path. From a distance, the temple appears to be nothing more than a great golden sphere. Upon closer examination of it, the globe is a temple of worship."

As they entered the edifice, Atira provided her guests with gold shoes for their feet. "I am going to offer customery prayers to the sun. Before I do I would like to tell you about Mu's ancient religion: sun worship. That circle over there, she said pointing, is a picture of the Sun. "Ra"is the Sun's collective symbol. We who worhip the sun look upon it as a symbol of Ra the Creator or infinite one. The Love and adoration of the Creator as the Heavenly Father and Love for all mankind (beings) as brothers is the basis of Mu's religion.4

In your time, 16,000 years into the future one can still see symbols of this religion in the records of ancient Egypt, India, ancient North and South America and elsewhere in the present day world where the ancient symbol of the sun is found.

"Tom knew that everything he'd ever learned about Sun worship came mainly from James Churchward's writings. "I've always regarded Churchward to be the ultimate authority on the subject. You and he seem to be in close agreement."

Atira smiled then gestured for her guests to be seated next to her on prayer rugs. Assuming the lotus position she said,"Today I pray for the universe, for the past, present, and future to be free of evil. I pray for Prince Sentius' release and for the complete restoration of the Golden Age."

Atira then shut her eyes and withdrew from her present surroundings until she was in deep meditation. When she'd finished meditating, she drank from a cup of sacred water. She then led her guests from the temple enclosure. She bowed in the direction of the Sun Temple before turning away. She then led her guests down a hillside and toward a small town.

"The village, with only a few houses, and one dirt road, appeared to be devoid of human occupants. A large dog, sleeping undisturbed in the middle of the road, opened his eyes long enough to see Atira and her guests pass by him before lapsing into sleep again.

"This place seems rather familiar", said Hal, who recalled having seen surroundings similar to the one he now saw, in photographs of 19th Century books.

"If the streets seem empty, if life's pace seems slow, that's the way things are here. Beings of the Golden Age are contemplative. They regard spiritual sustenance to be more important than food or drink, all of which is derived from vegetables."

"I was rather hoping I might be able to find a good hamburger here", said Hal.

"You'll find our vegetable products to taste as delicious as meat. I'll introduce you to them when we have a luncheon break."

"By the way" interrupted Tom, "Where are the people—beings?"

"Most of the population is either inside working or taking a day off by visiting other times in the past or near future. Sometimes school children are allowed to take field trips into the future but for only brief periods and under the most careful supervision."

"I thought it was prohibited for anyone to visit the future?" said Whitfield.

"It is prohibited. The future reality is carefully monitored. Beings only see the things the Martian and Venusian rulers want them to see."

"Until the tear in the fabric of the Golden Age is mended and beings are living peacefully again as brothers, the average being will have only the rare glimpse of what the future holds in store. Few if any of Mu's inhabitants have seen the entire picture. It has yet to be developed. The struggle among the powers that be for the outcome of that development is fierce. Saturn won't give up his supremecy easily, although Menelus and his followers are determined that he should."

"Do you mind if I ask you a rather personal question", asked Jaime, who until lately had always found Atira to be distant and remote. "I don't mind at all" was the reply.

"What do Mu's inhabitants pray for when they visit the Sun Temple?"

"Most, including myself, pray for peaceful solutions to the problems that confront the solar system. We also pray for peaceful solutions to personal problems as well."

Atira then gestured for her guests to continue following her along a beautiful path where purple wisteria, grew profusely in overhead trees, and perfumed the air with a delicate aroma.

Tom broke the silence by saying, "In more than one instance, Churchward's writings mention Queen Moo. I understand her to be one of your most famous rulers. Do you suppose you can tell us where she is today?"

"Queen Moo is visiting Atlantis on her way to the Mayax colony in Egypt. That is why we don't see her golden standard flying above city walls enclosing the palace where she resides.5

"Although you won't be staying within its walls, you'll have access to the palace library. Professor Whitfield might even discover some of the information he'll need to help with his research". Before any of you pass behind those walls, you should be counseled on the dangers of probing too deeply into mysteries there. Danger oftentime accompanies discovery".

"Do you suppose Menelus might then think that you're becoming a threat?" whispered Hal.

"If I play the game wisely, I'll make Menelus and his cronies feel that I'm inept compared to them. We want them to believe that they are winning, and that we are mere fools to be treading upon their turf."

Whitfield yawned as Hal congratulated his friend on his extreme cleverness.

"Allow me to show you Mu's great library", said Atira now standing upon library steps. Once inside the library, huge glasslike windows through which glorious daylight streamed in from every direction, made the library seem as if one were standing outside it. The illusion was heightened by the presence of flowers and plants dominating the library's interior.

"Where are the books?" asked Tom who kept looking in every direction for them.

"I'll show them to you later" said Atira leading her guests toward a panel where small rectangular devices protruded from the room's walls. Atira touched a device. The library's cataloging system immediately was displayed.

"All present knowledge of the universe may be found within this room. The knowledge of the past or future may be found in adjoining rooms", she said touching another rectangular device: "Here is a book on Mu's geography", she said handing it to Tom so he could inspect it.

"Why there's nothing to open here", he replied.

"There will be in a moment", she said placing the rectangular object inside another device protruding from a wall. Within seconds, a book popped out from the base of the device.

"Where did the book come from?" asked Tom.

"It was hidden in time and space. We don't have space to accommodate all books here in the library. We have to shelve them out to different time frames and dimensions."

Jeannie looked over Tom's shoulder as he thumbed through the book's pages.

"Is there anywhere else within the library where the information contained within this book is stored?" asked Tom.

"Yes" replied Atira, who leaning foward touched another device displayed upon the panel: Up popped a small screen upon an adjoining wall, Tom saw the first page of the book he held in hand displayed on a computerized screen.

"The book is preserved within cyber space", she said leading her guests from the library and toward their accommodations.

Tom lagged behind Atira and her other guests. His attention was diverted. Etched into the passageway's painted scarlet wall was a bright pastel terracotta diagrammatic representation of Mu as it appeared nearly 50,000 years ago. 6 Tom gently ran his hand over the diagram's smooth surface. He thought he'd recognized something of importance represented there. Seeing that Tom was straying behind his companions, Atira encouraged him to move forward.

"Whatever has caught your interest we can return to it later" she said taking his arm in hers. Whitfield, who'd been watching Atia and seemed surprised by her eagerness to move Tom away from what he was studying asked: "how private is one's access to the information here?"

"For security reasons some of the sensitive information contained within this library must be accessed only by the few. Queen Moo and her advisors are concerned with Menelus's increasing interest in Mu's Internal affairs. It has been said, that even as we speak, Menelus is attempting to usurp Myaca's power and place his son Mars upon the Martian throne. If he succeeds in doing so, Menelus is no fool-- he realizes he will face the ultimate challenge in having to overthrow Saturn in a fight to control the solar system.

Mars and the Earth settlements of Mu and Atlantis are allies. Menelus realizes this. He seeks to dominate the Earth settlements in any way he can. His spies are everywhere. Once the perfect equation is mastered, it is Myaca's hope to send her cousin's unwelcome cronies packing and back to Venus."

"Perhaps too much is resting on solving the equation", said Whitfield removing a pipe from his pocket and thoughtfully placing it in his mouth. "Queen Myaca seems like a courageous woman. There should be an alternate defensive plan ready so we might take action against Menelus if what you say about him is true."

Tom, who stood alongside Whitfield, nodded his head in agreement.

"Perhaps all parties should seek some sort of diplomatic solution to the problem."

"My father is working on the problem. He's a great diplomat. He's also is a master magician. By that I mean he is a devoted sun worshipper. Vorelis believes in the supreme power of a benevolent Source: Any evil attempt to overthrow the Source's power must ultimately fail. On more than one occasion, Vorelis has been forced to use his power to stop Menelus'evil intention.

Menelus, on the other hand, aligns his power with a personal sense of evil. Regardless of how many times Menelus challenges Vorelis he is destined to fail since his source is finite rather than infinite. Atira then proceeded to tell her listeners how Vorelis went about applying his skill.

"On one occasion, during parlor entertainment Menelus tried to use a device to transport Myaca into another dimension so he could imprison her there. Fortunately Vorelis was present at the entertainment. He quickly turned Menelus' device into a malevolent creature found only on the moons of Jupiter. The creature wrapped itself around Menelus' hand until he shook it loose and it fell to the floor. Vorelis then picked up the device. With a bow, he handed it back to him."

"That must have been a tense moment for everybody."

"It was" said Atira. "It was especially trying for Queen Myaca. In tears she started to leave the room but my father, Vorelis gently took her aside. He told her a funny story of how he'd once trapped an unwanted visitor in the same room with a huge scorpion, and left him there with it until it was time for dinner."

Hal and Tom laughed at Atira's account. Unlike Hal's laughter, Tom's was sobering. During his visit to the lost island, he shuddered to remember the time he and his companions had been the object of Vorelis' pranks.

*   *   *   *

After their visit to the sun temple, Atira led her guests across a bridge where steaming hot vapors curled around tropical plants defying description. Strange organisms resembling large shrimp swam amidst a primordial mud bath resembling an unappetizing soup.

"We link the past with the present here", she said directing her guests to their accommodations situated precipitously in the branches of trees resembling Cecropia and fig. The fruitful bounty hanging heavily from the tree branches made lunch seem unnecessary

Tom yawned and stretched then glanced upward. He happened to see Whitfield staring down at him "I thought you were going to stay at the palace so you could be in close proximity to the library," he said climbing stairs toward his treehouse balcony.

"Atira thought it would be more comfortable for me to remain here."

Tom finished climbing the treehouse stairs and stood upon his bungalow balcony. Whitfield left Tom standing alone. He retreated to his own treehouse hidden in branches, and shut the door behind him.

Tom then reached into his shirt pocket for his pipe. Placing the pipe stem in his mouth, he gazed at nearby vines hanging from huge trees. He tried to imagine what it would be like to swing through the trees just like Tarzan. Feeling a tap upon his shoulder, he turned. Jeannie was standing alongside him.

"Stop fantasizing. We're both too old to go swinging through the trees."

Tom placed an arm around her: "I rather like the way the treehouse steps wind precipitously into the tree's highest branches."

"Our nearest neighbors seem to be the birds of paradise," said Jeannie, who realized that the tree's heavy branches afforded them privacy in all directions.

Tom then took Jeannie's arm in his and pointed to a bird of paradise perched next to them. The bird whistled a welcome before he swooped down within the greenery to gather up fruits and berries fallen to the ground.

*   *   *   *

The following morning, Whitfield accompanied Atira to the library where he hoped to find out more about the library's function as a research facility. Everyone else took some time off to relax.

"Perhaps I should have accompanied the Professor", said Hal who lazily stretched out in a hammock, placed his hands behind his head and yawned. "This whole business of time travel is exceedingly exhausting. I'm sure Whitfield could have used a little time off—no pun intended, rather than being dragged off to a library where, if you ask me the books seem rather inaccessible. Even Murdock's library made more sense than the library's cataloging system here."

"I'm sure the library's cataloging system makes a good deal of sense to people who use it", contradicted Tom. "We both should have followed along with Atira and Whitfield so I could demonstrate."

"But, Grandfather, you know you've never used such a system. How would you know?" Tom really wasn't sure if he did know but he kept on talking as if he knew.

"I listen when someone demonstrates. You on the other hand, Hal never follow along with the demonstration. That's why a perfectly simple rather ingenious cataloging system doesn't make any sense to you. If your father Harry were here he would tell you the same thing."

"And by the way", said Tom who was feeling rather guilty for having left his son in law behind on an adventure of a lifetime: "Your father probably would have been here rather than stuck in New York during the heat of a 21st C summer if you had returned directly to the family business there and not taken a detour from work."

Jaime, who'd been listening to her father, interrupted him. "You know you were pleased that Hal introduced you first to Professor Whitfield rather than to Harry."

"You and Professor Whitfield are about the same age, Grandfather. I just thought you two would have more in common with one another and more to talk about as well."

"And besides" said Jaime bending over and whispering into Hal's ear, "somebody has to mind the family store. I'll talk to Atira. We'll find someway to get your father here through time and space."

"I'm not returning home-- not yet Grandfather", said Hal who saw Atira approaching them.

Jaime, who'd seen Atira walking toward them too, smiled and invited her to sit down next to her on a huge shaded mushroom. She began the conversation by saying, "You remember my husband Harry don't you?"

Atira smiled at Jaime and said, "Why of course, how could I forget. Harry as I recall, was all too eager to conquer a city that for thousands of years had been left abandoned by the outside world. He along with the rest of you left the premises rather quickly."

"We thought we would perish", said Jaime.

"But you didn't did you. And here you are again but this time without your leader to conquer all once more. I'm sorry", said Atira bursting into tears. "The day to day tensions involving the situation on Mars and Venus not to mention that of Earth's colonies has put me under a great deal of stress."

"I quite understand", said Jaime. "You don't need to apologize."

"I'm not apologizing", said Atira. "Professor Whitfield wants you here because he considers you friends and allies—fellow earthlings of the 21st C. We, on the other hand, merely tolerate your presence. We've allowed Professor Whitfield to include you in his momentous voyage in time because we were hoping you'd learn something from it."

For a moment, Jaime seemed a bit insulted but managed politely to ask the question, "Does that mean we may summon Harry here?"

Atira arose from the huge mushroom. With a mild look of distain, accompanied by a sigh, she remarked. "You may summon Harry here. My Father Vorelis always felt guilty for expelling you so suddenly from the lost city. We now will allow you to assist us in expelling evil from our midst."

"What do you mean by expelling evil from our midst? None of us is even sure what you're up against."

"What we're up against is what you're up against", replied Atira evasively. Settling herself once more upon the giant mushroom she said, "Please be reminded that we beings living during the Golden Age, aren't supposed to know evil. You, on the other hand, come from an age rampant with it. In our age we're not accustomed to intimidating people like Menelus and his son Mars. Queen Myaca is in peril. Those of us loyal to her are ready to fight in defense of Mars and the Earth colonies."

"Well, then said Jaime interrupting Atira, "I'll tell my father and Hal that you need all the support you can get and that Harry must be summoned here immediately."

No sooner had Jaime finished what she had to say to Atira when Whitfield approached them.

"Good afternoon, Professor. I hope your time in the library was well spent."

"I've made a little progress with my work if that's what you mean."

"I'm glad to hear that", said Jaime. "Now I need to tell you that Atira and I have agreed that Harry needs to be summoned here immediately. He must join us as we prepare to become part of the army Vorelis is assembling." Whitfield who'd always worked pretty much on his own found it hard to think of himself as part of an army. Nonetheless he followed Jaime as she led him to the place where her father sat with Hal who still was relaxing in a hammock.

"Atira is going to use the time machine to send Harry a message through time and space. Whatever business urgencies Harry has, must seem minuscule in comparison to what is confronting us here on so mammoth a scale."

Tom didn't need Jaime to explain the importance of Harry's presence. It was Harry's brilliant leadership in years gone by that had led them to the Forgotten Island and the city of gold.

CHAPTER FOUR

▼

Harry was sitting alone in his New York apartment and missing his family. He put aside the book he'd been studying on recent archaeological finds. He turned to his computer so he could check his email messages. He yawned a little and wearily thought about just deleting all messages and going straight to bed. On second thought he decided to read them.

One message in particular caught his eye. "Assistance through time and space will be given by a fellow traveler. Meet Marvelous Amelia at the Circus of Wonders as she demonstrates the talents of Fabulous Natasha the Elephant." A specific time for Harry to attend the circus was given so he printed the email message before deleting it. "What utter nonsense. Is this some sort of joke?" he thought, crumbling the paper and throwing it in the trash? After reconsidering his actions though, Harry retrieved the message. He would attend the circus on the date and time specified.

*   *   *   *

Amelia, the daughter of Gabrielle and John Pelletier, had been born and raised in San Diego, years after her parents' return from the Forgotten Island. After John abandoned her mother, and returned alone to the lost island, Amelia, a college student, had worked part-time at a used car dealership near San Diego. In between answering the telephone and doing some accounting for the dealership's owner, Mr. Jack Hopson, Amelia became especially fond of Natasha, a gentle rather intelligent pachyderm.

Hopson had purchased Natasha from a circus that had gone bankrupt. He displayed her to the public as a means of attracting people into his car dealership. At night the elephant wept inside the uncomfortable quarters of a truck once used for transporting her from city to city when the circus was on tour: She wept at the humiliation of being so forgotten and at the memory of her dear mother, who'd been shot and killed in a jungle by ivory hunters. Left to wander on her own, Natasha had been finally captured, sold to a circus, and then sold to the used car dealership.

Alone and frightened, Natasha's sole comfort in life was the attention Amelia showed her during lunch breaks, when she visited the elephant and brought her bags of carrot treats, apples or a delicious watermelon, Natasha's favorite food.

Following two years of college, Amelia decided to take a bold initiative. She dropped out of school so she could help her friend return to her former days of glory as a star circus performer. With all the money she'd managed to save, Amelia purchased both the elephant and the truck from Hopson.

"I hope you realize I'm practically giving you this elephant and the truck" said her former boss, who was tired of caring for Natasha and relieved that he was getting a little cash for the truck as well. The expense of feeding an elephant and new zoning laws that necessitated his getting rid of Natasha as soon as possible, had enticed Hopson into making a quick sale.

Amelia smiled to herself and hugged Natasha's trunk as the two of them prepared for what lay ahead. Their first circus audition was for a company called "The Circus of Wonders". The circus proprietor, a rather elderly man a little over five feet tall in height was also the circus' resident magician. "The name is Donald Forbush but you may call me Vorelis. That's the name by which I'm known in the circus world. I'm not surprised that you and Natasha perform so well together" he said after their audition. "Natasha comes from a long line of gifted elephants. It is said that her ancestors performed for the gods and carried them upon their backs to sublime regions of the universe."

Amelia listened with fascination as Vorelis continued to tell her of Natasha's distinguished pedigree. With wide eyes she encouraged him to tell her more but the magician, suddenly broke off from the recitation.

"It's difficult living out of a trunk, if you'll excuse the pun. We circus performers get used to it."

"Does that mean we're hired?" asked Amelia

"Yes", said Vorelis walking away and leaving Amelia standing by herself.

After witnessing an evening performance, when Natasha and Amelia had received a standing ovation, Vorelis came to Amelia and said privately, "I see great things ahead for you both."

Wondering if a talent scout had been in the audience. Amelia expected Vorelis to say more. He didn't elaborate.

Later that evening, when she was busy leading Natasha out of the ring, Vorelis ran into Amelia and said, offering her elephant a bag of carrots,"When the Circus of Wonders plays in New York next week, you two will be our star billing."

"Really" said Amelia stroking Natasha's trunk. "Thanks Vorelis."

Amelia then led Natasha to a comfortable barn prepared for her temporary stay in Pittsburgh. "I'll check on you later", she said after she made sure her pachyderm friend was sufficiently fed, watered and comfortable for the night.

She then headed to her dressing room, and got cleaned up before making her way to a nearby diner. On her way to supper she again ran into Vorelis.

"Excuse me for asking you this. I was just wondering. Do you ever see your father, John Pelletier?"

Puzzled to think Vorelis would even know her father, Amelia thought his question rather strange.

"No. Mom and I keep in touch with one another over our cell phones. My father disappeared five years ago."

"I see", replied Vorelis who didn't try to pursue the subject."Fabian the Lion Tamer and Garfield the Clown and I are going to have a bit of supper at the next door diner if you'd care to join us. I assume you're on your way there too."

"Sure, why not" replied Amelia, who'd decided she wouldn't mind having some company. As they walked together toward the diner, Vorelis struck up a conversation by telling Amelia about Harry Worthy.

"He's someone who tried very hard through the years to meet your father but never succeeded in doing so. He'll be present at the Friday evening New York circus engagement. I'm sure he'd be interested in hearing about your father."

At the mention of her father's name again, tears welled up in Amelia's eyes. She quickly tried to hide her emotions.

"My father was an archaeologist of great renown but somehow he couldn't settle down to normal suburban life", she said sounding upset. "He left my mom and all of us when he disappeared in search of a small Pacific island that doesn't even appear on any map. My mother was heartbroken. My father hasn't been seen or heard from since."

Vorelis wanted to tell Amelia that perhaps she was being too hard on her father. Instead, he simply nodded his head in sympathy. He then opened the door to the diner and they joined their circus friends who were already busy eating.

The waitress, poured coffee for them, and set a small plate of eggs and toast before Vorelis. Amelia took a large bite from the hamburger she'd ordered and gazed down at the small supper Vorelis was eating, before saying, "You certainly don't eat very much."

"My dear", replied Vorelis, "In the world from which I come one learns to live not by bread but by the inner spirit directing one to higher planes of consciousness. Food is sometimes a necessity but not the chief source of our nourishment. Your father felt the same way about food as I do."

"How well did you know my father?" asked Amelia seeming curious about the association.

"We're old friends and have been acquainted now on many planes of existence."

Amelia set aside the hamburger she'd been eating. "You sound just like my father. He was always talking about other planes of existence. He wanted to seek them out but my mother was always trying to discourage him from doing so."

"I believe your father has given into his wanderlust", replied Vorelis.

Amelia stared at the hamburger she'd been munching. Tears came to her eyes.

"I'll probably never see my father again."

"My dear, you mustn't be so pessimistic. Wait for further developments. Believe me all isn't lost."

"Hey", said Fabian the lion tamer, who'd been sitting across the table from Amelia and listening to the conversation. "Vorelis is right. All isn't lost", he said before handing her a tissue, "Your father could show up anytime. He's probably just on an extended vacation from life's problems right now."

Garfield the clown agreed and changed the subject by saying, "Say, by the way, you and that elephant perform pretty well together."

"Thanks" said Amelia. "Natasha does it all. I just follow along and let her do her routine which she remembers pretty well from her earlier years in the circus."

"Well, as the saying goes", said Garfield, "'elephants never forget.'"

"And speaking of never forgetting; I mustn't forget to make a detour tonight to the overnight grocery store so that I can bring Natasha a couple of watermelons for an after dinner snack. I'm always afraid she isn't getting enough fruits and vegetables."

"I'll help you carry the watermelons", said Garfield who paid his bill, thanked the waitress, and placed a tip on the table. Taking a last sip of water then setting the glass down, Vorelis followed along with them to the grocery store.

    *   *   *   *

The following morning, the circus was on the road to New York for its scheduled performance there. The truck, driven by Amelia, and carrying Natasha, bumped along the highway as the elephant placed her trunk on a steel compartment window and strained to see a world holding her captive.

When the truck came to a red light at an intersection, Amelia turned her head. She looked through a compartment window so she could check on her friend. She then shoved a bunch of bananas through the window, as the noises of honking horns and police sirens pierced Natasha's ears. Grateful for the snack and the diversion from the traffic jam, Natasha grunted a low rumble of thanks.

*   *   *   *

The Circus of Wonders opened with Amelia and Natasha ready to make their Big Apple debut with a brand new rountine. Harry Worthy gazed at a huge poster featuring them together. He'd already purchased his ticket for the performance, and was about to enter the building when he felt a tap on his shoulder. Upon turning, he found standing behind him, the figure of Vorelis. Immediately Harry recognized him as the same Vorelis who'd expelled him from the lost city so many years earlier.

"I see we meet again", said Vorelis extending a hand in greeting to Harry, who for a moment seemed lost for words.

"Where did you come from?" he asked uneasily, trying to hide his utter amazement at seeing Vorelis again.

"Where do you suppose I came from?" asked the elderly magician who told Harry that he'd been summoned to the Circus of Wonders so he could meet someone special."

"Summoned? Aggravated at Vorelis' use of the word, Harry said: "I came here of my own accord and only because I hadn't been to a circus in many years."

"Well then" said Vorelis trying to placate Harry's seeming indignation, "Regardless of your motivation to come, after tonight's performance, I want you to meet someone special."

Harry started to ask whom he had in mind. He was interrupted when the magician said, "I also have a matter of interest of the utmost importance I wish to discuss with you."

Seeming uncomfortable with his sudden encounter with the old man, Harry felt old resentments resurfacing. He wanted to tell Vorelis to take a walk. On second thought, he decided he would ask him how he managed to end up in a circus.

With a mild look of satisfaction, Vorelis placed his hands together and smiled.

"I have an eternal mission in life. That mission at all costs must be accomplished."

Harry wanted to ask Vorelis to elaborate but an usher, who stood nearby, showed Harry to his seat. Before Harry was whisked away, Vorelis whispered to the usher, "See that Mr. Worthy remains on the premises until after the show so I'll have a further chance to talk with him."

Harry, who'd watched the performance impatiently, could hardly wait for the final act to end so he could escape from the Circus of Wonders. He was disappointed. Once again he found himself trapped by Vorelis.

"Please come", he said. "I want you to meet Amelia and Natasha. They worked hard tonight to deliver a good performance. Amelia has something of interest to tell you."

Harry reluctantly followed Vorelis backstage where he also met Fabian the lion tamer and Garfield the clown.

"I must admit you guys weren't bad", said Harry.

Amelia was grooming Natasha after their evening performance together. She had carefully removed the elephant's decorative costume and was leading her toward an elephant shower when Vorelis and Harry approached them.

"Allow me to introduce someone special": "Amelia, this is Mr. Harry Worthy. He tried many years ago to meet your archaeologist father, John Pelletier. Unfortunately the acquaintance never was made."

Amelia breathed a sigh of dismay. "Please don't remind me of father just now. He's brought enough sadness into my life and into my mother's as well. Mr. Worthy, I don't mean to sound critical of Father. He's let a great many people down in life."

"He's let many people down in life including me", replied Harry. "I don't see how anyone who is perpetually absent from life can let so many people down."

Looking Harry directly in the eye Amelia said, "It's a pity you even tried to meet with Father. Such a meeting could only prove to be a waste of time. Whatever answers to archaeological mysteries my father holds in regard to his discoveries, he holds secret."

Having been listening to their conversation, Vorelis interrupted it by saying, "You hold an unfair opinion of your father. Actually, he's a man of unselfish endeavors. He carries within himself a knowledge of the universe few, if any ever will attain or even understand."

"How do you know that?" asked Amelia. Harry answered the question for the magician.

"Once you get to know our friend Vorelis, you'll see him as a man of great talent and judgement. His skill and understanding of the universe surpasses anything I've seen demonstrated by others."

"How do you know that?" asked Amelia softly. "How many people do you know that well?" She then stared inquisitively at Vorelis.

"He knows a good many", replied Harry.

"And if I may interrupt" said Vorelis. "If you and Mr. Worthy would be interested in getting to know John Pelletier better than either of you has done so previously, I'm prepared to help you make that better acquaintance."

Amelia was hedging. She wasn't sure whether she wanted to see her father: "My mother tried to find Dad after he abandoned us. All attempts failed. She ended up broken hearted. Thank goodness she's now happily remarried."

Then looking at Vorelis directly she said, "Nevertheless, it might be interesting to find out where father is. I'll take you up on your offer to visit him."

"Does that mean you're ready to visit with John Pelletier too?" asked Vorelis turning to Harry.

"I don't see how such a visit could be really profitable at this point in my life. I'm ready to give it a try. I have few business matters I need to attend to first."

"Oh, don't worry about them" replied Vorelis. "I can put your entire life on hold for you as you seek out another dimension."

"But time doesn't stand still" replied Harry.

"Oh yes it does" he explained. "Once you enter that other realm, you'll see exactly what I mean."

Harry's love for adventure had been peaked. He was curious to see where the road would lead him.

"When do we leave?" asked Amelia feeling skeptical. She felt as if she were being pulled into a tidal current from which there was no escape. "Are you sure we won't be missed", she said uncertainly.

"My dear friends, the wonders of the universe await our discovery. How can you doubt my sincerity in wanting to take you on a riveting journey?"

"May I take Natasha with us?" asked Amelia.

"Why of course" replied Vorelis. "I'm sure you wouldn't want to leave her behind and frozen in time until you get around to returning to her."

*   *   *   *

It was later that evening, after the circus arena had become empty and everyone had left for the day, that Vorelis sent word to Fabian the lion tamer and Garfield the clown telling them of his extended absence.

"I'll need one or both of you to carry out my administrative duties. And by the way, for a month or so, the circus will need to hire a temporary replacement act for Amelia and Natasha the elephant."

It was half past midnight when Harry, Amelia and Natasha stood in the midst of an empty circus arena. Vorelis began going through his famous light show routine. On ordinary occasions, midway through such a routine, people would have been brought to their feet with cheers and applause. Now there was no audience. Vorelis stepped beyond what he ordinarily did during a show. The light performance quickly became something else. Suddenly the arena disappeared. Harry, Amelia and Natasha found themselves standing in a field. It was daylight and in the distance, there were cows grazing.

"This is the way this area looked 150 years ago before it went commercial", said Vorelis who waited to see if Harry and Amelia, not to mention Natasha wished to continue the journey.

Natasha's response was an elephant wail of approval.

"Well, I guess that does it. We're on our way to higher planes."

Amelia stroked Natasha's trunk and gazed around in awe as she watched the sky change different hues and the moon and stars whisk by in a spectacular array of color and cosmic splendor.

"Are we almost there?" asked Harry, taking a deep breath. He stretched out his arm. He attempted to touch images that seemed to melt before his gaze as they rapidly appeared then disappeared along time's passageway.

Amelia thought she was going to faint as she watched the dizzying spectacle of color and light whisk by her. She tried to hold fast to Natasha's trunk. Instead the elephant swept her up and placed her behind her ears. In exhaustion, Amelia leaned over and grasped hold of Natasha's neck.

"Sometimes the journey into the unknown has its anxious moments", said Vorelis. "Don't worry, we're almost there."

Suddenly the sky stopped moving. Time's passengers found themselves becoming part of a solid and stationary landscape again. Amelia uncertainly loosened her hold on Natasha's neck. The elephant then gently lifted the girl up before setting her upon the ground.

"Where are we?" asked Harry.

"We are where you have always longed to be."

"Is this Mu?' asked Amelia who'd once heard her father describe such a place.

Vorelis didn't answer her. He waited instead for the next part of the journey to unfold.

"I see people over there" said Harry walking toward them.

Natasha again lifted Amelia up and placed her behind her ears as the travelers walked toward a gathering of familiar people laughing and talking together. Seeing her husband accompanied by a girl riding a circus elephant, Jaime could only stare in astonishment. She started to ask the question "Where did you come from?" She'd hardly gotten the words out when Harry took her in his arms and kissed her. Despite their many years of marriage the spark of romance between them hadn't died.

Jaime had hardly noticed Vorelis standing alongside her husband until he answered the question she'd asked Harry: "I make it my business to overcome the obstacles of time and space".

"We never would have made it here had it not been for him", said Harry complimenting Vorelis on his superb light show.

Hal had been lazily lying in a hammock, but rolled out of it and gave his father a welcoming embrace. "No apologies necessary for taking so long to join us" he said.

Tom placed a hand on his son-in-law's shoulder and said. "Taking off into the unknown without a major research partner, was a mistake. We're glad to see you made it here safely."

"And who are your friends?" asked Jaime referring of course, to Amelia and Natasha.

Amelia, who'd introduced herself and Natasha as Circus of Wonders performers wondered why her time traveling father hadn't been there to greet her. "We've come such a long way", she said trying to fight back the tears.

"In time you will meet your father" said Vorelis. "Be patient".

Seeing that she was visibly disappointed at not having her father greet her upon arrival, Jaime said, "Please tell us who you are dear?"

Vorelis answered the question for her by announcing to everyone that Amelia was indeed the daughter of the one and only John Pelletier. Stunned by the announcement, there was silence. Tom started to make an unkind remark about Pelletier but he was interrupted.

"She looks like top circus billing to me", said Hal who couldn't help but notice how pretty Amelia was with her soft brown hair and blues eyes. "I see she's brought along a circus elephant too."

Vorelis spoke for both Amelia and Natasha. "Amelia is a gifted animal trainer and talented circus performer. Her elephant's talents had been forgotten until Amelia again introduced the elephant to the circus world.

"Natasha is a healthy, intelligent pachyderm. It would have been unfair to leave her behind. Besides, she comes from a very distinguished line of elephants. Her ancestors carried Mu's rulers upon their backs."

"Natasha and I have become inseparable", added Amelia, who suggested that the elephant might be hungry after her journey through time and space. "Right now, she probably would enjoy a delicious meal consisting of oats and pasture grasses. She also likes large quantities of fresh fruits and vegetables, if someone would be so generous as to offer them to her." No sooner had Amelia finished speaking than Atira appeared with an entourage bearing food for Amelia's pachyderm companion.

Harry had no difficulty recognizing Atira. He extended a hand in greeting to her then asked after her sister Ramira. Jaime, who'd always been slightly envious of Atira's eternal beauty and mystifying charm, watched closely as the two struck up a conversation.

"Ramira is fine. She would be here today to greet you but her duties within the lost city prevent her from joining us. I'll tell Ramira that you asked after her."

Jaime quickly took Atira's arm in her own. Then, leading her from Harry's presence, she said. "I've always admired you and your sister so much. Your sense of style and the wonderful way in which you make visitors feel at home are attributes any hostess should wish to emulate."

"Thank you" replied Atira, who knew that Jaime, as usual, was watching Harry's every move out of the corner of her eye.

When Jaime turned again in search of Harry, she found him helping Hal and Amelia spread around the food that had been brought for Natasha's consumption. "Our lunch is waiting for us under those trees" he said, as he watched Hal and Amelia roll a couple of watermelons to Natasha.

"She also likes oats", said Amelia laughing as Natasha rolled one of the watermelons back in Hal's direction.

Taking her arm in his, Hal then led Amelia to where his parents and grandparents were already seated beneath a protective canopy and enjoying the mid-day meal.

"Isn't it lovely the way Atira just wheels everything outdoors so we can enjoy feeling at one with nature" said Jeannie. "Why she does this little a fresco get together perfectly. I haven't even seen one fly yet", she said brushing away an imaginary insect.

"Where's Dad?" asked Amelia, who although she found herself swept away by Hal's undeniable charm, also felt she'd been cheated. "Weren't we supposed to meet father here?" she tearfully asked certain that once more the great John Pelletier had skipped out on her.

"In time, you'll be reunited with him," replied Atira, who now sat at the lunch table too. "Right now your father is concerned with urgent matters in another dimension."

After listening to the explanation regarding John's absence, Jeannie injected her own comment regarding her ex-husband's behavior. Turning to Amelia, she said,"Well, you certainly can't say that John Pelletier isn't predictable."

Tom put a protective arm around his wife. "My dear you mustn't concern yourself as to John's whereabouts."

Hal poured Amelia a glass of wine while she tried to fight back tears. In between sobs she managed to say, "Other dimensions! How absurd. This whole trip to over the rainbow land is just another illusory escapade. I feel like Dorothy in the Wizard of Oz. 'There's no place like home'. Right now I want to be there. I want to be surrounded by real things and not this charade you people are putting on for my benefit."

"Bravo" remarked Jeannie who applauded Amelia. "I think we've all had enough of Vorelis' unwelcome tricks at the lost city".

"Well then" remarked Vorelis. "I'd be happy to return you to your 21st C. reality of wars, turmoil and floods. I was just trying to offer you a pleasant diversion, a chance to play a game that might for the better even change the whole course of history."

"The course of history has already been decided and playing this game of wanting to go into the past to change things is utterly impossible", said Jeannie

"No it's not", said Hal, who'd been listening to the conversation. "When Professor Whitfield and I stepped into his time machine at the Global Trade Mart, we changed the course of history. We prevented a catastrophic event from happening by simply erasing it from time's record."

"How may a mere machine transport one from the grips of destruction?" asked Amelia.

"It didn't entirely. We believed that the time machine played a role in our escape from an inferno. The fact is that both Whitfield and I remained calm in the face of catastrophe—confident that somehow the universal power of good would prevail that day and it did. Our heroism saved not only ourselves but those around us as well.

"I won't ask myself any more questions about what I think may have happened to us at The Global Trade Mart. I won't try to explain to myself why I'm here with you in a place that was supposed to have disappeared from the Earth thousands of years ago."

"Good" said Professor Whitfield who'd just returned from the library and had overheard the luncheon conversation. He set two heavy volumes he'd been carrying, down upon the table then said. "I'm too busy just now to answer any more questions regarding the phenomenon Hal and I experienced on that momentous occasion or how we managed to transport ourselves through time and space to the planet Mars."

"You mean that happened to you too" said Amelia turning to Hal. "Yes" he responded. "I believe Mars is where your father is right now."

"Oh, now I'll never see father", said Amelia dissolving into tears again.

"Oh yes you will my dear", said Vorelis who'd placed a comforting arm around her shoulder. "Right now John's presence upon that planet is indispensable. He's there to protect Queen Myaca from being overthrown by her evil cousin King Menelus of Venus. Menelus would control the solar system if it weren't for the valiant effort of people like your father. In fact, he would annihilate Earth's colonies of Atlantis and Mu too."

"Pelletier has joined the struggle to save the Solar System's Golden Age, and to prevent evil from taking over lives in the 21st century and beyond," interrupted Whitfield.

Amelia gazed at Vorelis and Whitfield. She bent her head, placed her hands over her eyes and shut them. Then looking up she said softly, "I don't believe in time travel. We're all just playing some kind of game. Sooner or later it will be over with and things will be back to normal again."

"My dear" said Whitfield, "An object's speed through space is cancelled when one crashes the light barrier. There is no passage of time at light speed: To go beyond the speed of light and survive, is to grasp the infinite possibilities for the past, present and future. We have a responsibility facing us now though. Since the possibilities for the past, present and future are wide open—we must discover a perfect world," said Whitfield.

Vorelis, who bowed slightly in acknowledgement of what Whitfield had said, simply uttered. "Yes".

After listening to the professor, Amelia finally replied, "I don't think I want to find myself groping for higher realities. I want to catch up with the lower realities confronting me right now."

She then stood up from the table where she'd been sitting and noticed that Natasha had been wandering far afield amidst dense brush. "I think she may hide or disappear completely if I don't catch up with her."

Hal who'd whistled in hope that the elephant would return to them ran alongside Amelia as the two raced to catch up with the slowly moving elephant.

Just as Natasha was about to disappear into thick brush, Hal whistled again.

Natasha then obediently wandered over to Amelia, lifted her up, and placed her behind her ears before picking up Hal as well.

"It looks as though she's retrieved us and not the other way around," said Hal laughing.

Natasha slowly made her way to the tree house accommodations where everyone was staying. She stopped only momentarily, to pluck some luscious fruit from tree branches so she could carry it with her to eat later.

When she reached the stable prepared for her beneath Amelia's tree house home, Natasha dropped the fruit. She gently set Hal and Amelia upon a tree house balcony.

"You and Natasha seem to need each other", said Hal patting Natasha's trunk.

"We're best friends" replied Amelia. "I give Natasha the care and sustenance civilization has denied her."

"Well, it looks like we're next door to one another", said Hal opening the door to his tree house.

"Good night", he said as Amelia disappeared into her own tree house.

*   *   *   *

The sun was beginning to set. In the distance the sound of chanting was heard coming from those who offered prayers to the sun.

Harry and Jaime, who'd been visiting the temple, were walking along a path together when Harry said, "Time's reality may have been suspended in this wonder world. I still feel the pulse of a normal earth day descending upon me."

The couple then paused to greet Whitfield who was returning from a visit to the Imperial Library. A mild tropical breeze blew from the ocean and rocked the palm trees as the world rested and became still. "Good night" said Whitfield as he continued on his lonely way.

The following morning as everyone met over a luscious breakfast of tropical fruits and freshly made whole grain breads, Atira announced: "I have good news. This morning as I was looking at my time screen to see if I had any messages, I received a message from John Pelletier. Queen Myaca feels confident that she will be able to block any attempts Menelus might make to kidnap her and throw her into an undesirable dimension. She insists that John should be reunited with his daughter. Pelletier will be joining us within the celestial hour."

The clouds above began to gather and darken as the sun retreated behind them. Within seconds a low rumble of thunder was heard followed by a sonic boom that shook the Earth. A tremendous flash of lightning lit up the sky. In the distance, a figure approached the group of people sitting at breakfast under a protective canopied patio.

Amelia stood up from the table where she had been sitting and cautiously approached the figure she saw walking toward them.

"It's been so many years since—we last saw you", she said looking at her father.

Pelletier, who seemed stunned to see his daughter, could only stammer. "How did you get here?"

Amelia gazed at her father and said through her tears, "Vorelis insisted I travel through time and space to meet you." She then turned away from her him. She tried to hide the feelings of insecurity she felt, before she blurted out in anger, "How could you abandon us?

"Mother waited years for you to return to us before she had you declared dead. She's remarried to someone else now."

John, who'd always known he'd failed miserably as a husband and father, wanted to take Amelia aside and apologize for the lapses in the family relationship. He started to tell her why he'd abandoned her mother. He knew any explanation he could give in that regard wouldn't make up for years of neglect.

"I just got lost in time. The years went by so quickly before I realized I'd lost you entirely. Did you come here to bring me home?"

"No" she replied. "I came here to find you. I knew I could never bring you home."

Pelletier turned away from Amelia. He was speechless, sad and proud all at the same time. He was proud that his daughter had managed to find him through time and space but sad that she'd made the journey to meet him totally on her own or almost on her own. What he hadn't expressed to his daughter was the inner sadness he felt at his own personal failures.

"Life's obligations can be overwhelming", he said apologetically as he watched her turn away and walk from him."

"What's wrong?" asked Jaime, who put her arms around a weeping Amelia.

"You know, your father has the worst reputation for walking out on people when they need him the most. That doesn't mean he doesn't love you though", she said trying to comfort the girl.

"That's right", said Jeannie who'd realized that the father and daughter reunion wasn't going as smoothly as planned. "You know before I divorced your father and he married your mother, I made up my mind that I would never let anybody hurt me again. Your father's not a bad person. He's just a man who's totally wrapped up in his work and his own life. That's the way it's going to be whether anybody likes it or not. Believe me, he loves you and wouldn't want to hurt you."

When John finally met with Vorelis and told him how the meeting with Amelia had gone, Vorelis made it plain to John that it was he who'd convinced Amelia to accompany him through time and space. "She was reluctant to come"

"I guess she didn't want to confront me with all my personal inadequacies", he said sadly.

"You mustn't say such a thing".

John sadly gazed around at the landscape. The sun that earlier had peeked through the clouds had disappeared from the face of a lush, peaceful landscape. John Pelletier, the brilliant time traveler felt guilty. He suddenly felt himself being overwhelmed by an unseen storm sweeping him into oblivion and away from others. Within moments, he'd disappeared.

Vorelis shouted, "He's gone", as Harry, who'd heard his cry came running to see for himself.

"Can't you summon him back?" asked Harry.

"No" replied Vorelis. "I think John has returned to Mars so that he may first face his own inadequacies. Once he does, perhaps he'll rejoin us again."

"We all have shortcomings", said Harry gazing down at the spot where John had last been seen.

"Right now it may be too difficult for both John and Amelia to be together. It takes time for old wounds to heal."

"Right" said Harry, who wondered how her father's disappearance would affect Amelia. Later when Vorelis met Amelia he said, "You mustn't take your father's disappearance to heart. You'll see him again."

"Thanks for trying to help" said Amelia as she shuffled away from his company and the company of everyone else. Followed only by the loyal Natasha, the elephant insisted on picking the girl up and placing her behind her ears. She then foraged for fruits and nuts so abundant in Mu's forests.

Tears streamed down Amelia's face as she lay down between Natasha's comforting ears and sobbed. Although she wouldn't admit it to anyone, Amelia felt humiliated to think she'd traveled all this distance to find her famous archaeologist dad only to realize he was still a rolling stone.

Amelia was unaware that Natasha understood her thoughts and emotions and that she was sympathetic to her. "If only we elephants ran the universe. Everyone might be delivered from the pain man inflicts not only upon himself but upon other living beings."

Natasha then raised her great trunk and trumpeted a wail as she remembered her mother's tragic death. Amelia momentarily forgot her own problems. She gently caressed and patted her friend's head. "You're trying to tell me something aren't you", she whispered. The elephant grew calm again.

Natasha then flicked away a few flies with her tail, and the two friends continued to journey along life's trail together.

Chapter Five

▼

Murdock, who'd greeted John upon his return to Mars, couldn't help but notice his friend's melancholy spirit.

"What brings you back so soon, John? We'd expected that you'd want a little more time to get to know your daughter."

Feeling that Murdock was prying into his personal business, John wanted to tell his furry friend to go bury his head in his burrow. On second thought, he didn't want to hurt Murdock's feelings. He said nothing.

When John didn't offer an explanation for his sooner than expected return, Murdock tried telling him a few Martian jokes. When that didn't work, Murdock finally said, "Don't be downcast. Your daughter must find her own way through life's labyrinth. Once she gets her bearings and is headed in the right direction, you'll meet again. When that happens, you'll both have something worthwhile to say to one another."

"My daughter sees right through me", said John who hung his head in despair. "She's made me take a hard look at myself. What I see isn't what I wanted to find. My two failed marriages happened because I quite frankly had the wanderlust and couldn't settle down to a daily routine."

When I returned to the Marquesas and the house my missionary parents had built and raised me in, I became so obsessed by the legend of the Forgotten Island, I could think of little else. I knew that the island was hidden from the world, that only a handful of people had ever visited it, and I was one of them. I forgot about my friends, my family and the life I'd left behind. That was the price I paid for finally returning to the island and becoming a time traveler."

Murdock studied John's face before he said. "You may have left your family behind when you went in search of the island and the city of gold.

Once you achieved your goal, you made new friends. Those friends, I might add, have taken you to the far reaches of the universe."

John, felt guilty for sounding so ungrateful for the experiences his journeys through time had given him. "When I confront Amelia again, I want to have conquered my weaknesses."

"Right now you've had the strength to confront your past and your shortcomings. Once you conquer them, you'll be strong enough to take on other foes and win. First you must look beyond the selfish confines of your own world and embrace a world in desperate need of your attention. The 21$^{st\,C.}$ world is riddled with pockets of want and poverty. I nearly wept at the image of Darfur where people are forced off their lands. Starving and poor, these people have no place to go. If the 21st C. is to be remembered as a great era for man then the fate of those poor people and others must not end in death or in poverty. Any age is only as good as the individuals who comprise it."

"Correct", responded John. "I don't want to face that one alone. I don't want to think that I've in any way contributed to such 21st C. misery."

Murdock thought of the necessity of bringing more individuals such as himself and Pelletier into the cause surrounding the overthrow of want and misery. "We'll never win if we don't change our concept of the world and others. The Golden Age will never be realized in the 21st C. unless men become less selfish toward other beings including us animals."

"I think we've got a long way to go in that regard," replied John who watched as Murdock poured himself a good strong cup of pomegranate tea, gulped it down and then asked John if he'd like a cup too."

"No thanks" he said slipping past Murdock and disappearing into the shadows.

After his friend left him, Murdock walked down the hall of his palatial burrow and gazed at the time travelers' mirror. "Look at me" he said addressing the mirror. "I'm a mere descendant of a mole-like creature who managed to pull himself up the evolutionary ladder by denying his shortcomings."

"Did you say something to me?" asked John who'd overheard Murdock's conversation with the mirror. Turning from the exit, John now stood before his friend.

"Try looking for the positive side in others as well as yourself", said Murdock trying to hide his own sense of insecurity.

Still despondent, John shuffled past his friend and made his way to the door again. "I'm feeling a bit weary right now. I'll consider what you've said to me later.

"Good" said Murdock as his voice eerily echoed down the hallway of his burrow. "We'll shoulder our responsibilities together."

No sooner had Murdock finished speaking when a heavy fog engulfed the Martian landscape. The dense clouds of mist hung over the Sun Temple and even crept inside cracks in the door and beneath the temple's enclosed area where John and Murdock had been talking.

Seeing that the fog had crept under the door to his burrow, Murdock thrust his weight against the heavy gold and silver door and opened it. His first reaction to what he saw was that he was seeing a perfectly natural phenomenon. The Sun Temple wasn't far from the Martian Sea. It was quite possible that the pink fog enveloping everything around them was fog rolling in from the ocean.

Then Murdock heard a terrible scream. The scream echoed within the halls of the Sun Temple and reverberated on the early evening air. The scream seemed to be coming from more than one direction and defied discovery.

John, who'd heard the same scream, opened the door to his accommodations and, quickly tried to find his friend Murdock.

Seeing that Murdock was fine, John said, "I don't think there's any point in our looking for the origin of such a terrible cry until the fog has lifted and there's plenty of daylight."

Murdock nodded his head in agreement but still gazed around the corridor.

"Please don't forget that Morning repast is at 8:00AM", he said to John as he watched him turn and begin walking along a corridor.

Smiling, John thanked Murdock for reminding him. As he made his way toward his rooms, solar panel lighting streamed down from above. John gazed upward at the dizzying serpentine forms represented on the ceiling of Murdock's burrow. For a moment he felt weak and disoriented. When he reached his room, he noticed that the door to it was open. A pot of tea a butler had brought to him earlier was sitting on a small table next to a bed. Ignoring the calming brew, John yawned then threw himself across the bed and went to sleep.

His rest went undisturbed until he was awakened during the middle of the night by the same shrill scream he'd heard earlier. Bolting out of bed, John opened the door to his room. Stepping into an empty hallway, he listened again for the scream. He heard and saw nothing. Trying to convince himself that what he'd just heard had to be part of an unpleasant dream, John returned to his room. Closing the door behind him. He then gazed down at the teapot still full to the brim with the calming liquid. "Perhaps I should have had some of that before I went to sleep", he thought climbing back into bed.

John's rest went undisturbed for the remainder of the night. In the morning, after he'd met Murdock for morning prayers and breakfast, he was shocked to learn that in the middle of the night, Queen Myaca had mysteriously disappeared.

"We must find the Queen at all costs", said Murdock. John only wished that it had been he and not Queen Myaca who'd disappeared. He and Murdock agreed that they shouldn't waste any time in making inquiries into her disappearance.

"Rest assured" replied Murdock. "Everything is being done to find her. I have the worst suspicion that her cousin Menelus or his son Mars have the dear lady in their clutches and won't let her go", said Murdock anguishly ringing his paws.

"Has Vorelis been informed of the Queen's disappearance yet?" asked John.

"This morning, I sent Vorelis a message telling him of it. I'm still waiting to hear from him.

"Don't fret. I believe, with Vorelis' leadership, any effort we put forth to rescue Myaca must have positive results.

CHAPTER SIX

▼

The dark especially cloudy Venusian sky took on a strange purplish hue as Vorelis, having transported himself through time and space, set foot upon that planet. The rumble of thunder shook the planet as an unhealthy rain imbued with pollutants and gases, pelted down upon the once pristine Venusian landscape.

Having studied Menelus' evil mind, Vorelis instinctively knew where his adversary was hiding the beautiful Queen Myaca. "Menelus wouldn't dare send her off to some hostile dimension" he thought. "He knows he would have civil war on his hands if he did."

The magician returned the intricate time traveling mirror to his pocket, and made haste. He knew Menelus and his cronies were fortified in a palatial Venusian fortress. "Menelus must be confronted at once", thought Vorelis sweeping unseen past sentinels who guarded the fortress. Menelus will have no choice but to free the Queen once he realizes I'm about to bring his fortress plummeting down around his ears if he doesn't do so."

The steep winding steps of palatial apartments were connected to a large room where Menelus was busy greeting guests and visitors. A huge intricately carved wooden door, inlaid with semi precious stones and dragon images swung open as the magician entered the reception area.

Vorelis, who'd remained invisible until now, stood before Menelus and the assembled guests. With a sweeping bow and confident smile, he said, in a courteous manner, "It is always such a pleasure to pay a visit to such a distinguished personage as you".

Menelus wanted to say, "How dare you come here uninvited". Instead he said rather meekly, "Surely it can't be the Venusian climate that has brought us the unexpected pleasure of your visit."

"No, your majesty," replied Vorelis. "I understand you have a distinguished guest staying with you. Although I'm sure you are treating her with the utmost hospitality, her friends and subjects miss her. They would like for Queen Myaca to return at once to her Martian home." Menelus was already feeling the discomfort of a warmer than usual Venusian day. He now seemed even more uncomfortable with what Vorelis had just told him. Menelus didn't want to appear a coward. He rose from where he was sitting and bravely confronted Vorelis face to face. He smiled uneasily and his hands shook when he said, "My cousin Myaca and I have been friends since childhood. She and I grew up together here on Venus. I missed her when she returned to Mars so she might marry Prince Sentius. Now that she is queen I see even less of her. I realize she's been under great stress ever since she lost her dear father. Now her husband is missing, trapped in the dark dimension, unable to extricate himself. I was only trying to offer Myaca a little escape from her ordeal--a diversion from the daily worries and suffering she lately has undergone."

Vorelis listened to Menelus's explanation for Myaca's abduction. He searched the frightened faces of the room's assembled guests. There was a deathly calm. Then Vorelis said quite decisively, "Now that the Queen has partaken of your hospitality, I have come to transport her home to her people at once."

There was an embarrassing silence. Menelus seemed unable to reply to what had just been said to him. His face darkened with a look of deep discontent. With a nervous laugh, and knowing that Vorelis had just given him an ultimatum he said, "I'll take your request that the Queen be released into consideration."

Vorelis was silent, the expression on his face stoney. The room began to tremble as if the floor was about to give way directly beneath Menelus. Trying to appear nonchalant, he nervously laughed saying, "I believe Myaca told me just this morning that she missed her Martian friends and would like to see them soon."

Vorelis smiled a look of deep satisfaction to think that he'd actually backed Menelus into a corner. His calm diplomatic maneuvering, coupled with a mild tremor or two, had won the Queen's release.

Menelus could hardly mask his fury behind a look of detached calm. "I'm just glad I was able to provide my dear cousin with a short vacation from her responsibilities." He then excused himself so he could invite Myaca into their presence.

Upon entering the room, Myaca appeared cheerful and composed. She greeted Vorelis by saying, "Why, what a lovely surprise. Your visit is so unexpected. First I experienced the unexpected pleasure of having Menelus summon me to his side. Now your arrival upon the scene has given me even added pleasure."

Vorelis breathed a sigh of relief when he was told that arrangements for Myaca's return travel to Mars had been made.

"Won't you please join us first for lunch though", said Menelus gesturing for the assembled guests to follow him into the dining area for a sumptuous meal. Myaca politely settled herself between Menelus and Vorelis. After a toast from wine distilled from the leaves of a rare Venusian palm tree, Myaca raised a gold fork and began picking at her salad.

Vorelis calmly complimented Menelus on his choice of wines and took pleasure in the food too. He started to tell Menelus how much he'd enjoyed seeing him again but wasn't sure under the circumstances, how the Venusian king would react. Vorelis knew he'd forced his foe to return a precious commodity. He'd done so without violence.

Menelus' hands quivered in anger as he watched Myaca and Vorelis leave his presence bound for Mars.

*   *   *   *

The news of Myaca's abduction and rescue traveled quickly within the solar system of 16,000 years ago. When Atira and Ramira heard that their father had successfully rescued the Martian Queen, they weren't surprised.

Atira had been assisting Whitfield with his library research when a message was received from Ramira giving the reason for Myaca's abduction: In recent years, Venus had become such a threat to Martian security, that important information once filed in Martian libraries was now filed only in the lost city.

"When Menelus realized he couldn't crack a secret code, accessing information, he wanted, in retribution he decided to abduct the Queen and hold her prisoner until the information he wanted was handed over to him. It seems that his attempt to steal information hasn't gone unnoticed. A footnote to the historic attempt has been placed in our special filing system."

"Do you think anyone else knows about the footnote?" asked Whitfield sounding rather shocked.

"No" replied Atira. "Only my sources that keep the system updated have that secret information."

Ramira, who'd continued to send her sister and Whitfield information, suddenly broke off in mid sentence saying, "I've just received another coded message from our sources. Menelus has incapacitated normal time travel to the lost city: His spies have set up confusing detours, ultimately leading nowhere. My Father was no fool when he allowed Tom Daudelier and Harry Worthy to visit the lost city during the 1960's. The sundisk hieroglyphics they deciphered may be our only blueprint for gaining physical access to the Lost City."

Stunned by the information he'd just received, Whitfield asked Atira to find Harry and bring him to them. Within seconds, Harry stood in their presence. The first thing Whitfield asked him was, "Did you bring the sundisk with you?"

"I think Jaime brought it with her. She's always believed that some of the sundisk's symbols remained untranslated or have been mistranslated. She thought that during our visit here we might be able to obtain a complete translation."

"Where is Jaime now?"

"She and Jeannie went to watch Amelia put Natasha through her circus routine. Since Natasha is grazing in a field now, they're visiting a teahouse adjacent to the field."

*   *   *   *

"Of course I've got the sundisk", said Jaime as Harry and Whitfield, on either side of her sat down next to her on a prayer rug. "Hush", said Harry, who realized that their conversation had been overheard by people trying to meditate

"Why would you even ask such a question?" she said lowering her voice.

After they'd left the tearoom, and were walking alongside together, Jaimie asked Harry why it was so important that she'd remembered to bring the sundisk.

"Menelus has blocked all time passages leading to the lost city. Further deciphering of the disk's hieroglyphics may be our only means of discovering the city's whereabouts in time and space."

"I find what you're saying hard to believe", said Jaime,"I thought Vorelis had everything under his control in the lost city. Surely he hasn't relinquished his responsibilities."

Atira who'd been closely monitoring everything Harry was telling Jaime, and had been following unseen behind them, interrrupted their conversation."Vorelis hasn't relinquished anything. Father can't be two places at once. He left the Forgotten Island so he could help Queen Myaca. Unfortunately she doesn't have everything under control". Atira then turned a corner and disappeared.

*   *   *   *

When Myaca had heard that the key to the Forgotten Island had been lost, that the file containing the code enabling one to discover the island's whereabouts in time and space was missing, her displeasure was immediate and apparent.

Vorelis, who'd been with her when she'd received the news, tried to calm her. Myaca's indignation was such that she picked up a piece of priceless Titanian pottery Menelus had given her, and smashed it upon the floor.

"How dare Menelus tamper with the Imperial Library records or intrude upon me. If he thinks that Mars is his so easily, he'll soon be surprised."

"Please, my dear", said Vorelis gazing down at pieces of the shattered, priceless urn, "you mustn't be upset." She'd hardly noticed that Vorelis, with his ingenious power for putting things back together again, within seconds had the urn sitting back upon a table in its usual place.

"I'm not upset", said Myaca still sniffling. "I'm just a bit enraged to think that Menelus could steal from me so easily."

"Here" said Vorelis handing Myaca a handkerchief so she could blow her nose. "You must compose yourself."

"Menelus has allowed his planet to become an ecological disaster. The temperatures on Venus are unbearable. If he gains access to the Forgotten Island or precious real estate here or on Mu or Atlantis, he'll destroy them too.

I've contacted my sister Queen Moo. I've warned her not to trust Menelus. In the past, she unwittingly has been drawn into his schemes. She's told me that Menelus wants to form an alliance with her against me. I've warned her that to do so would be utter madness, and would only end in some terrible confrontation. Fortunately Moo is taking my advice. A family confrontation must be avoided at all costs. There is tremendous strength within the solar system. For any of us to unleash its destructive power would be foolish."

Vorelis appeared to take the information Myaca had given him without alarm. Inwardly he was upset."As a friend and advisor, I would take care in confiding in your sister. Free exchange of information regarding your dealings with Menelus should remain confidential. As for Menelus's attempt to abduct you, I would advise you to tell your sister, you merely had been enjoying Menelus' hospitality. If Moo thinks that Menelus had been planning to exile you to another dimension, she might become too fearful to confide in you lest a similar attempt be made by him to abduct her as well."

Myaca apologized for her tirade. "I feel so desolate since Prince Sentius disappeared. I used to be able to deal with the everyday pressures of living. Without him, I feel weak and especially vulnerable to hostile threats of any sort. I used to enjoy venturing into the public domain. Now my spirit has been crushed. Even the will to live has become a daily task. My position is a lonely one. I sometimes feel, there is nobody I can trust."

"Madame" said Vorelis, appearing a little embarrassed by the queen's utter honestly, "I can assure you no harm will come to you. Menelus and his cronies may feel they are superior in power to you but there are those of us who believe that within their company are those who would betray. Trust me when I say, you are fortunate to have around you only those who are loyal."

Myaca then took Vorelis's arm and led him to a balcony. She pointed in the distance to craggy volcanic mountains. Beyond the mountains was a rough forbidding seacoast. "It is whispered that strange sea beasts come ashore there to bask in the warm Martian sun. They then disappear into sea craters of a seemingly bottomless ocean, and prompt speculation: The sea beasts aren't beasts at all but are amphibious robotic spy submarines employed by Menelus to scan the lonely and desolate Martian coastline."

Myaca left Vorelis standing alone on the balcony. She then wearily leaned against an indoor pillar and closed her eyes. When she opened them she found Vorelis standing beside her. "You mustn't overtax yourself with worry", he said as a robot butler entered the room, wheeling a teacart. Myaca smiled a reasuring smile. "I'm quite all right", she said sitting down on a divan before offering her friend a cup of tea. Vorelis sat down on the divan next to her. He took the cup from her hand as Myaca, leaned over, picked up a tray from a nearby table and offered her friend a piece of cake flavored with pungent pomegranate juice. The warm liqueur flavored icing oozed from the deliciously textured cake as Vorelis imbibed the calming tea, and with satisfaction bit into the cake.

*   *   *   *

"Plans must be made at once to return to the Forgotten Island", said Atira who'd delivered a message to an assembled group of time travelers. Present within that small assembly, was the stalwart Tom Daudelier, Harry Worthy, their wives, Jeannie and Jaime, and the youngest group members, Amelia and Hal.

Amelia smiled cordially at Hal who had taken a seat next to her. A mild tropical breeze blew the palm trees aligning the portico in front of Mu's famous library. "Why did Atira choose to have the meeting outside?" whispered Amelia to Hal.

"She knows we've been enjoying ourselves trying to pretend we're on vacation. She didn't want to spoil our escape into paradise by telling us about the problems that come with ruling an empire."

"Hush", whispered Amelia giggling. "Atira might hear you."

Hal looked up and smiled. He'd seen Atira glance in his direction. Then whispering to Amelia he said, "Dad says Atira is afraid Menelus may have succeeded in having the library's main interior rooms bugged. She's taking no chances on him learning about our expedition plans. We're all sitting here out of earshot."

As Hal spoke, Natasha, who'd been grazing in a lush meadow adjacent to the library, wandered over to them. On bended knees, she extended her long trunk so that Amelia could hand her a bunch of bananas, one of the elephant's daily intermittent snacks.

"Natasha hates being by herself too long. I think she's trying to tell me that it's time for her daily slosh in the river too." Emitting a low rumbling sound in response to Amelia's remark, Natasha patiently settled herself nearby as Atira lectured to the assembled audience.

"As some of you may know, with Harry and Tom's assistance, I've managed to decode the remaining sundisk symbols. It is now of the utmost importance that the sundisk be protected so that the decoded message remains inaccessible to those who would pursue us in our journey to the Forgotten Island."

Atira continued to emphasize the gravity of the situation but was interrupted when Whitfield, arriving late for the meeting, burst in upon them. He immediately apologized to Atira for his tardiness but interrupted her again when he said: "In studying the sundisk hieroglyphics this morning, I've come to the conclusion that what we may have decoded is also a mathematical formula. I won't be sure of my hunch until we visit the lost city and I can look for records supporting my hypothesis."

"The sooner we leave for the Forgotten Island the better" said Atira, stepping down from the platform so she could confer with Whitfield. Before she did though, Harry asked, "The last time we accessed the Forgotten Island, was by water: Are we to journey there in the same manner now?"

"The Forgotten Island in your time is an island. In our time, 16,000 years ago it is a peninsula. After studying the sundisk hieroglyphics, I've decided the best way to access the Forgotten Island's lost city is to journey to it over land. I've contacted Deiphos of the Cloud Temple. He will protect us on our pilgrimage to a sacred place."

Will Natasha be able to accompany us too" asked Amelia who didn't want to leave her friend behind and unattended. "Vorelis told me that Natasha's ancestors once carried the rulers of Mu upon their backs. Shouldn't she now have the added honor of carrying our equipment and supplies to the lost city? She has a keen nose for spying out fruits and vegetables and in locating fresh water sources too."

Atira knew that traditionally elephants led important processions. "Of course Natasha should accompany us." Understanding what Atira had said, Natasha rose from her great knees, raised her trunk, and trumpeted an elephant wail of triumph. At last she would be traveling the path of her mother's ancestors.

"When do we leave?" asked Jaime holding the precious sundisk and gazing down at it as if she were seeing it for the first time.

"As soon as possible" replied Atira.

*   *   *   *

The following morning, after dawn had enveloped the sky, Atira offered prayers to the sun. Then rising from the lotus position, she led the expedition team into the wilderness. Huge colorful butterflies of every imaginable description surrounded the procession as the team followed a path running parallel to a river. Weaving like a green serpent slithering through the jungle's interior, the river's gurgling sounds were enhanced by the croaking of frogs, and birdcalls from inhabitants living in branches bending low over river's edge.

Walking together, Jaime and Harry lagged behind the rest of the party. Jaime was convinced their companions had taken the wrong path: A butterfly had come to rest on her hand at precisely the moment she and Harry would have accompanied the others along a path following the river. Harry called to Tom and told him to wait. Jaime raised her arm. Another path was just feet from where she and Harry stood. Their companions quickly glanced back in their direction and watched as the butterfly, fluttered around Jaime, then marked out the correct path for them to follow. Atira, who'd stayed just ahead of the rest of the party, glanced over her shoulder. She watched as the butterfly fluttered around Natasha's head until the elephant turned and took the correct path.

"The ancients believe that butterflies are sacred, and will guide pilgrims through the wilderness," said Atira.

"I hope the butterfly has scoped out this territory before", said Hal watching as the beautiful green and white butterfly settled between Natasha's great ears.

"The path the butterfly has chosen is hidden in time. According to the sundisk's hieroglyphics, that you didn't translate, a butterfly will lead us to a sacred temple sanctuary." As Atira spoke, Natasha passed under a moss enshrouded ancient tree where myriad species of insects and forest creature's slept beneath the rotting tree's silent veil.

"I don't hear any noises at all", said Jeannie gazing in several directions, and expecting some creature, sight unseen, would emerge from the brush. Tom assured her that silences were to be expected in any rain forest environment.

Soon the silence was broken. Atira raised her hand and signaled for everyone to listen. Low chanting accompanied by the steady muffled beat of drums permeated the air. The chanting continued to grow louder as the group approached an edifice partially hidden by jungle growth. Natasha continued to move forward but stopped in her tracks when the butterfly flew from her ears.

"We're not going anywhere now Natasha", said Amelia."You can put me on the ground. I believe were here for a temporary stay."

"Look" said Hal, standing on the ground next to Natasha with Amelia still on board. "Somebody's coming to meet us."

A monk with shaven head and clothed in a simple woven garment approached the visitors. Atira, who customarily wore beautiful ceremonial robes depicting her high status within Mu's hierarchy, wore a garment of similar weave. Deiphos bowed slightly to her: "We trust your journey has been an uneventful one. We've been watching your progress from a high vantage point within the forest. Our prayers for your safe arrival have been answered." As Deiphos spoke, Natasha gently placed Amelia on the ground next to Hal.

Atira bowed in acknowledgement of the greeting: "We are thirsty. We have traveled a great distance and wish to drink from the sacred waters here. Deiphos knew that the waters Atira wished to drink from not only would quench her thirst. The waters of the subterranean river would bring her tranquility as well.

"Come" he said. "A little food and drink await you and your companion."

Deiphos then led the way through the jungle to the base of a steep stone stairway gradually winding toward a stone structure affixed to the temple's highest level.

The Cloud Temple was open and accessible to pilgrims who came for prayers and meditation. A monk, with a large silver cup, met Deiphos and his guests at the temple's base. The water cup was handed first to Atira then to each one of her guests. After drinking the water, Atira motioned for her guests to follow her example: Sitting upon the ground, she assumed the lotus position. Then falling into deep meditation, she offered prayers of thanksgiving.

Rising from meditation, a monk offered Natasha sacred water from a huge wooden bucket. The elephant then stood still beneath a huge rainforest tree. She watched as Amelia and the other pilgrims followed Deiphos into the temple structure reaching into the clouds above.

When they came to a mid level sanctuary, Deiphos gestured for the pilgrims to follow him. A thanksgiving meal celebrating their safe journey had been prepared for them. Before she sat down to eat with the others, Amelia stood alone in a huge temple window. The pungent fragrance of flowers and ferns surrounded her in the early evening stillness. As she gazed downward, she saw Natasha with the messenger butterfly still poised between her ears.

With a swing of her trunk, Natasha reached into the trees above, and partook of the abundant rain forest vegetation.

Deiphos and the monks with him curiously watched their guests eat. They politely waited until the visitors had finished their meal, before they inquired as to the nature of their pilgrimage to the Lost City.

As if anticipating their questions, Atira gazed at the onlookers and said. "Our journey concerns time's mysteries and the problems facing the future of the Golden Age. We are weary but today time retreated when we penetrated these sacred jungles and found the Cloud Temple. We'll need your support and prayers as we journey to our destination."

Atira then showed Deiphos the sundisk. He knew Atira was the lost city's guardian. Her right to enter forbidden passages there could never be denied. He recognized the disk's hieroglyphics indicating the existence of a hidden path ultimately leading to the lost city. "A safe and easy journey to the Lost City lies ahead for you and your companions", he said bowing politely.

Following the evening meal, Atira and her companions were shown to simple, comfortable accommodations within the temple. Once again the monks' chanting resonated as the pilgrims drifted off to sleep in the early evening stillness.

Only Natasha remained awake as darkness fell upon them. Standing directly beneath the place where Amelia rested, she raised her great trunk in a wail of farewell. As the last light of day faded from the sky, she too shut her eyes in sleep.

*   *   *   *

The following morning, Deiphos showed the pilgrims the sacred path under which the sacred subterranean river reputedly flowed. Amelia and Hal sat atop Natasha as the elephant led the way. The rest of the party, including Atira walked behind them. After the pilgrims had followed the path for several hours, Atira raised her arm and said,"We'll rest here".

Nyas, the monk Deiphos had sent to accompany them, spread rugs upon flat rocks so they could sit down for a midday repast. Crusty bread, dried nuts and fruits were handed to all. Atira took a sip of sacred water from a silver cup. Then looking up from where she sat upon a rock she said,"We're nearing the Bridge of Clouds. We must hurry if we are to reach it before nightfall."

"Nyas pointed to traces of the bridge just above the trees. "The sacred hawk is guardian of the Cloud Bridge. He is also a time traveler. Brother hawk knows the bridge connects the civilized word with what lies unseen and beyond the normal reach of man. In your time, after the destruction of Mu, such birds served as messengers from the lost land. Their ancient effigies are found in the forms of monoliths and ancient symbols throughout N. and

S. America and elsewhere. The American Indian's great thunderbird is such a symbol as are the bird symbols of ancient Egypt and the great soapstone bird carvings of ancient Africa.1 Pilgrims who traverse this pristine wilderness look upon this land as sacred, a shrine that mustn't be defaced or destroyed by man."

The bridge, suspended in space, loomed before them. "It reached high into the mountains above the rain forest and bridged the gap between the rainforest and the mountains surrounding them". Atira raised her arms in salutation. As she did, the hawk came and perched upon her shoulder. He then perched upon her wrist as she released him and he soared into the clouds above.

"Come" she said turning to her companions, "we will cross into the clouds now."

The hawk continued to soar above them until he swept downward and surveyed the passage before the travelers. After stepping onto the Cloud Bridge, and walking upon it for several hours, the bridge dipped downward. The pilgrims found themselves nearly walking across the tops of trees. Nyas said they were descending into the rainforest canopy where they would rest amidst the shelter of fragrant flowering trees and feast on an abundant array of fruits and nuts. During the rest period, Jaime turned to Nyas. She asked him who built the Cloud Bridge?

"There are those who will tell you that the gods of ancient times built the bridge. That information is incorrect. The answer to your question is rooted neither in the mythology of Mu nor in the history of the Chucaran Empire. The Cloud Bridge was formed neither by god-like beings nor humans hands."

Nyas then sat down, took a small drum in hand, and began to beat upon it. As he chanted along with the drum's rhythmic beat, his chanting gradually turned into a narrative. The recitation told the tale of the snow spider that once having become entrapped in mountain snows, had to escape from them. The spider, nearly starved and frozen, began spinning a diaphanous web across a seemingly endless sky. As the spider's effort and determination grew, so did the spider's size so that she might be equal to the task of bridging the gap between the natural and celestial world.

When she had finished the task of spinning the web, the snow spider shrank in size and became an inhabitant of the rain forest where she remains today. Whenever the winds blow her above the trees toward the snowcapped mountains surrounding the rainforest, the spider spins again.

Having listened to Nyas's account of the Cloud Bridge's tale, Jaime said to him, "I really find your story rather hard to believe. Nyas bowed his head politely saying, "When one becomes less restricted by the laws we impose upon our existence, the glimpse into unseen worlds will become available to us. One will step from the ordinary into the extraordinary."

Gazing at the Cloud Bridge once more, Jaime said, "Haven't we already bridged the gap between the ordinary and the extraordinary?"

Nyas didn't answer her. Instead he rose from where he'd been sitting and again mounted the great diaphanous bridge that spread across the sky.

Atira wrapped her woven cloak tightly about her shoulders and said turning to her companions, "Come, we must hurry. The Bridge may disappear by nightfall or be lost to us by daybreak."

"I feel as if I'm floating in a hot air ballon", said Jaime.

"We're higher up than we were before", said Amelia as she and Hal, hurried to catch up with Natasha and Nyas. Once they were with them, Natasha swept Amelia and Hal aboard her.

"There's no turning back now", said Atira.

The sun in the sky was beginning to set, and the clouds that looked like pink cotton candy, made Amelia feel as if she and Natasha were doing some sort of extraordinary routine for the Circus of Wonders.

Nyas, who walked steadily alongside Natasha, signaled for everyone to halt. Atira stood next to him.

"There is a continent of trees and wildlife beneath us here. The bridge has closed the gap. We may descend from the bridge now. "Ramira is preparing to meet us through time and space. Time's passage has opened for her to enter it. At present she's still in the 21st C. I've sent the messenger hawk ahead to summon her here to meet us."

When Ramira received the messenger hawk she knew Atira and her companions had safely concluded a portion of their journey, and waited for her to meet them. Reaching into the pocket of the simple woven robe she wore, Ramira removed a time traveling device. Using the strange mirror to employ the sun's rays as energy, she and the hawk, were transported backward through time's current.

Within seconds, she found herself with the hawk perched upon her shoulder, embracing her sister and greeting Nyas and Atira's companions.

"I trust your journey across the Cloud Bridge was a pleasant one", said Ramira turning to Nyas, who politely bowed and assured her that it had been. "Your skill at being able to form a protective barrier around the portion of rainforest where the Cloud Temple and Cloud Bridge extends, enabled you and your companions to travel here with relative ease. Had you been unable to access the Bridge, you and your companions would have had to pass through dangerous terrain. There are still many large reptilian beasts that inhabit the portion of the rainforest you crossed. Menelus, who has little if any appreciation for the natural world, treats these magnificent inhabitants of the Jurassic era with distain. He sees them as objects to be hunted rather than as rare representatives of a species needing to be preserved.

Ramira searched the weary faces of her guests. "You must be tired. We're within close proximity to the lost city. Perhaps you might first enjoy the comfort of Vorelis's castle. If we wander along this mountain path, we'll reach the castle within the half hour." The turquoise sea seethed violently against the high precipice where the castle was situated. Amelia glanced downward at the ocean. She then gazed uncertainly at the steep pathway leading toward the castle: "Will Natasha be able to make it through that narrow passageway?" she asked

"Of course", replied Ramira. "The path leads to a comfortable stable for her situated near the castle. Your room will overlook the stable so you can see that Natasha is being accorded proper hospitality"

Later after Ramira's guests had arrived at the castle, Natasha, like her human companions, dined on vegetable delicacies of every conceivable description. Unlike her human friends though, Natasha didn't sleep on finely spun gold sheets nor did she drink the rare and exotic palm wine that made her companions dream mysterious dreams.

The following morning when everyone was awake and refreshed, Ramira led her guests toward the entrance to the lost city.

Upon entering the city, Ramira turned to Whitfield and said, "We'll examine the library later. Perhaps the additional information you'll need to solve the perfect equation might be found there."

"Perhaps?" the very word seemed to throw doubt upon the prospect. Suddenly Whitfield was feeling he might have made the journey to the lost city for nothing.

"I was hoping you'd show me where the library was first". Questions began to run through Whitfield's mind. "Was Ramira going to be of assistance to him or would she seem as evasive as Murdock had been at the Sun Temple? He was beginning to think he'd come to the lost city only to experience a replay of a familiar situation. His hopes slowly were being dashed. He was further disappointed when Ramira left him alone within the lost city's library. He was sure she knew where the most vital documents important to his research were to be located, yet she left him with the task of going through a mountain of unessential information.

*   *   *   *

When Queen Myaca received a coded message from Ramira telling her that Whitfield and his companions were within the lost city, she seemed fearful and preoccupied. Pelletier had informed her that he'd recognized some of Menelus's spies lurking outside her palace.

"I don't think it is safe for you to remain here. The volcanic fortress of Nurablia is a more secure haven for you right now. From there, Vorelis or I can travel and meet clandestinely with Whitfield on the Forgotten Island."

"Who will guard my kingdom while I'm gone?" pleaded Myaca, who in her anxiety thought perhaps Pelletier was trying to seize the reins of power from her. Pelletier's reply was immediate and decisive. "Why Murdock, who else—he's already shown himself to be loyal to you in so many ways."

Myaca turned from Pelletier. She stepped onto a magnificent balcony and gazed at a lush and green landscape. Her gaze fell upon a distant Martian city where inhabitants lived and went about their daily business, unaware of the power struggle within the Chucaran Empire. "I am the only one who should guard my kingdom. I refuse to flee my palace like some frightened hermit for a fortress from which there is no escape."

Pelletier, who knew Myaca to be a difficult woman to sway, knew there was no point in further discussing the matter with her.

"I need to be here. When Mars and Menelus see that I have the loyalty of my many subjects, he'll think twice about opposing me, at least outwardly", she said.

Myaca then gazed into Pelletier's face. He felt uneasy and uncomfortable with the eye contact. He dared not admit to himself that perhaps she thought his loyalty to her might be waning. "I've never had the strength of character to hold my position within any organization very long", he said humbly. "My former wives will attest to that."

Myaca smiled an understanding smile indicating that she'd won. Her decision to remain at the palace would go unchallenged.

Frustrated that his advice had been rejected, Pelletier excused himself from Myaca's presence. He left the palace and wandered like some vagabond through busy Martian streets where beings went about their business unaware of the distinguished time traveler's presence.

During the day, when he became hungry, Pelletier purchased food from Martian street vendors. At night, he slept undetected in alleys where loitering wasn't encouraged. During the time he wandered, Pelletier could think only of his last meeting with his daughter Amelia. Haunted by Amelia's tears, he could still hear her words.

"How could you desert mother the way you did, not to mention me? Before mother declared you missing, she said you'd come back to us but you didn't."

John hung his head in despair. Perhaps Amelia was right. He was nothing better than a rolling stone, always seeking greener pastures when life got too rough.

Exhausted by his own unproductive, negative self-pitying thoughts, the great John Pelletier, finally fell asleep behind a pile of Martian trash. On any ordinary day the trash collectors would have relegated the mess to some other place in time. Today, for some reason, the pile remained uncollected.

When John awoke, he was startled to see standing over him Menelus' notorious son Mars, who by reputation was nothing better than a pirate.

"Well" said Mars staring down at Pelletier. "Perhaps you drank too much Martian wine or did you become disoriented, and lose your way through time and space," he said laughing. "Allow me to offer you my hospitality. You look as though you could use a good meal not to mention a bit of cleaning up and fresh clothes."

John remained motionless, almost unable to move. Mars was right. He had drunk too much wine. He'd also been drugged and Mars knew it.

"Pardon my saying so" said Mars a little sarcastically: "You really seem to be at the end of your tether." Mars and his cronies lifted John up and placed him in a hovercraft. The craft then sped off to an undisclosed location where John soon found himself behind four solid walls.

"We'll soon see, Professor Pelletier, just how much loyalty plays a role in Martian politics. I doubt if Queen Myaca will be willing to pay the handsome ransom we Venusians are about to place upon your head. I doubt if any of your friends, including that ridiculous mole Murdock or that mechanically malfunctioning robot Sarius or even Vorelis himself will be able to get you out of this predicament".

John stared at the floor. He raised his head and gazed around. His utterly luxurious surroundings were comfortable in every conceivable way.

"I trust you will find everything here to your satisfaction" said Mars who made his way to a door before he turned and said, "Just ring should you need anything else."

Once Mars had left the room, Pelletier tried to stand but still felt weak and disoriented. He glanced again at his surroundings to see if this time he could detect any available means of escape. As he did, Mars opened the door again and said, "By the way, John, I wouldn't try to escape if I were you. We've planted force fields around the building, making such an attempt quite impossible."

Mars then closed the door, sure that Pelletier's ability to travel though time and space had been blocked. John reached into his pocket. The mirror he'd carried with him so that he could transport himself through time was missing. In despair, he placed his hands over his face. His head ached and his legs felt so weak that when he rose to his feet, they buckled under him. John lay on the floor. Light from the ceiling above streamed down upon him. He knew he had to devise an escape plan and he had to do it immediately.

When the drug's effect had worn off, John opened the door to an adjoining room where he bathed and changed into fresh clothes. He then returned to the room where he'd lain on the floor and sat down at a table where he stared at food prepared for him to eat. Picking up an eating utensil, he was about to start eating when he felt a hand upon his shoulder. Dropping the fork, he turned to see who it was.

"Don't say anything", said Sarius dressed in the manner of a Venusian officer of the guard. "I told the robot gatekeeper that I was here on business and that I had a special message to deliver to Mars from his father Menelus. When the guard became suspicious of me, I caused him to malfunction with a device I carry with me. He admitted me without a struggle and has granted me access to all rooms within the building. Hurry, let's get out of here."

As John and Sarius turned to leave the room, they heard voices just outside the door. John's heart pounded. He knew if someone opened the door to the room and discovered Sarius, neither of them would be able to explain their way out of the situation.

The talking stopped. The semi transparent door started to move but remained unopened. "I need to adjust the force field lock in the room upstairs first", said the voice on the other side of the door.

Sarius, who was close to experiencing malfunction caused by the stress he was under, handed Pelletier a device so he could reboot him. "Thank you—I can breath more freely now. Let's go."

How are we to get by the force field", asked John.

"Don't worry about that. Murdock has planted an electro magnetic jamming device near the garden. We'll make it out through the red beets and cabbage patch."

John and Sarius quickly moved toward freedom. The third floor where John had been held prisoner, quickly gave way to the second floor as an invisible flight of stairs merged one floor with another and the two found themselves running for safety.

Murdock's hovercraft, quickly appeared and an invisible vacuum net swept John and Sarius safely into the craft

"Duck down" said Murdock, who sat at the craft's control panel, and pushed a throttle forward for maximum exit speed. "They've spotted us". Electronic rays and jamming devices were directed at the craft's controls in an attempt to bring it down.

"Thank heavens I had the latest anti-jamming devices installed or we might be sitting in the middle of a red beet and cabbage patch." No sooner had Murdock gotten his words out when a ray grazed the craft. "Keep your heads down", said Murdock, who with a paw tightened his anti-force field helmet.

Within minutes, the hovercraft was circling Queen Myaca's palace. "We have our instructions to remain in the air until security gives us clearance to land. I doubt if Mars or any of his cronies would dare pursue us in such close proximity to Myaca's palace."

Murdock's assessment of the situation was wrong. Within seconds he saw one of Mars' crafts approaching them. Murdock pressed a lever forward and released a missle. A humming noise was heard followed by a sonic boom. The pursuing craft neither blew up nor fell to the ground. It simply evaporated in mid air leaving no trace of ever having existed.

Once they had safely landed and were in the walled enclosure of Myaca's palace, Murdock said, "You have some explaining to do. You've caused Myaca embarrassment by wandering off the way you did. Now Mars will try to defend his reason for abducting you by saying he was trying to rescue you from your own miserable degradation."

"Perhaps he would be right," said John, who despondently hung his head in shame. He then extended a hand in gratitude to Sarius. "I'll never be able to thank you enough for undertaking such a brave rescue of me today. I know you're programmed for courage. Your actions went well beyond the call of duty." Sarius beamed in response to what John had just said. "You and Murdock are my friends. As such, I had no other choice than to help Murdock rescue you."

"We both thank you", said Murdock, who knew that without Sarius' help, penetration of Mars' compound would have been impossible.

"If you thought no attempt to rescue you would be made, you were wrong. As soon as you were reported missing we traced your whereabouts with an electronic probing device, and that device, directed us to Mars' compound. We then made immediate plans to free you from your abductors. If Sarius and I had failed to accomplish your rescue, Myaca's forces were ready to infiltrate Mars' compound. There's no telling how many lives might have been lost if such a maneuver had been undertaken."

John hung his head in despair. Murdock's tone was harsh and unforgiving.

"Fortunately the time traveling device Mars stole from you has been completely destroyed. The mirror's tracking device allowed me to locate the mirror's whereabouts, electronically activate a tiny detonator contained within it, and shatter the mirror into a million pieces.

"For the time being, I don't think you'll be issued another time traveling device-- at least not until Myaca decides that she can trust you not to get in another predicament."

"When am I to see Myaca?" asked John.

"I don't think the Queen is too eager to see you right now. You'll know in a few days when she's going to grant you an interview. For the time being, your activities are restricted. In other words, you're grounded."

"Thanks for telling me", said Pelletier sarcastically.

With nose held high in the air, Murdock started to leave the room but hesitated.

Turning to his friend his said, "Please don't think of me as unsympathetic. We all have moments when life's problems weigh heavily upon us. You'll work things out."

*   *   *   *

Having heard the news of Pelletier's daring rescue, Queen Myaca congratulated Sarius and Murdock on a job well done. She also silently congratulated herself on her choice of allies. Without doubt, Murdock and Sarius had proven their loyalty to her by undertaking Pelletier's rescue. She had reservations regarding John's loyalty. Although she refrained from criticizing him, secretly Myaca now regarded him as someone she couldn't fully trust.

Chapter Seven

▼

After Murdock and Sarius left Myaca standing alone in the reception area, she wandered along a forbidding and empty corridor. The sound of her footsteps echoed in unison with silent murmurs of the past as the ancient floor creaked beneath her feet. Myaca turned as if she'd heard a voice. Seeing no one there, she continued walking. Every now and then she would stop momentarily and gaze at portraits of her Martian ancestors staring down at her from their silent place in Martian history.

"I won't step back in time to find any of you today" she said aloud. "I doubt if any of you would be eager to share my world or to solve the problems facing this time in history. I only wish father were still here. He'd know how to confront Menelus and foil his attempt to access this planet."

Myaca then bravely ventured into an unfamiliar part of the palace. Since childhood she'd heard that one palace room held secrets of the universe and of the future. Even though Myaca had been warned not to approach the room, she was curious. Why was the room always locked? Why shouldn't she enter it?

"I must know what lies ahead for me and the future of the Martian Empire", she thought a little desperately. Myaca took a key from her pocket. She stared at the archaic wooden door resembling something manufactured during the 20th Century.

"How strange", she thought staring down at the brass doorknob and unlocking the door. "I don't want to step into the 20th C."

No sooner had Myaca unlocked the door than she felt a hand upon her shoulder. Frightened, she turned to find nobody there at all. Feeling bewildered and very much alone, she quickly started to retrace her steps but stopped upon hearing a voice but seeing no image.

She placed her hands to her ears. "I must be hearing things". The voice grew louder. Myaca started to move away from the place where she thought she'd heard the voice. She tried to ignore the voice entirely but when it addressed her by name she courageously turned and asked, in a very firm voice. "What do you want?"

At first there was no answer. Myaca was quite sure she was going insane. She started to run from the room and find the corridor where the haunting portraits of her ancestors gazed down at her. She started to weep at her own fragile vulnerability. Then she heard the voice again.

"Myaca, Myaca, I love you", said the voice repeating her name again and again. Finally Myaca recognized the voice to be that of her husband Prince Sentius.

"Where are you?" she asked gazing around but seeing no one.

"I'm lost to you now. Menelus still holds me prisoner. Somehow I had to find you through time and space and warn you not to explore the forbidden room. You mustn't be frightened."

"Trust those including John Pelletier, who have proven their loyalty to you. I must leave you now. Don't try to pursue me-- to do so could be dangerous and might result in your own imprisonment. Perhaps someday I'll find my way back to you. Perhaps someday I'll be able to help your friends discover the key that will unlock the mystery they want to solve. I must go now."

"Wait" said Myaca. "I want to be with you."

"No" answered the voice. "You must stay where you are and help those who are struggling to release us from the cursed rule of your cousin Menelus."

With that said, the voice was heard no more. Myaca dissolved in bitter tears as she made her way alone along the empty palace corridor.

For the remainder of the day, she remained in isolated seclusion and received no visitors. She ate nothing and drank only a calming bitter tea that neither quenched her thirst nor lightened her spirit.

The following morning when she met with Murdock she said. "I feel I must be under the most extraordinary pressure to act according to my position. Yesterday I doubted my own sanity. I even thought the realm might best be governed by someone other than myself."

"I'm sorry to learn that you weren't feeling well yesterday". "I do hope you're feeling better today."

Myaca wanted to open her heart to Murdock. She wanted to tell him about hearing the voice of her husband but she thought it best to keep that extraordinary experience to herself.

Instead she told Murdock, "My husband has been gone so long. I was just feeling lonely and vulnerable. Memories of him overwhelmed me. I had to have some time alone."

Murdock nodded his head in sympathy as if he understood Myaca. Inwardly he thought her to be silly and sentimental for being unable to get on with her life.

"Surely your grief will pass in time".

"I'm sure it will. I'm also sure that whatever prompted your visit to me today wasn't motivated by an excuse to inquire about my health."

"You are without a doubt a great judge of character, madam" replied Murdock who'd come to request that John Pelletier be fully reinstated as a time traveler. "There is nobody more loyal to you than he," said Murdock.

Myaca gazed downward in embarrassed silence before saying, "Perhaps I was a little too harsh in my criticism of John Pelletier. I've had a great deal on my mind lately. This morning, I had a chance to think things over. I came to the conclusion that despite Pelletier's obvious shortcomings, his assets outweigh his liabilities."

"Does that mean I can tell John he's free to travel throughout time and space?"

"Yes, but you mustn't allow him to wander off alone again. If he's to be part of my team, he must stay with the team."

"I'll see that Pelletier remains with us. In fact, I won't let him out of my sight."

"Good" replied Myaca. "I'm glad we understand each other. Please tell Professor Pelletier that he's to stay with you and Sarius at to your burrow in the Sun Temple."

"I'll be more than happy to do so", said Murdock who wished the Queen good day.

After he'd left her, Myaca decided to retrace her steps of the previous day. She left the empty room where she'd had the interview with Murdock. She began walking alone along the long corridor. When she came to a magnificently woven tapestry, she stopped, stood in front of it and gazed at the design of an equilateral triangle. The tapestry, a gift from the people of Mu, symbolized that Earth continent's natural division into three separate islands. 1

Myaca turned from studying the tapestry and walked past the portraits of her ancestors. She continued to move forward until she stood once more before the door where she'd heard Sentius' voice. Had the voice really been his or had it been one of trickery conjured up to confuse and frighten her? Myaca continued walking. Perhaps the voice was Menelus' doing she thought to herself a little angrily. Only he could be capable of concocting such trickery meant to confuse and frighten her. But then she remembered the voice saying that he loved her.

Only Prince Sentius could have told her that. With that thought in mind, Myaca returned to her study and began studying pertinent state papers.

*   *   *   *

When Murdock told John that he was free to travel again through time and space, John received the news with mixed emotions. "There's no place I want to visit right now. I've always used time travel to escape from my problems. When Myaca decided that I shouldn't be allowed to travel through time, I was almost grateful to her. I thought at last I'd have to face the man I'd become since I couldn't run from him anymore."

"You mustn't be so hard on yourself", said Murdock. "There are few humans I respect more than you. One reason I feel that way is that you don't try to patronize me because I'm a member of the mole family. I respect Sarius, for the same reason you respect me. I feel that it was loyalty and mutual respect that enabled Sarius and me to work together and to foil Menelus and his cronies."

Pelletier hung his head in shame. He realized how selfish he'd been. He had friends who'd risk their lives to save his "I shall always be grateful to you, Murdock."

"No" replied, Murdock. "It is I who should be grateful to you. You and a handful of other humans recognize us animals as having qualities of loyalty, strength, kindness and generosity that often go unnoticed or unappreciated by humankind. If I had to do it again, I wouldn't hesitate to rescue you. Don't ever run from your friends."

*   *   *   *

"Something must be done immediately to normalize time travel between Mu and the Forgotten Island", said Vorelis who'd been studying the problem from every possible angle.

"I quite agree", said Myaca placing her hand on Vorelis's arm and walking along a palace corridor with him.

"Have no fear", said Vorelis still trying to convince himself that everything was under his control, "I shall succeed in foiling Menelus' attempt to block normal time travel between the Forgotten Island and Mu. My absence from your Martian domain will be only temporary. As soon as I've finished the job, I'll return to you."

"Thank you" said Myaca who was grateful to know she could depend on Vorelis. She started to tell him about hearing the strange voice from behind the forbidden door but suddenly felt foolish.

Instead she said, "My position is a lonely one. Without Prince Sentius, I find life's burdens almost unbearable."

"Trust me", said Vorelis, "I'll be at your side as soon as I've finished the task I am undertaking. In my absence though, I would advise you to stay at the volcanic fortress of Nurablia where the force fields are strong and will repel any unwanted visitors."

Myaca suddenly felt guilty for not heeding Pelletier's earlier advice for her to go into temporary seclusion there. "I'll do as you say", she said.

Offering her his arm, Vorelis told Myaca that Murdock and Pelletier had a hovercraft tethered in the garden ready to take her to the retreat."

*   *   *   *

Pelletier held open the door for Myaca, as she and Vorelis stepped inside the craft. Murdock then quickly released the air anchor and the craft sped skyward toward the castle fortress.

To onlookers, the castle's thick fortress walls presented a forbidding presence. An electronic eye situated in a fortress tower, scanned the surrounding sky and countryside: It penetrated the far reaches of outer space in anticipation of uninvited visitors.

"I'll miss my garden", sighed Myaca stepping from the craft and gazing at the jagged, forbidding rocky landscape surrounding her. A spectacular bolt of lightning lit up the sky as a Martian crash of thunder shook the very foundation of the fortress.

Myaca shuddered then gazed down at the seething Martian sea surrounding the fortress. She watched as a robotic serpent, guarding the base of the fortress, slithered along before it raised its head and signaled for the giant gold and iron door to swing open for the distinguished guests.

Myaca sighed with resignation. "This place seems so dark and inhospitable. I suppose all secret doors are locked" she said half murmuring to herself. "Prince Sentius would never be able to find me here."

Now that Myaca was safe within the fortress, Vorelis took leave of his friends. He crossed a bridge connecting the fortress with the outside world. He made his way up a sloping path until he stood high upon a precipice where he gazed at the world beneath. For several moments he hesitated to move. He waited until the sky's turbulence became such that the Martian downpour rained upon him heavily. A streak of lightning lit up the sky. Vorelis raised a device he held in hand to the sky's lightning bolt. Instantly he was transported through time to another place.

Mu's familiar landscape now surrounded him, and Vorelis made his way down a steep mountainous slope toward a cave. Upon entering the cave he switched on a small lantern he carried with him. He then glanced upward and saw colorful stalactites of a crystal like substance hanging from the cave's ceiling. When he gazed downward, Vorelis was careful not to stumble upon the beautiful stalagmites rising from the cave's floor. Then hearing a voice addressing him, Vorelis turned in a semi-circle. Standing before him was a monk clothed in a woven robe.

"Welcome" said Deiphos extending a hand in greeting to Vorelis. "Please follow me along the passageway" he said pointing. "The passage passes directly beneath the Cloud Temple. It also leads to a subterranean river that connects Mu with the Forgotten Island."

"We'll rest tonight at the Cloud temple", he said leading Vorelis along steps winding precipitously from the cave's floor and ending at a door opening into the temple's main enclosure.

The sound of chanting and drumbeats could be heard reverberating throughout the temple, as Vorelis temporarily settled himself into the monastery's daily routine. Following prayers to the sun, Vorelis joined the monks at their evening repast. He imbibed the river's sacred waters and ate the crusty bread and rain forest fruits before retiring for the evening.

"Good night my friend" said Deiphos bowing politely "We shall leave at first light for the Forgotten Island. Rest well-- our journey may be arduous."

Vorelis knew that it might be days before he and Deiphos stood within the lost city on the Forgotten Island. The following day, when they began their journey along the subterranean river, Vorelis had high hopes for any new discoveries they might make.

With pole in hand, Deiphos carefully guided the boat through the river's passageway. He hesitated to move forward only when he came to a place in the river where it separated into two branches. Taking up a pole as well, Vorelis started guiding the craft along the less explored branch. Deiphos knew the branch Vorelis had chosen, would take them away from the direction leading toward the lost city.

"We can retrace our path if necessary". Vorelis knew that a being equal in power to him was rumored to inhabit this subterranean world. Vorelis also knew if Menelus truly had succeeded in blocking normal passage through time to the lost city, he would have had to confront the power of the one who ruled this subterreanean world.

"She sings the song of the siren", he said. The craft, caught by the river's current, now drifted toward the sound of a singing voice that caused quartz like crystals hanging from cave walls and ceilings to vibrate. Vorelis reached up, touched one of the hanging crystals and noticed that placed between it was a solar mirror. The mirror, powered by sunlight from above, illuminated the river passageway and revealed the image of the one who sang the siren song.

Narena's face shone as light piercing the darkness of the subterranean world, as Vorelis and Deiphos stepped from the craft and politely bowed to her.

"Your visits here are rare." she said addressing Vorelis. "As for you Deiphos, you've never dared venture into my realm before."

"I respect the privacy of your realm", said Deiphos who waited politely for Vorelis to tell Narena the reason for their visit.

"I have come to ask a question. Those who live in the upper reaches of the solar system have been blocked from normal time travel to the Forgotten Island and lost city. It is said that Menelus and those who abet his bid for power within the solar system have succeeded in creating the blockade—is this true?"

Narena, whose long golden locks fell about her shoulders and hung to the waist of her silver gown, smiled knowingly. "Menelus flatters himself if he thinks he has succeeded in creating a blockade. Only I am capable of doing that. The blockade was created so that pilgrims would find an alternative route to the Forgotten Island. In doing so, it was hoped that their strength and resolve would be tested."

"Did the pilgrims succeed?" asked Vorelis. "Only in part" replied Narena. "Hal and Whitfield must again prove their worthiness before normal travel to the Forgotten Island is resumed."

Dissatisfied with Narena's selfish and evasive answer to his question, Vorelis said, "The Golden Age can't be saved by them alone".

"I can tell you no more."

Disappearing into thin vapor the woman whose sweet voice had captivated Vorelis' imagination left him and Deiphos standing alone.

"Now I understand why you are considered to be one of the great masters of the universe. Only the few has ventured near Narena's realm and heard her voice. None that I know has ever seen her."

Smiling at Deiphos' recognition of the accomplishment, Vorelis said "We must return to where the river branches."

Once they had crossed into the smooth dark waters of the other river branch, Vorelis gazed upward. Gold stalactites, hanging from the ceiling of the subterranean world led them to a gateway marking a steep passageway. Steering the craft toward shore, Deiphos and Vorelis then disembarked.

The quarter mile passageway wound its way in a gradual and serpentine ascent. Steps laden with gold and semi precious stones reflected the opulence of a subterranean world where solar light transported from above streamed down upon them.

A huge gold door with solar light panels on either side swung open for the travelers as they stepped into daylight. Knowing that her father's arrival was eminent, Ramira embraced Vorelis then welcomed Deiphos, who with a bow was met also by Nyas. "Food and drink has been prepared for you. The comforts of the Sun Palace are at your disposal."

*   *   *   *

When finally alone with Vorelis, Ramira urgently whispered, "Whitfield thinks he needs your assistance."

"No, he doesn't. Whitfield has been admitted to the lost city. That's as far as the journey will take him. As for his companions, they've passed the preliminary test but their presence here is unnecessary."

"But father, they've just arrived. What am I to tell them?" she whispered.

Seeming rather unconcerned about the matter, Vorelis replied: "Trust me, my dear, you'll think of something." Vorelis then disappeared around a dark corner of the Sun Temple with Ramira still in pursuit of him.

"Where are you?" she called searching every nearby nook and cranny."Father, we need to talk". Little did she know, that just inches away, practically in front of her nose-- was Vorelis.

"He must be feeling poorly", she thought. "Father only disappears like this when he's not feeling well." Ramira knew she must be close to the place where Vorelis hid. She knew he was depressed. So much depended on Whitfield finding a solution to solving the perfect equation that Vorelis was beginning to feel unnecessary.

Just as Vorelis was about to take the entire day off from daylight and friends, an amicable Whitfield appeared. Embarrassed that she couldn't find Vorelis, and knowing he was trying to avoid Whitfield, Ramira calmly took Whitfield's arm in hers: "Perhaps you and Deiphos might enjoy a city tour. Father always insists that I show guests around the premises before any serious business is conducted," she said smiling. "Only father is skilled enough to guide you through the library's intricate labyrinth leading to clues that might aid you in your research."

Having overheard his daughter's remark, Vorelis smiled. He would confront Whitfield. Emerging from shadow, and wearing a mask of silent reserve Vorelis now stood before him.

"To solve the perfect equation is to hold the very grail in one's hand" he said loudly.

With tears in her eyes and feeling quite helpless, Ramira listened as Vorelis ranted on about the subject "Only the few should know of the grail's potential for power".

Sensing that his old friend might not be feeling well Whitfield politely remarked, "I really prefer the serenity of my office at the Primary Institute of

Study to wandering around here for gracious knows how long. To be perfectly honest, I hate being thrust backward and forward through time as if I were a tennis ball flying between two opponents."

"Are you suggesting that we're opponents?" asked Vorelis

"Of course not", replied Whitfield. "It's just that you don't seem especially eager to introduce me to any of the fabled mysteries here within the lost city."

"Only the few should ever know the city's potential for power", said Vorelis, who although he admired Whitfield, wasn't sure if he wanted to trust him with the realization of that power.

"I ask for little assistance in my quest to solve the perfect equation. I'm here only because Queen Myaca insisted I show up."

Relieved to see that her father finally had received his friend, Ramira was disappointed in him. He'd assigned her the task of showing Whitfield through the library.

"Ramira knows as much about the lost city's library as I do. She will show you what you need to know so that you can complete your work."

Whitfield politely followed Ramira around as she showed him library documents few had seen. When she felt that she'd shown Whitfield almost everything he should see, she allowed him to gaze upon a huge wall map.

The map, beautifully painted upon a terracotta surface, revealed the solar system planets in orbit around the sun. The map also represented the colonies of Mu and Atlantis outlined in vivid colors upon a world map of Earth. In the map's center was an almost indiscernable diagram of the of the Dark Tower's mysterious interior chambers leading to distant dimensions.

"Do you see anything unusual depicted upon the map?" asked Ramira who waited for Whitfield to reply.

"No" he answered hesitantly.

"Very well", she said, "I've shown you all the resources you should need to help you in your research."

"I'm growing tired of this little charade", said Whitfield interrupting Ramira. "If you don't mind I'd like to get back to the real world."

"Very well" said Ramira, "I'll tell father how you feel."

Having eavesdropped on their conversation, and still invisible, Vorelis quickly exited the library. Knowing Whitfield's departure was imminent, Vorelis cheerfully made his way to the lost city's great meeting hall where he revealed himself to his other guests. He was busy conducting a seminar on the history surrounding the great meeting hall, when Ramira, accompanied by Whitfield, found him and interrupted him.

"Professor Whitfield has found his visit to the lost city to be unproductive. He must be getting back to his research at the Primary Institute."

"You mean you didn't find anything here that would help you in your research?" asked Hal with disbelief.

"Correct", replied Whitfield quite emphatically.

Amelia patted Natasha's head and ordered her to set her down upon the ground. "Natasha and I were about to rehearse our old circus routine", she said. "We've never performed together in such a huge arena."

"Well, it looks like the booking is cancelled," said Hal "If Professor Whitfield is going home, I suppose we can go home too."

"Oh, please don't feel you have to leave" said Vorelis. "The elephant needn't go. She already understands the lesson the rest of you should have known or failed to learn long ago."

"And just what lesson are you referring to?" asked Tom.

Harry put a comforting arm around Jaime who had started to weep.

"Well, I'll put it very simply" said Vorelis. "Elephants and other animals have always lived in harmony with their environment. They take from their planet, only life's necessities. Men, by contrast, take from each other and from other living beings. Menelus is probably one of the worst offenders in that regard. The perpetual need to have more and to acquire more has pushed us all to the limit of endurance. Even as I speak, final clouds are gathering. We must prepare for the battle.

"What battle is he talking about?" asked Hal turning to Whitfield.

"I think it's time for us to go", said Harry turning to Whitfield. "Can't you find a way to summon that time machine of yours through time and space?"

Reaching into his pocket and removing the time machine's remote, Whitfield pointed it in an upward direction. Within seconds the time machine stood before them.

"I'm not leaving without Natasha", said Amelia. Within seconds, both Amelia and Hal found themselves atop the elephant and deposited in a pasture behind his family's homestead.

"How did you manage that?" called Amelia. Whitfield and the rest of Hal's family stood only a hundred feet from where she and Hal were.

Later when Amelia was standing next to him, Whitfield truthfully confessed, "Vorelis must have arranged for your homeward passage."

"Won't you stay for supper?' asked Jaime eager to get back into a normal routine.

Graciously declining the invitation Whitfield said that he needed to return to his work at the Institute. Within seconds his time machine whisked him away to his desired destination.

"Well, how about that" said Hal scratching his head. "The adventure of a lifetime just dissolved. Now I've got to figure out what happened to us."

"Don't try" said Harry who was standing beside Jaime with his arm around her.

"By the way "said Hal standing next to them. "Amelia says she doesn't want to return to the circus as a performer anymore. She wants to offer Natasha sanctuary from the unnatural life the elephant has led so far. She was wondering if we could rent some pasture land from you so we could open a sanctuary for her and needy elephants too old to perform."

"Of course" said Harry. "We'll even donate the land for the sanctuary. The office adjoining the barn is vacant. You and Amelia can use it to conduct sanctuary business."

"Thanks Dad" said Hal giving his father a hug.

"That's wonderful news", said Amelia. "Your family has been so generous. I never dreamed our friendship would lead to a home for Natasha and me or the establishment of an elephant sanctuary."

"When I first met you, that was the farthest thing from my mind too" said Hal with a laugh. He then gazed at Amelia and wondered if she felt as deeply about him as he did about her. Sensing that the couple might want to be alone, Harry took Jaime by the arm saying, "I think Hal and Amelia might want some quality time alone together."

After a quiet stroll, the couple stepped onto the porch and was met by Hal's grandfather. They then followed him inside where other family members gathered for supper. Following the meal, Hal and Amelia excused themselves from the table. They left the house and walked toward the barn where they sat down on nearby bales of hay. Hal took Amelia's hand in his and said, "I'm glad Vorelis and the Circus of Wonders brought us together."

Amelia looked at Hal and said,"If for no other reason my journey into time and space was to meet you, then it was entirely worthwhile." Hal kissed Amelia. The couple then rose and walked hand and hand toward the trees growing at the edge of the pasture. Late afternoon light touched the trees' leaves making them seem nearly transparent in the sun's waning brilliance

"I never thought when I agreed to accompany Vorelis on a journey to meet my father so much would happen.

"Neither did I" said Hal who thought they'd been destined to meet. "Life has its strange experiences. I can't accept that what happened to us was real but it certainly made a huge impact on my life. After we met, I discovered my life's calling. I've always wanted to help animals ever since Dad sent me to Kenya one summer so I could help out in Edgar's veterinarian clinic. When I tell Edgar and Simone that we're opening an elephant sanctuary here, they'll be pleased. By, the way, he added, I want you to meet Edgar's mother Lillie. She and Bill practically raised me.

Amelia listened to Hal. She wanted to tell him that he'd changed her life. He'd made her impossible dream of wanting to start an elephant sanctuary a reality.

"Natasha and so many animals like her have been crowded out of habitat. Until attitudes toward wildlife change we'll have done our part in saving a species by creating a modern day Noah's Ark."

"Creating an elephant sanctuary isn't enough. I want to do more. I've already talked with Fred Hinson. He's working on a plan to restore wetlands around the world. He's also working with Edgar and others in an effort to stop the African trade in bush meat and ivory. Right now Edgar and Simone have eight baby elephants in their care. Ivory hunters killed the mothers. I've promised Fred that I'll do what I can to help him and Edgar."

Tears came to Amelia's eyes. "Natasha's mother had been killed for ivory." Hal put his arms around her and held her. The two then rose from where they sat and began strolling back to the house. As they walked together, Amelia said, "For years your parents tried but were unable to meet my father, John Pelletier. Now we've been brought together because of the meeting. I'm sure he would be pleased to know that your family had taken me in and provided shelter for Natasha too."

"Don't be silly" said Hal. "We're not just taking you in—you've become very special to us all, especially to me. I love you. You need stability in life, Amelia. I'm going to see that you and Natasha get it. Once we get the sanctuary established, who knows where the road might take us. Someday I want you to be my wife."

Amelia placed her arms around Hal's neck and gave him a big hug and kiss. Gazing into his eyes she asked, "Is that a promise?"

"That's a promise".

Hand in hand the couple continued walking back toward the house where they found Hal's family sitting and talking with friends. Having just dropped by for a visit, Bill and Lillie appeared much grayer than they had in previous years. They were in remarkably good health though. After Hal introduced Amelia to them, he then sat down next to her on the living room sofa.

Jaime, who was serving iced tea, offered Hal and Amelia a glass before saying,

"Bill and Lillie finally spotted that ole gator in Harrison Lake."

"I sure did", said Bill. "I laid a trap for the critter and captured him too. The fish and wildlife people came this morning and picked him up. They're going to transport him to a place where he won't be bothering anybody. I was just worried about my farm animals", said Bill. "There's no telling when and if that ole gator might have gotten a hankering for a taste of one of them."

"I can't say I liked the thought of a gator watching us as we fished either", said Lillie. "I'm glad the critter's safe from harm and has a new home."

"Yeah" agreed Bill, who said they needed to be getting home.

"As they were getting up to leave, Lillie turned to Amelia: "We've always heard so much about your famous father. Since we never had the pleasure of meeting him, we were delighted to meet you instead."

CHAPTER EIGHT

▼

It was only a few days after Hal and Amelia had discussed their future together that Fred Hinson extended a hand in greeting to Hal.

"Sit down" he said directing him to a comfortable office chair.

"I spoke with your father over the phone this morning. He's told me you've been on an adventure similar to the sort of thing your father and I experienced years ago. Your Dad didn't say too much over the phone. He mentioned Mu and the Forgotten Island. I assume you got swept up in some kind of time warp."

"I'm not sure what happened to us."

"Say no more" interrupted Fred. "I've always been the pragmatic sort. I've never had the desire to probe the world's mysteries. When I returned from the Forgotten Island, I decided I'd put the whole surreal experience behind me and try not to analyze it. Years have passed. The island experience changed my life in many ways, I can't say that I've ever believed the things we saw or experienced there were real. To do so would be like labeling myself a kook.

"I don't know whether your father feels the same way about the experience as I do. We've never really talked about it. Sometimes I think your father's reaction to some of the things we saw and did on the Forgotten Island had something to do with what we were going through. When I first met your father, I found out he'd been through some bad times. I was going through some tough times too.

"You can only imagine how stunned I was to be assigned as bodyguard to someone as wealthy and important as your father. When I happened to save your Dad's life one time, and when he invited me along on that surreal little adventure to the Forgotten Island, my ego really was boosted. The best thing that ever happened in my life happened to me while I was working for your Dad. I met my wife Sophie. I nearly lost her when she headed home for Australia, and I found myself on some wild goose chase tagging along with your father and grandfather who were looking for ' the place where the serpent coils in the sun.' We nearly died on that island as I recall--but we all kept hoping and trying to find purpose and meaning to our lives while we struggled to survive.

"I swore that if I ever got off the island alive, the first thing I would do would be to head straight to Australia and bring Sophie back to the U.S. with me. I'd told her that I loved her and wanted to marry her. Thank God, she believed me and waited for me.

Sophie has helped me sort out my life's problems. I quit smoking because of her. I also started this firm because she insisted that the lesson I'd learned, and the things I'd been shown while on that island had to be important not just to me but to the rest of the world.

"By the way", said Fred, "I want you to meet my wife Sophie", he said opening an adjoining office door, where a tall, attractive middle-aged woman sat at a desk and behind a computer.

"So you're Harry Worthy's son", said Sophie. "I've heard so much about you," she said shaking Hal's hand. "Your parents have been a great inspiration and help to my husband in starting this firm. We welcome you as a support member of the team."

"Thanks" said Hal. "I've heard a lot of good things about you too. Fred said you were the girl of his dreams, and that you kept him going when things got rough."

"When I got on the ship to return to Australia and he left with your father and grandfather on that expedition to the Forgotten Island, I wasn't really sure if I'd ever see Fred again. He found me. We're still happily married after all these years."

As Sophie continued to talk, she suddenly looked at Hal and said,

"We'll, I've had plenty to say about myself. What about you and your family's recent adventure-- I understand from what Fred has told me, that your father finally met the elusive John Pelletier."

"Yes, we met Pelletier", said Hal. "I'm afraid the meeting was a bit of a disappointment though."

"He didn't stay around long enough for any of us to get to know him. As usual, he took off for some unknown destination. We haven't had any word from him since. I met Pelletier's daughter, though. She's become the girl of my dreams."

"How wonderful for you" said Sophie, "I hope you two will be as happy as Fred and I have been."

"Thanks" said Hal who added, "I want Amelia to get to know my son,

Nick. He's visiting the farm with Mom and Dad right now. I spoke with him over the phone today. Amelia gave him a ride on Natasha."

"Who's Natasha?" asked Sophie. Hal then told Fred and Sophie how Natasha had inspired him and Amelia to start a sanctuary for elephants.

"How did you three happen to meet?" asked Sophie with a giggle.

"Well, it's a long story", said Hal. "It might take an entire afternoon to tell you how it happened.

"The important thing is that we met. I thought I might never care for anyone after Amanda and I divorced. But when Amelia walked into my life that feeling disappeared. Amelia feels the same way I do about animals and the environment. Amanda used to make me feel like a fool for wanting to protect wild things and the environment.

Amanda didn't care about quality of life for the Earth".

Sophie listened to what Hal had to say about his former wife, then abruptly interrrupted him. "You sound bitter Hal. Just because Amanda didn't appreciate the same things in life as you do, doesn't make her a bad person. Obviously, you two weren't meant for each other. It's too bad you didn't find that out sooner instead of later. You mustn't think about the past though. You've learned from your mistake. Now you must look forward to the future."

"That's right", said Fred, who'd been listening to the conversation.

"I'm a city person. I'd never experienced much of the great outdoors until I visited the Forgotten Island. If the outdoors had any purpose in life, I thought it was strictly for hunting and fishing and not for appreciating Nature just for its sheer beauty. Frankly, I'm ashamed I held that attitude for so many years. I know such an attitude isn't unlike that held by millions of people who've been leading deprived existences in that they've never been close to nature.

"After Sophie and I were married, and I brought her back to the States to live with me, I decided I would devote the rest of my life to making the Earth a more beautiful place in which to live. The bottom line is that I don't care what the rest of the world thinks of me. I don't care if they think I'm foolish for trying to save wetlands and rainforests. I know that in my heart what I'm doing is the right thing and may be the only thing that will ultimately save our planet."

After reflecting on what Fred had told him, Hal said, "If we can't save a rainforest or wetlands from annihilation, how are we to save an urban city? Both require care and planning?'

Handing Hal a list, Fred said, "I believe these companies and people will listen to us and give us their support if we approach them in the right way."

"By the way," said Hal starting to leave, "I want you and Sophie to meet

Arthur Whitfield. I've invited him to join us for dinner when Amelia visits me in New York."

"Thanks for the invitation. I think I speak for Sophie when I say we'd love to join you."

Hal then closed the door behind him. With a strange look on his face, he stepped alone into the elevator and muttered to himself. "Perhaps someday I'll have the pleasure of introducing you to Murdock and Queen Myaca."

*   *   *   *

It was early evening when Hal wearily opened the door to his New York apartment and set his briefcase aside containing the list Fred had given him. Picking up the remote, and flopping into a chair, he turned on the television set. Hal was comfortable and half asleep in the chair, when he heard a knock on the door.

Muttering aloud about the inconvenience of having to answer the door, Hal rose and crossed the room. Upon opening the door, he was surprised to see gazing back at him the familiar face of Vorelis.

"I thought I'd find you home now. I have an important matter of the utmost urgency I need to discuss with you."

Hal's first instinct was to tell Vorelis that whatever he had to tell him could wait until the morning. Instead he invited him inside.

"Have a seat", said Hal directing him to an easy chair opposite the one in which he'd been sitting. Hal then picked up the remote and switched off the game.

"Would you care for a beer?" he asked leaving the room momentarily and returning with two cans of the beverage.

"Hmm, don't mind if I do" said Vorelis, who having been handed a can, opened it then savored the beer's malted aroma before imbibing the liquid. With a slight burp followed by "excuse me," Vorelis set the beer can aside.

"I'm aware, through my private sources that you'll soon be visiting a number of large corporations in the U.S. and around the world on behalf of an environmental campaign set in motion by Fred Hinson."

"Knowing that the master magician was living up to his reputation as a snoop, Hal asked, "how did you obtain that information?"

"Ignoring Hal's question, Vorelis said, "If I may be quite honest in saying so, you're plans appear to be quite inadequate."

"I'm afraid I don't understand what you mean", said Hal.

"Well let me put it this way, Hal. Your appointment to the lecture circuit must reach a much larger audience than the one upon which you plan to focus your environmental campaign. I too have an important list I'd like to present you with so that your lecturing engagements will take you to places not just upon this planet but elsewhere within the solar system."

"No, absolutely not" said Hal sounding decisive. I've already visited Mars. I've no desire whatsoever to schedule other visits."

"I'm sorry to hear that", said Vorelis who reached into his briefcase and produced his time traveling mirror. "Allow me to provide you with information on climate change. Temperatures are changing not just on Mars and Venus but temperatures are dropping below normal or soaring on the moons of Jupiter and Saturn too."

Hal started to leave the room. "Please remain seated in your chair", said Vorelis. The room where they were sitting soon was encompassed by a three dimensional video revealing how devastating the effects of war and pollution had become on planets during the era known as the Golden Age. If all planets are to be saved during the Golden Age and beyond it, your work is cut out for you."

Hal took a sip from the beer can and followed it with two more gulps. Drained of its contents, he set the beer can down on the coffee table and looked Vorelis straight in the eye.

"Listen, I don't think it's possible to zero in on every solar system planet that needs saving during the Golden Age. Even if they could be saved, I'm not the one to take on the mission for salvation."

"I'm not asking you to visit these places one by one", said Vorelis. "I'm asking that you join the brotherhood of which I'm sole leader and help search for the perfect land. During your conversation with Fred and his wife Sophie, I heard you talk about making the world a better place in which to live. It's a place we all want to find and need to find if this age or any age is to prosper."

"How would you know what I said to Fred and Sophie? You weren't even present when I was with them today."

"Don't be silly Hal. I haven't earned the title of master magician for nothing. If I want to overhear something someone is saying or doing, my ubiquitous presence makes it entirely possible."

"But why would you care to overhear something I said?"

"My dear Hal, we who are interested in saving the solar system from total annihilation, make it a point to search out new talent like yourself so that we might enlist them in our cause. The negative past must be canceled in order to insure a stable future for the solar system."

"I've been acting as a talent scout. You may not make it to the final competition: You really are using your positive inner energy in the right way. The train has jumped the tracks, if I may use an archaic cliché. We must set it back on the right path toward a bright and pristine environment."

"Surely you don't think I'm capable of doing all that."

"You're right, my boy. I don't expect you to do all that single handedly. If you and I and countless other beings align our thinking with the perfection and spiritual beauty of the great Source, we will succeed in saving the Golden Age from annihilation at the hands of such individuals as Menelus.

"I must admit, I was impressed to learn how well you conducted yourself within the Dark Tower when you and Atira were contacted by Menelus. Most find him intimidating."

"I don't find anyone intimidating until I get to know them. Menelus seemed to think I was trespassing on his property. I wanted to get to know Menelus so I could ask him a few more questions. Atira was afraid I was getting in over my head. I didn't want to end up like Prince Sentius so we left.

"I commend you on your clear thinking. You exited the tower at just the right moment. You made an impression on Menelus. You drew him into a conversation, asked him an important question and got an honest answer. That is something not everyone gets from him.

"If the Golden Age is to be mended we must somehow bring people like Menelus to the side of reason. That may not be done without a struggle. We must persuade Menelus and his cronies to see things our way."

"You mean you're planning to attack him?" asked Hal seeming rather stunned. "I don't want to be pushed into some outrageous scheme that might get me swept away like some obscure entity lost in time and space."

"Trust me Hal. I assure you that nothing like that will happen."

"And why not?" he asked.

"It's because I will be with you at all times."

"Really. We both already know that. You're always there even when you're not there."

"I don't appreciate you talking to me like that", said Vorelis pretending to be hurt. I assure you I'm not planning to coerce Menelus into any sort of weak peace treaty with Mars. Such an action wouldn't be in keeping with my principles. Queen Myaca would never consent to such an action either. There are other ways Menelus can be persuaded to see things our way."

"Such as"—said Hal, waiting for Vorelis to answer

"I'll simply present him with a three dimensional panoramic view of the future. After Menelus sees his planet with cities devastated, rivers and seas dried up, and images of beings unable to breathe the foul atmosphere surrounding them, he'll see things our way."

"You're assuming too much", said Hal. "If what you've told me about Menelus is true, he doesn't want peace. He doesn't care if he ruins his planet's environment. He wants dominance. The images of a future world in devastation will never convince him otherwise."

Gazing at Hal, Vorelis said, "Even if we fail, we'll have strengthened our position. Beings throughout the solar system and elsewhere in the galaxy will be aware of our efforts to save dying planets from impending doom."

"How is anyone to know of our efforts to reform Menelus if our interview with him is private?"

"Well, if I may remind you Hal—you've said so yourself on several different occasions. My presence is ubiquitous. What I know in private will soon be made public if my enemies don't cooperate with me."

Hal rose from the chair where he sat. Lookly directly at Vorelis he asked, "Does that include me?"

"You've been entrusted with an important responsibility. I've shown you that I have complete trust in you. Yet you want to back off from that responsibility."

Hal sat down again. He felt weak and nauseous. He saw himself standing once more in Whitfield's office that momentous morning months ago when he and Whitfield got swept up in a time warp, ending up on Mars. He could almost feel the building sway beneath his feet. Hal swallowed then wiped his forehead with a handkerchief. He got up from where he'd been sitting and crossed the room.

"I've been sitting in the time machine too long," he said. "I'm a failure", he whispered.

Vorelis behaved as if he hadn't heard the remark.

"We both know you'll succeed with what I'm asking you to do if you'll only put your heart and mind into the effort."

Hal appeared as if he were in a daze. He'd hardly noticed that in Vorelis' hand was a time traveling device enabling him to temporarily step into the dimension occupied by Menelus.

"We won't actually confront him physically. That would be too dangerous", explained Vorelis.

"That's the biggest TV screen I've ever seen", said Hal. The image of Menelus now encompassed the entire room.

Menelus was sitting alone in a room within his Venusian Palace. He was casually glancing through a volume of Venusian history, when he came to a blank page. He stared down at the page still unable to admit to himself that it was blank until instinct told him that it surely was. Menelus started to shiver. He then let out a scream that reverberated throughout time itself. He saw the image of Vorelis beamed down at him from a time traveling screen installed in the room where he'd been reading.

"How dare you interfere with my plans for the future", he said shouting at the image of Vorelis. Knowing that Menelus would stop at nothing to get his own way, Hal, shuddered listening to the confrontation between the two adversaries.

Vorelis folded his arms and raised his voice—just a little—to insure that Menelus heard him and knew he was totally serious.

"Your plan for the Venusian domination of the solar system is nothing better than a blank page in history if you continue down the same destructive path you've been following. In fact, my friend Hal who stands by my side, is ready to challenge your supremecy."

"Oh, please don't tell him that", said Hal trembling. He was remembering his last meeting with Menelus inside the Dark Tower. Hal was ready to back down the stairs again.

"Get out of here at once" shouted Menelus, who taking the time screen's remote in hand threw it at the screened images of Vorelis and Hal.

Ignoring the tirade he'd just witnessed, Vorelis said, "The motives for cruelty and revenge must be blocked—erased from the record. History then will take a new turn. The Golden Age will live on as a shining example of unblemished peace in the face of intolerance, misery and war."

After witnessing the terrifying encounter between the two adversaries, Hal was relieved to see that it was over with. Stunned and unable to say anything in reponse to it, Hal simply stared at the magician.

Vorelis looked at Hal and could see that he'd overstayed his welcome. Hal was quite pale. When he tried to get up from where he now was sitting, Hal looked as if his knees might buckle beneath him.

"Are you sure you're alright?"

Hal managed to mumble not too politely, "I'm fine".

"Well then, thanks for the beer" said Vorelis. "I'll let myself out—Oh by the way," he said turning around before he closed the door behind him. "Tomorrow morning we have another scheduled meeting with leading participants of the Golden Age. I'll see you then. Good night."

After Vorelis left him, Hal tried to get up. He was exhausted. He collapsed into a chair and closed his eyes. Groggy and almost half asleep, he started to recall Colonel James Churchward's last meeting in India with the old Rishi. 1 For years, the incident hadn't meant much to him. Then Hal began to recall the account in vivid detail. What he remembered weren't just words jumping out at him from a book's page. The Rishi, who had taught him to transcribe the temple's secret tablets, carried Churchward on a journey to Mu. They floated across a great flat land, over cities and open plains. Days and weeks seemed to pass before Churchward's life on that plane of existence suddenly dissolved.

Hal sat upright in a chair. He could hear Vorelis talking to him even though he wasn't present. "I've scheduled another meeting for you tomorrow. It's my hope that tomorrow's journey through time and space will be sufficiently real enough to draw attention to the matters that are urgent and must be addressed if the Golden Age is to survive."

Hal fell asleep again. When he'd opened his eyes, it was morning. Sunlight streamed in from a glass balcony door. Hal opened the door and stepped onto the balcony. He gazed downward. Below him, people busily went about their daily business. Car horns blared, and in the distance he could hear the shrill whining noise of a police siren. Lost in thought and for a moment absorbed by the activity he observed below him, Hal almost didn't hear the knock on his apartment door. When he opened the door, he found staring back at him the familiar face of Vorelis.

"I've brought coffee", he said taking off his coat.

"It looks as though you've brought breakfast too" said Hal who thanked Vorelis for his generosity, and then unwrapped a ham, egg and cheese biscuit before taking a sip of coffee.

Vorelis seated himself comfortably in a chair. Then taking out his time traveling device, in hand he announced: ' Let the games begin.'"

Hal, who'd been busy eating, had forgotten to close the balcony door. The wind was blowing the balcony curtains around. He started to get up so he could close the door but Vorelis signaled for him to remain seated.

The room darkened. There was a sound of thunder. Outside a midmorning rain started to fall. Suddenly a tremendous bolt of lightning streaked across the sky followed by the sound of thunder so intense that it shook the room.

Vorelis closed his eyes. Hal, who'd momentarily put his coffee and biscuit aside long enough to notice that Vorelis appeared to be asleep, realized he was wide awake but in a trance.

Before Hal could cross the room so he could shake Vorelis awake, Vorelis blinked his eyes and opened them. He explained to Hal that he was just taking a little catnap from the rigors of living on more than one level of consciousness.

"Rather than going directly to bed as I should have last night, I took a flight into other worlds so that I might directly contact those whose presence at today's meeting is most desired. It has been many years since I last saw Jove. When I entered his presence last night, I saw he was surrounded by the symbols of his power, thunder and lightning. Present with him too were none other than the infamous Titans and Giants who'd once challenged his bold rule after Jove usurped his father Saturn's place within the cosmos.1 When I reminded Jove that such an attempt had only brought the anathemas of the solar system down upon succeeding ages he agreed to new terms. Jove has decided to join a solar system alliance.

Just as Vorelis was about to tell Hal of the conditions under which Jove had agreed to the peace pact, a huge clap of thunder was heard. The bolt's intensity was such that the room shook. A lamp sitting atop a table fell over and crashed to the floor

"I believe we've just experienced divine intervention," said Vorelis. "Jove has not only agreed to a pact, he has thrown down the gauntlet."

Hal had a mouthful of biscuit. He tried to swallow and talk at the same time.

"What gauntlet?" he asked nearly choking.

"If the events of history are to be mended and the mistakes of the past erased, the challenge is for your generation", said Vorelis picking up his coffee cup and taking a sip from it

Vorelis bent over and picked up the glove lying upon the floor. The glove bore the symbols of power, the royal escutcheons of Mu, Atlantis and the ruling orbs of the solar system. Handing the glove to Hal he said,

"The grail isn't for immortal Jove to discover, it is for you as a member of your generation to do so."

Hal gazed at the glove, then dropped it on the floor.

"I can't do this", he said. "I'm just an ordinary businessman and if I might add a rather bumbling one too."

"No you're not", said Vorelis. "You, as much as Whitfield were responsible for turning around the events that day at the Global Trade Mart. You were determined that the event couldn't happen. Since you've visited the dimension where there is no evil, you're ready to erase the evils that for centuries have plagued men but for which they've found no remedy.

"Passage through the gate of the sun awaits you. The great Ra Mu, the light of the universe encompassing all things has touched your life. Now you must let your light shine by discovering the grail and bringing it home to the 21st century."

No sooner had Vorelis gotten his words out than Hal was transported back through time and space. He was no longer sitting in his New York apartment. He found himself standing once more within the Martian Sun Temple of 16,000 years ago. In his hand was the glove Vorelis had passed to him after Jove had thrown it down.

Quickly gazing down at the glove then muttering a few obscenities under his breath, Hal knew he must somehow contact Vorelis and demand that the magician transport him back to New York. Upon turning around, though he found himself facing Murdock.

"Welcome back", said Murdock extending a furry paw in greeting to Hal, who in stunned silence shook it. He was about to ask Murdock the question.

"What are you doing here?" Knowing the remark would sound silly since Murdock lived upon the premises, he said nothing and continued to stare.

"I see that Jove has thrown down the gauntlet", said Murdock examining the glove Hal handed it to him: "I can't accept this challenge. It's not for me to undertake."

"On the contrary" replied Murdock, "You have to finish the job you've started. Whitfield has undertaken the task of solving the perfect equation. That proof will be meaningless unless it's actually put to the test.

"Throughout mythological history, men and gods have taken on ambitious challenges. Phaeton, who drove Pheobus' chariot in an attempt to prove to others he knew how to handle it as well as his father, met with disaster. This time the ride mustn't fail. The gauntlet Jove has thrown down to earth is given only to the most heroic.

"Your ordeal will not be unlike that of knights of old who found themselves confronting evil on more than one level." Murdock then pointed to a stained glass window representation of a symbol reputed to be over 35, 000 years old .2

Light streamed down through the window into the Sun Temple as Hal gazed at the cosmogonic replica and diagram of the land of Mu. 3 An exact replica of the stained glass window had been given as a gift from the beings of Mars to the settlers of Earth's Mu.

"The ribbon falling downward from the stained glass window diagram symbolizes the qualities one must have in order to attain the perfection symbolized by the central symbol, Ra the Sun. Courage isn't enough. Like the knights of old, men must be tested to the core of their being if the golden age is to be won and peace established throughout the solar system."

"I could never be a knight of old. I'm sure I'd fall under the weight of a coat of mail or fall off my horse."

"You misunderstand me Hal", replied Murdock. "The knights of old had to display many qualities other than strength. Courage and physical strength manifested by them was secondary to qualities such as right action, right living, meditation and adoration of a Source that knew no evil or cruelty but only good."

"Although he didn't believe in cruelty or violence of any sort, and he loved and respected all beings, Hal still felt unworthy.

"Ah, yes" said Murdock. "Like many people of your time, you feel unworthy. That must change. You must let your light shine. You must love the universe. Perceive universal beings as you wish to be perceived—for the great source of all—the great Ra perceives creation in that way."

"When may I return to Earth?" asked Hal.

"Just as soon as you're ready to take on the task that lies before you", said Murdock, who told Hal he would accompany him on the first part of the journey. "Today you'll be introduced to a replica of the chariot Phaeton drove."

"I don't know how to drive a chariot", said Hal admitting he'd flunked his driver's test twice before passing it. "I think you've seen that film 'Ben Hur' too many times". He was sure Murdock had no idea how to drive a chariot either.

"I assure you, although I don't know how to drive a chariot, I handle a hovercraft quite deftly" replied Murdock.

"I've driven with you before. You enjoy a little speed and are reckless at times. You're not a bad driver," admitted Hal

Deciding not to reply to Hal's remark regarding the way he maneuvered his hovercraft, Murdock said, "I'd like to take you for a ride in my hovercraft not to demonstrate my driver efficiency but because we both need to keep an important appointment."

"What appointment?" he asked sounding exasperated.

"I'm afraid I have no time to explain to you the nature of the appointment. Trust me, it's one you wouldn't want to miss."

Within minutes, they'd stepped from the craft and were meeting with a fairground's representative in the middle of a field. "There's an apartment adjoining the fairgrounds where you'll be staying", said the representative handing Hal some clothes. "You can change there," he said pointing.

Once inside the apartment, Hal spotted an open window. Thinking he might flee from the apartment undetected he was disappointed. A robot guard posted just outside the window, discouraged Hal from implementing such a plan.

"There'll be another opportunity to get away from here", he thought after he'd changed into the charioteer's uniform and was ready for his first lesson.

"I'm not going to drive that thing", said Hal inspecting the chariot.

"Please, you mustn't make such a hasty decision", said Orbutus who having been introduced to him was ready to give Hal a lesson.

Despite his reluctance to take the reins from Orbutus, Hal was spellbound by the chariot's amazing design and the horses' rare beauty. He stepped forward and gently patted a sleek black stallion tethered to the chariot. He then petted the other horses. "I've always liked horses", he admitted

"The horses are no ordinary horses", said Orbutus who with his gold locks, deep tan and piercing blue eyes looked like some mythological hero. If you learn how to handle the horses, they will take you into unknown dimensions."

Hal was intrigued. Then almost in a daze, he mounted the chariot. With Orbutus standing behind him, Hal took the reins of power.

Chamelon, the beautiful black stallion whinnied then reared joyfully as he led the other horses in an even rhythmic canter around the fairgrounds.

"You must get to know them", said Orbutus. "You have harnessed great spirits.

Hal held his breath in anticipation of what would happen next. Chamelon, the undisputed leader of the team snorted as he and the other horses pulled the chariot upward until it was now running ten feet or so off the ground.

Hal almost panicked when he saw they'd defied gravity. He quickly allowed Orbutus to take the reins from him. Orbutus then encouraged the horses to climb higher into the sky. Hyacinth the gray mare who steadied the other horses kept apace with Chamelon as the graceful Aleria, and the indomitable Ariel all raced against time itself.

"Obviously Mars' gravitational pull isn't as strong as Earth's" said Orbutus who also knew that the horse's levitation skills had nothing to do with the law of gravity. The team was now gliding between thirty and fifty feet off the ground.

Hal felt weak and looked quite pale. Orbutus thought he might have to hold Hal up to keep him from falling out of the chariot. "I think you've seen enough for one day." Hal didn't know what to say. Instead, he simply watched in stunned disbelief as Orbutus slowly reined in the horses until they were cantering smoothly along the ground and around the fairgrounds.

Once he'd brought the team to a halt, Orbutus asked:

"Did you enjoy the ride? If you did, you must let the horses know."

A fairground's attendant, carrying a silver tray, waited for Hal and Orbutus to step from the chariot. Taking the tray from the attendant's hands, Hal gave each horse a carrot treat. "One day you'll find yourself driving the team alone. You won't need any help from me", said Orbutus patting each horse separately.

"Let's not fool ourselves", thought Hal. "I could never do that in a millions years."

Unaware that Orbutus had read his thought, Hal was astonished when Orbutus replied "We're not going that far back in time".

When Orbutus finally led the horses away for watering, Hal called after him: "Even the horses don't think I'm the guy for the job."

"I spoke with Orbutus" said Murdock, who later met with Hal. "You must concentrate on the task before you."

"And what task might that be?" asked Hal a little sarcastically.

"You must bond with the horses. The magnificent creatures that you look upon as mere animals demand far more than a smooth rub down, a carrot treat or a reassuring pat for a job well done. The horses must grow to like and trust you. You must prepare for the journey.

"These riders of the sky will take you where they alone have been once you've decided within your heart that your motives for advancement are genuine. If you want to rise above the earthly pull of gravity and see the place where the heavens encompass the Earth, then the restrictions of time, like gravity will slip away. Nothing will hold you back.

"First you must learn to believe in yourself. Align your spirit with the resources of the infinite. See yourself and others as never having fallen from grace."

Clearing his throat, Murdock had nearly choked thinking that he was encouraging Hal to do something he personally hadn't done himself.

"Thank goodness Vorelis told me what to say to him" he thought as he continued to drone on with his sales pitch for riding into the beyond.

Murdock then held a time traveling mirror up to the light and showed Hal the awful scenario of what might happen if he didn't help stop approaching doom.

"Witness the war in heaven, the fall of the Giants and the Titans not to mention man. See Earth's destruction by asteroids, the obliteration of Earth's continents of Mu and Atlantis as well as destruction to the planets of the solar system. The train is rapidly approaching us: You must prevent it from making its final stop. First you must learn how to handle the chariot by conquering the limitations and fears within yourself."

"I'm not ready to take the ride right now. I must admit it felt pretty exhilarating when the horses pulled the chariot off the ground this morning."

"Ah so you enjoyed the ride" said Murdock interrupting Hal.

"I guess you might call it some kind of power ride. I'm really not sure if I truly enjoyed it. I'm not sure if you've selected the right candidate for preventing Mu, Atlantis and the solar system planets from becoming toast. Perhaps you need to find someone else to do the job. One thing I'm sure of though. I'm ready to go home."

"Very well" said Murdock, "Neither Vorelis nor I have ever forced anyone into doing something against his will. If you feel you're not cut out for the mission. If you feel you have neither the courage nor strength of character to cope with the demands of the job, we'll simply recruit someone else."

"That's fine with me" said Hal.

*   *   *   *

Within an instant, Hal found himself sitting alone in his New York apartment with the wind blowing the curtains around the balcony door.

"I was hallucinating", he told himself unconvincingly. "It was all just a dream."

Hal then reached for the cell phone he always carried with him in his pocket and started to call Amelia. As he waited for her to answer the phone, he happened to glance down at the floor. The glove that Jove had thrown down to him was there.

"Hello" said Amelia. "Hello, hello, are you there?"

For a moment Hal said nothing. He picked up the glove and almost dropped his cell phone before he mumbled. "I'm here."

"Of course you're there", said Amelia sounding a little impatient, "and you're calling me from your New York apartment too."

"I knew that", said Hal sounding uncertain.

"How's your new job?"

There was a pause. Hal wasn't sure which job she meant.

"Umm, it's going along just fine", he said still sounding uncertain.

"Are you sure you're okay" she asked sounding concerned.

"I'm fine—just a little tired"

"By the way" she said. "Natasha loves her new sanctuary and she couldn't be happier especially since I've taken in another needy elephant with a new baby. They get along super well."

"Listen" said Hal "I want you to know that I'm on my way home. I'm booking an evening flight to Atlanta. I'll see you later tonight."

"That's great. Do you want me to pick you up at the airport?"

"No, a limo is going to meet me and drive me home. I need to work on the presentations I'm planning to give to the corporations. This city is too hectic. I want to trade in the traffic noises for the peace and quiet of the farm so I can get some work done."

"I've missed you", she said. "It will be great to see you."

Hal continued to stare at the glove even after he'd gotten off the phone with Amelia. He then walked over to the balcony and watched the wind blow the curtains around as if the wind were trying to throw them away so that something else could take their place.

Hal closed the balcony door and locked it. "I'm going home", he thought picking up his laptop and his small carryon. Then closing his apartment door, he walked toward the elevator. Once he was standing on the pavement outside his building, he raised his hand as if he were reaching out to the world and asking it to stop all the noise and to listen instead for the silence and peace from within.

Hal knew the challenge offered him, had to be fought on the home front. He was feeling better now. He had a grip upon life. "There's work to be done.

The train mustn't jump the tracks", he said with a muttered laugh. Then, after hailing a cab, Hal headed for the airport.

*   *   *   *

When Myaca heard that Hal had backed off from the job as charioteer, her first reaction was to tell Murdock that a replacement needed to be found.

"Of course", replied Murdock, who lying said "There were several candidates just waiting in the wings to be tested."

"I've been in touch with Vorelis", said Myaca. "I've told him he needs to temporarily undertake the role of talent scout. Obviously he had a good eye for talent when he signed on Amelia and Natasha. I watched them through my time traveling screen as they crossed the Cloud Bridge. They made it look easy."

"Are you suggesting that I try to enlist Amelia in the role of charioteer?"

"Of course not" replied Myaca thoughtfully. "You might consider having her give Hal special coaching for the job."

"But Hal's already declined the offer to become a charioteer."

"Perhaps if Amelia boosted Hal's confidence, and showed him that by working with her and Natasha that he had the special qualifications necessary for the job, she might persuade him otherwise."

"But how are you to lure Hal away from giving all those speeches to 21st C. corporations? He likes being in the limelight."

"I have an excellent idea on how to do it. Hal hates to write speeches. To put it bluntly he's the sort of man who usually hires other people to do that sort of thing for him. From what you've told me about Hal and from what I've been able to observe about him, I've come to the conclusion that the heir to the Worthy Fortune is a bit of a drop out in more ways than one. "Not only did he just get by in college with all those gentleman C's, his record for being a procrastinator surprises even me since I'm a bit of one myself. I must admit. Hal has a good mind. If he wants to accomplish something nothing will stop him from doing it."

"Well, then" replied Murdock, "How are we to block Hal from calling upon all those corporations?"

"I don't think that will be difficult when you persuade Vorelis to allow Hal to step into his shoes as chief circus administrator. In that way, Hal will have the feeling of being in the office while taking a vacation from the everyday activities he finds to be such a grind. Amelia will do the rest for us. Hal hates to be separated from her. When Hal realizes that Natasha loves being with him too not to mention the other woman in his life, he'll be ready for the big top— big time. In fact, if push comes to shove we can banish

Orbutus from his duties at the celestial fairgrounds and send him on leave of absence to Earth where he'll have the opportunity to work with Hal, Amelia and the fabulous Natasha."

"You're not expecting the elephant to make a glorious ride into the sun with Hal at the reins are you?" asked Vorelis when Myaca told him of her plan.

Myaca gave Vorelis a knowing look. "Love conquers all" she said smiling. "Dear Hal, Amelia and Natasha are going to be part of a little love triangle that may bring the solar system into our grasp."

"You mean for better or for worse?" asked Vorelis who could see the look of self-satisfaction upon Myaca's face.

"I mean for better not for worse" she replied. "Menelus is a fool if he thinks he and his cronies are soon to be supreme rulers of the solar system. Why, when we were children, Menelus couldn't even beat me at mehen let alone monopoly."

Thinking of how recently he'd had to rescue Myaca from her cousin's clutches, Vorelis replied politely, "I'm so glad you have such a resilient spirit. Regardless of what your cousin's evil schemes may be, he never seems to win."

"At least not over me" said Myaca smiling.

Chapter Nine

▼

"I'm so glad you're home", said Amelia embracing Hal. The couple's moment of contentment was short lived though. Amelia told Hal she'd received an urgent call from Vorelis telling her that their services at the Circus of Wonders were indispensable. "The Circus is in a financial rut. Vorelis is fighting to keep it afloat. My act with Natasha has been missed. There's been a marked drop in circus attendance since we left. He wants us to return for a limited engagement, at least until the circus can find a decent replacement act for us."

"Do you think it's fair to put Natasha back in the circus arena again?"

"I really don't want to do it. This is an emergency. Vorelis also wants you temporarily to step in as manager, and see if you could help out with the circus finances. Starting next month, the circus will begin permanent engagements in Atlanta. If we do well there, Natasha can spend a few days each week here at the sanctuary. I was hoping this could be a permanent retreat for us but the jobs of Garfield the Clown and Fabian the Lion Tamer, not to mention all the other circus performers, are at stake if we don't help out."

Hal hated to think that the circus people might be out of jobs if the circus couldn't turn a profit. He was also flattered to think that Vorelis wanted him to act as the circus' chief financial officer. "Vorelis may be a great magician. I don't think he has much of a head for figures."

*   *   *   *

Amelia knew she and Hal had made a mistake in wanting to take Natasha out of retirement. When Amelia tried to coax the elephant into the circus transport truck, she wouldn't budge.

"It's no use Hal. I can't uproot Natasha and force her to return to circus life. It just wouldn't be fair. This is her home. The sanctuary was created for her."

Hal gently patted Natasha's trunk as Amelia fed her some carrots.

"I'm going to get in touch with Vorelis to see if there isn't someway he can find a replacement act for her"

"The act will have to be super", said Amelia sighing.

"I'm sure Vorelis can arrange for that".

*   *   *   *

Murdock was sitting and working in his Sun Temple office when a furry butler interrupted him, and told him he had a message. "The message better be important", said Murdock who disliked being disturbed. With a sigh of resignation, he followed the butler into the room where the time screen was located.

The screen's video message was from Vorelis: "The charioteer, horses and gleaming chariot are required as a replacement act. Please make the necessary business arrangements so that Orbutus and his spendid team will be ready for transfer to the Circus of Wonders."

"Hmm," mused Murdock before replying to the message, "I suppose Amelia and her pachyderm friend just don't have the necessary charisma to get the Circus of Wonders out of debt."

Later when Murdock met Orbutus at the fairground's training track, he told him he was urgently needed in another time zone.

"Why would anyone require my services elsewhere?" he asked."I like my job here." Murdock assured Orbutus that the work assignment was only temporary.

"It seems that Earth's Circus of Wonders is running into some financial problems. They need an act that's going to get the circus out of debt. With your unparalleled skill as a charioteer, we thought you and your horses might be just the act required for the job."

"I can see you now with the audience on their feet applauding you as you make your way into the arena so that you may show off your talent and your horses' great skill" he said trying to pump up a crestfallen Orbutus

"I've never played the 21st C. before", said Orbutus who was unsure how his horses would react to being put on display before audiences that had never seen celestial levitation. "I'm not sure I want to step into a century where the finite solid world is the only reality most beings know anything about. I hesitate to show off my skills and those of my horses to an audience that might not understand how our ability is achieved."

"Obviously, nobody is going to understand how you do what you do", replied Murdock. "Just go out there and ride your horses around the circus track. When you've consistently stunned audiences from performance to performance, Vorelis will just inform them that it's all done by optical illusion."

Feeling he was lowering his standard of excellence by accepting such an offer, Orbutus muttered, "I'll think about it."

Murdock removed the time traveling device he carried with him. Within seconds, Orbutus, his chariot and horses all found themselves center ring at the Circus of Wonders.

*   *   *   *

"Ready for rehearsal?" asked Vorelis, who knew Orbutus was furious at being catapulted through time and space where he found himself in unfamiliar surroundings. Orbutus was about to utter a few unkind words to Vorelis for the inconvenience but anger was abated when the welcoming committee converged upon them.

"So you're the new act", said Garfield extending his hand in greeting, before introducing himself and Fabian the Lion Tamer to him. "Vorelis has been telling us about you. I understand those horses of yours are pretty good."

Orbutus said that his horses weren't just pretty good: His horses' ancestors carried Phaeton into the sky for his final ride.

"Do you suppose we could include that item in the program?" asked Garfield who thought such a headline would draw customers into the circus. Fabian, who'd been standing alongside Garfield and listening to the conversation said, "I headline my lions and tigers as descendents of those that performed in the Circus Maximus. They didn't, of course, but that adds to the excitement."

Patting Chamelon's head, Orbutus assured Garfield that his horses didn't need to be headlined. "Come" he said, calling them together. "Show them what you can do." Ariel quickly left her place alongside the other horses and began cantering around the circus arena. Her hooves never touched the ground, as she effortless circled the arena before stopping in front of Orbutus.

"I've never seen a horse do that before", said Fabian who marveled at the horse's display of grace and agility.

"Ariel's talent for levitation isn't learned. It's inherited. She alone guides the rest of the team when they reach for great heights and other dimensions."

"What do you mean by other dimensions?" asked Garfield.

"Well", replied Orbutus, who was relieved to see Vorelis approaching them, and didn't want to reveal too much about the horse's secret power of levitation: "She simply imagines that she can do what you or I are incapable of doing."

"I hope you'll help Orbutus get acclimated to circus life", said Vorelis patting Garfield on the back.

"You mean you haven't acted in a circus before?" asked Fabian whose jaw dropped in disbelief.

"Well, to be perfectly honest, my horses have always trained for a different sort of exhibition. They're riders of the wind. They train at the fairgrounds where they race only on special occasions."

Not wanting Orbutus to reveal too much about himself, Vorelis asked Fabian if he could go over the accounts with the new accounts manager.

Hal was concentrating on his new job when Vorelis and Fabian entered the room.

"Perhaps you can answer any questions Hal might have" said Vorelis leaving them alone. Harry extended a hand in greeting to Fabian. Then pulling up a ledger on a computer screen, he said, "I think we can increase our nightly audience and get out of the red if we can line up a few more decent acts. For the time being we're calling Atlanta home. We won't be incurring any unnecessary travel expenses here."

"Good" replied Fabian who'd found traveling with his cats to be burdensome. "They need more freedom from circus life. Being cooped up all the time isn't good for them."

"I realize that", said Hal. "Dad and I have made arrangements for you to take your cats to a sanctuary where they can have some freedom, and where you can have a vacation. Since your act is one of the circus' main attractions, we're also giving you a raise and a promotion. You and your cats will perform alternately, one week at the sanctuary and one week at the circus. In that way, you'll be able to act as advisor to the sanctuary and perform as well."

Smiling and thanking Hal, Fabian said: "I've always dreamed of being able to give my cats the sort of life you're providing them."

"When people learn that the sanctuary is an extension of the Circus of Wonders, a place where animals are loved and humanely cared for, the good publicity will only enhance the Circus of Wonder's image," said Hal.

"By the way, while you're at the sanctuary, you'll be with a friend of mine, Edgar Joyner. He's a veterinarian who lives and works in Africa. He'll be working with you and your cats so you can get them back in shape."

*   *   *   *

The sanctuary was situated on an old farm outside Forsyth, Ga. and was about 40 miles from Atlanta. It was late afternoon when a trailer carrying Fabian's cats pulled into it. Edgar, who'd only days before arrived from

Kenya, greeted Fabian and helped him get the cats settled in their new surroundings.

"My veterinarian practice utilizes some of the wonders of African bush medicine: Age old cures are important. I've also found that proper diet, and good exercise work wonders in a majority of cases."

After several weeks' stay at the sanctuary, Fabian and his cats returned to the arena, and performed with an ease and skill previously not seen before. Brutus, Fabian's star performer, not only jumped through a hoop at the end of a performance, he managed to turn somersaults before he stood on his hind legs and took a bow.

Later, when Fabian and Hal were studying the circus ledger, Fabian happened to mention: I don't know what's come over my cats. Since they've been visiting the sanctuary on a regular basis, they get along better than ever. During leisure time together they display a spirit of playful camaraderie usually seen only among their species' younger generation.

"I think it's a too bad, Amelia and Natasha are no longer part of our circus family. The other performers tell me that they miss their spirit and sense of fun."

"Eventually Amelia and Natasha may be back in the circus arena. Right now I think they're enjoying farm life too much to trade it in for a circus routine."

"And speaking of routines", said Fabian, changing the subject, "When are Orbutus and his famous Sky Riders going to perform?"

"Orbutus and the horses are working on a routine with Garfield the Clown. Vorelis wants Garfield to introduce Orbutus and the horses to the audience. He'll then step in and become part of the routine."

The following evening, Hal and Fabian watched from the wings as Garfield with Orbutus standing next to him in the chariot, drove the team into the Circus of Wonders center arena.

Garfield brought the chariot to a halt, stepped down from it and then introduced Orbutus and his act. Taking the reins in his hands Orbutus and his magnificent horses began circling the arena just as Vorelis entered the act too. He combined his brilliant light show with the horses' unsurpassed skill and grace. When the team appeared to be soaring ten feet off the ground, the audience wasn't sure if what they were seeing was actual or just illusion.

Hal and Amelia, who'd been watching the performance from the wings, knew what they'd witnessed had been circus genius. "Only Vorelis could have made that happen", said Hal taking a bite of pink cotton candy.

"Did I hear someone mention my name?" asked Vorelis on his way backstage to his dressing room.

"The performance was amazing", said Hal. "It never occurred to me that you were in the chariot riding business."

"I've never been a professional charioteer if that's what you mean. I'm in the business of screening candidates to take that glorious ride into other dimensions. I'm not sure if Orbutus has the right qualifications for the job. For one thing, he has no idea where Prince Sentius is hidden, and even if he did know of his whereabouts, I doubt if he'd have the courage to confront Menelus. You, on the other hand, are the supreme candidate for the job. You found the door to the dimension where Sentius is hidden."

"I may have found the right door but it's closed and I have no idea where Prince Sentius is hidden."

"That knowledge is unnecessary", said Vorelis. "You need only to take the ride into the final dimension and doors will open to you that for centuries have remained closed."

"If you want me back on the job. If you think I'm still a candidate for it the answer is still no."

"My Worthy", he said patiently. "You've already told me your answer is no. I'm a reasonable man. I can take no for an answer. All that I'm asking for you to do is to help the trainer train the trainee."

"And who might that be?" asked Hal

"Well, right now I'm not sure. I'm still looking for your replacement. All that I'm asking of you is to temporarily fill in—just for a while. I'm sure you wouldn't mind if Amelia helped out too. She has great skill and expertise in working with animals. You both would make a marvelous team. Picture yourself in the role of supreme charioteer."

"I've already said no to the challenge. I don't want to get burned. Thunder and lightning couldn't make me do it. Just as Hal was speaking, a nearby lightning bolt hit the ground followed by an enormous clap of thunder. For a moment, the circus lights went out. When they came on again, Hal found the glove at his feet. He bent, picked up the glove, then slowly handing it to Vorelis, he said "No, absolutely not."

"I think Hal is right in rejecting the offer said Amelia. Hal's not a circus person. Hal's never performed in the big top before."

"Now wait a minute", said Hal. "I may not be ready for the big time, big top but I did a pretty good job in crossing the Cloud Bridge. We arrived at the lost city on schedule. Even you said you didn't know how you and Natasha could have done it without me."

"I'm sorry, Hal", said Amelia a little teary eyed. "It's just that I've had so many absent people in my life. First my father walked out on me. Now you seem ready to take the big leap too."

"You can help him succeed", said Vorelis. "Hal only needs a few people to believe in him. Then the wings of Pegasus and all the great horses of history will sweep him to victory."

Amelia stopped sniffling. She knew Hal needed to experience success.

"All right" said Hal still seeming reluctant. "I'll give it a try. I must admit that being at the reins of one of the chariots of the gods is a heady experience."

"Just remember to keep your feet on the ground", said Amelia. "Just because you're in the company of great charioteers doesn't mean you don't need a little earthly coaxing from people sitting on the sidelines."

"Does that include you?" he asked.

"Well, I've worked with animals before. I think I understand where their heart is. I know that as long as Natasha is eating pasture grasses and roaming in the sunshine, her desire to return to the circus arena is at its lowest ebb. The horses are no different. They've been trained to surpass the endurance and speed of ordinary horses but their ability to do so depends largely upon the freedom they feel. If they are surrounded by darkness and confined to a barn, the spirit within them is crushed. The horses will never allow you to obtain the gold ring."

"Do you think I'd regard them as carousel horses?" said Hal who'd remembered riding one when he was a kid. "I never managed to capture the gold ring", he said thoughtfully.

"But you will" said Vorelis who impressed upon Hal that he was destined for great things.

Hal gazed down at the glove. "I realize the chariot team is fast becoming a star attraction for the circus. I need to take the team home where I can practice with it on my own turf. Right now the team responds best when Orbutus holds the reins in his hands. Under my direction that could change."

"Of course it could change", said Vorelis. "You'll discover your own pace and establish a harmony and rhythm with the horses that is uniquely your own. Only Orbutus has ever driven the team into the heavens. The sun blinded him though. He turned back. To have continued in the face of the sun's brilliance might have brought certain death not only to the horses but to him as well."

"Suppose the same thing happens to me too" said Hal who admired Orbutus's skill, and felt sure he could never surpass it.

"You and Orbutus will work together as a team. He'll school you in the finer points of being a charioteer. Then he will hand the reins to you. You see, Hal, it is you who must assume the great ride into the heavens because you and Whitfield together have taken the first step in solving the perfect equation."

"Well then, why doesn't Whitfield take the ride?"

"He's doing his part in solving the mathematical portion of the equation. You, on the other hand, are involved in the equation's practical application."

Gazing at him, Amelia could see the lack of confidence reflected in Hal's face. "Don't doubt yourself. You took the lead the day we crossed the Cloud Bridge. The way across the bridge was solid and secure."

Hal remembered that day and the moment when he'd leaned forward, peered over Natasha's great ears, and saw only a mist-covered rain forest. In the distance looming ahead of the Cloud Bridge were the mountains from where the snow spider had once come. Her web, so finely spun that even man's finest fabric could offer only an inferior comparison, had covered the heavens for them that afternoon. Once upon a time one small spider had been blown by the breath of the wind into the heavens, and then forged a passage through forbidden terrain. Hal recalled the moment so well that he hardly heard Amelia whisper.

"You can do it again".

Later that afternoon, four horse trailers pulled up in front of the family farm. Behind the trailers was a car: Stepping from it was Orbutus, Hal and Amelia.

"Mother will show you to your room" said Hal introducing Orbutus to Jaime. "After you're settled, Amelia and I will show you around the farm."

*   *   *   *

Myaca was sitting upon a comfortable divan and eating delicious Martian chocolates laced with sherry from Murdock's vineyard when she heard that Hal was in training with Orbutus. Turning to a robot butler who'd served her the treats, and brought her the news, she said. "Please inform Vorelis that I congratulate him on a job well done."

She then sighed, got up from where she'd been sitting, and walked over to a balcony. A sultry afternoon breeze blew the leaves of a tree resembling a gingko. Myaca gazed downward at the tree and recognized a familiar visitor perched upon a tree branch.

The pigeon's gold and silver feathers indicated he was no ordinary bird. Hadrian cocked his head to one side. He cooed a soft sweet song carried upon the cool breeze and captured Myaca's heart.

"Hadrian" she whispered reaching out to him with outstretched arm. Immediately the bird flew to Myaca's hand and perched upon one of her fingers. After stroking his soft feathers she noticed Hadrian carried a message for her. Dropping the message in front of her, Hadrian quickly flew to Myaca's shoulder. He remained there until she left the balcony and crossed the room to her desk.

The message was from her husband Prince Sentius: "I dared not contact you sooner for fear that my message might be intercepted. Now that Jove has become our ally and friend, perhaps he will be able to assist us in bringing about my release. Until I'm able to win my release and return to you, Hadrian will act as our messenger. Let him remain with you until you are certain it is safe for him to return bearing your message to me. Signed—your loving husband Sentius."

Myaca read the message several times. She studied its handwriting to be certain the letter was genuine. Then ordering one of her servants to bring her a large gold cage, she watched as Hadrian entered the cage and dined on delicious fresh grains and fruits there.

Hadrian flew from the cage to an open window and down to a garden pool. He then bathed and carefully preened his feathers before returning to Myaca's shoulder.

"You have been the bearer of great news today" she said as he hopped from her shoulder to her hand. Hadrian then flew from Myaca's hand before comfortably settling himself upon the highest perch situated within his gold cage, and went to sleep.

Evening had settled upon the palace once more. Myaca picked up Hadrian's cage and opened the door to her bedroom. She then placed the cage containing Hadrian on a table next to her bed and fell asleep.

When she was awakened the following morning by Hadrian's cooing, she yawned then stretched before she stepped from bed and walked over to a shuttered door opening onto a balcony. Sun streamed in from the balcony. Myaca knew she must make haste or she would be late for morning prayers.

Hastily she changed from robes of gold to a simple long dress of white muslin. Then followed by Hadrian, who flew behind her, she hurried across the garden to the palace sun temple.

Following the prayer service, Myaca sat in her garden and enjoyed a morning repast in the company of Hadrian. Perched upon her shoulder, the little bird enjoyed the luscious scraps she fed to him from her plate. His attention to that diversion shifted only when he spotted gaudy butterflies to chase around a garden pool before plucking fruits and nuts from a golden plate Myaca had set before him. As Hadrian played and flew amidst the garden shrubbery, Myaca called for her royal stationery, so she could write her husband a letter. When she had finished writing it and had folded the letter into a small bundle, she gave it to Hadrian. "You must again be lifted up by the morning wind."

Then, stretching out her arm Myaca let Hadian courageously fly toward the sky's highest reaches. She anxiously watched her little friend become a mere speck in the sky until he'd disappeared from view. When Hadrian passed a migrating flock of sacred white geese, Hadrian watched as the exhausted birds descended to a pristine volcanic lake. Upon hearing their honking amidst the welcome retreat, he too wanted to rest. He knew he must continue. It was only after he'd searched for a high thin vapor, and found it that he realized he was nearing his journey's conclusion. Entering a small vortex, he finally was swept into the dimension where Prince Sentius awaited his return. Seeing the bird approach his high prison tower window, Sentius stretched out his arm in welcome. Quickly, Hadrian flew through the barred window and landed upon Sentius' shoulder. Then dropping the folded letter before him, and with head cocked curiously to one side, Hadrian watched as Sentius' trembling hands opened it.

"Plans for your rescue are being made. Until then, you must protect yourself and Hadrian at all costs. Destroy this message from me at once and remember that I love you always—Myaca"

Ready to obey whatever order Sentius gave him, Hadrian gallantly perched upon his master's shoulder. "You are a brave soldier", he said stroking the bird's feathers and feeding him scraps he'd save from his most recent meal. Your loyalty and service is recognized. Sentius decided that after Hadrian had sufficiently rested, he would free the bird and send him back to Myaca.

Picking up Myaca's message, Sentius walked over to the hearth, and threw it into the fire. He sadly watched as flames consumed his precious secret. Then turning, he walked over to Hadrian, picked up the little bird, and placed him in a cage where there was sufficient food and water for him. "Rest my friend", he said covering the cage.

Sentius then left the room. Stepping onto a balcony, he gazed down at a turbulent sea where serpents raised their ugly heads searching the sea's cold depths for pray. The healthy algae that once had sustained the serpents, was now tainted and poisoned. The once harmless serpents now were flesh-eating monsters, ready to consume any living thing. Sentius knew that Myaca's father had met his death trying to escape the tower. He felt like a coward for not trying to succeed where King Aurelius had failed.

Cut off from the rest of the world, Sentius sometimes thought he'd rather die than suffer a slow death of isolation. Myaca's message had given him hope. Perhaps someday he would escape the Dark Tower. Then Sentius hung his head in despair. The Tower's darkness surrounding him contrasted deeply to the light he'd once shared with Myaca. He gazed at the cage where Hadrian peacefully slept and envied the bird's gift of flight. Sentius longed to accompany Hadrian on his journey homeward.

The following morning when Hadrian was freed from his cage, he came and perched upon his master's shoulder. "Soon you'll be surrounded by her love and I'll still be longing for her sweet embrace," he said.

When it drew time for Hadrian to depart, the bird, always loyal to his master, was reluctant to go. Although he had been coddled and spoiled by Myaca, who saw him as a precious pet, Sentius saw the bird in a different way. In his imprisonment, the bird had become his only companion. He was the messenger from the lost land, a world where he'd known love and happiness. Determined to return to his master through time and space, Hadrian would find the means to come to Sentius.

Finally Sentius walked onto the balcony. With outstretched arm he released Hadrian, and allowed him to fly into the deep reaches of time and space. The precious message for Myaca was held fast within his beak as the majestic little bird first circled the forbidden tower then flew high into the heavens and away from the tower.

Vultures soaring above the jagged rocks and waters of the Forbidden Sea had tried to follow Hadrian and to close in on him but he flew beyond them. The sky at sunrise burned with crimson brilliance yet Hadrian flew above the scorching sunrise. His silver wings carried him into the cooling currents of beyond where the sacred eagle, guarding the dimension into which Hadrian flew, greeted him. The two then flew together: The eagle gently hovered beneath the little carrier pigeon, and insured his safe return home.

*   *   *   *

Myaca, who'd summoned Murdock to her side for consultation on matters of state, sat opposite the mole in a huge drafty sitting room where the balcony door had been left ajar. Anticipating Hadrian's return to her, Myaca wrapped herself in a shawl and glanced anxiously at the balcony in hope that Hadrian soon would return bearing a message from Sentius.

The Queen hardly appeared to be listening as Murdock told her that the annual Martian wheat crop had failed in certain planetary regions. Pacing back and forth with his paws nervously clasped behind his back, Murdock said, "I've been told that Mars may have had a hand in the crops' failure."

"Sources have told me that Menelus' spies have come ashore in submarines disguised as beached aquatic beasts, traveled inland throughout our dear Martian landscape and introduced a blight that has destroyed some of our vital agricultural crops. Menelus realizes that if our crops fail, we'll have to import inferior Venusian wheat. As you know, the Venusian wheat isn't selling well within the solar system. The moons of Jupiter and Saturn have stopped importing it. Although Menelus won't admit it, his wheat crop is inferior to ours because the Venusian environment is failing and the wheat crop has been affected by environmental contamination."

Murdock continued to drone on about the problem. He only looked up when Myaca announced a tea break. Sitting down in an intricately designed Martian antique chair upholstered in the finest brocade, Murdock accepted a cup of pomegranate tea from the Queen. Then taking a bite from the delicious fruit nut cookie offered to him from a silver tray, he set his teacup aside. He continued talking once more about the state of the wheat situation and remarked that if Venus succeeded in blocking Martian wheat imports to the moons of Jupiter and Saturn, the Martian economy would be severely affected.

The Queen, who'd idly poured herself another cup of tea, had hardly listened to Murdock's rantings about the sorry state of the wheat crop or the economy. When she saw his teacup was empty, she leaned forward and poured Murdock another cup of tea. "It will calm your spirit", she said, offering him another fruitnut cookie.

Murdock, who'd felt slightly disconcerted to think that the Queen appeared not to have heard a word he said, started to tell her so but on second thought decided to keep quiet. To tell the Queen that she wasn't interested in the planet's wheat crop would neither be a wise nor a diplomatic thing to do. Murdock was no fool. He knew Myaca's thoughts were elsewhere. She was absorbed by personal problems and that concern threatened the well being of the Martian domain. Prince Sentius was missing, and the chances of him ever returning to Myaca, seemed to Murdock to be rather slight indeed. He wanted to ask her, "Have you thought of remarrying?" He knew under the circumstances such a remark would probably only add to Myaca's misery. Besides, she might think such a suggestion too impertinent coming from a mere mole.

Instead he said, "I hear the weather along the seacoast near the craters of Arturias is splendid this time of year. Have you thought of taking a vacation away from the cares of state? A short stay in your castle there might be just what you need to reinvigorate your zest for life."

Murdock was now embarrassed. He'd said too much. He'd reminded the Queen of her shortcomings. He wanted to slip out of an embarrassing situation by asking the Queen's permission to leave.

"If you don't mind, Madame", he said setting his teacup aside, "I haven't been feeling too well lately. I suppose I've been working too hard. My friend Rupert, who's from Venus, and owns several farms there, came for a short visit recently. His crops aren't doing well, and he's told me that the blighted Venusian environment has taken its toll on the growing season there. I suppose I've overreacted to Rupert's rantings. His fears that a similar catastrophe is befalling our Martian agricultural industry, has rather overwhelmed me."

"That's quite all right", replied Myaca, who didn't want to admit to Murdock that she hadn't heard a word her old friend had said to her, other than something about her taking a vacation near the seacoast of Arturias.

"I'm afraid I have too many matters of state with which to contend with right now."

With that said, Myaca led Murdock to a huge door of beaten gold which opened for them. She accompanied him down the hallway past the portraits of her ancestors. She then watched as he descended palace steps and headed toward his hovercraft parked amidst palace gardens.

Myaca slowly wandered back along a palace corridor, past the portraits of her ancestors. When she returned to her sitting room, the wind was blowing the balcony curtains around. Myaca started to close the balcony door so that no more rain could sweep across the already wet floor. No sooner had she started to draw the balcony doors together when she noticed a very wet Hadrian perched beside a balcony balustrade.

"Hadrian!" said Myaca, scooping up the little bird and rescuing him from the rain. "Where have you been?" Hadrian flew from Myaca's gentle grasp and landed directly upon the Queen's shoulder. "You have something for me don't you?" said Myaca sitting down at her desk. Hadrian then hopped from her shoulder and dropped the message in front of her. The latest message from Sentius advised Myaca to keep the little bird with her. "It is much too dangerous for him to be carrying our messages back and forth to one another. Send him to me with a message from you only if the situation is an emergency—signed you loving husband, Sentius."

Myaca then placed Hadrian in his huge gold cage where he had sufficient food and water at his disposal.

*   *   *   *

It was early evening when Murdock and Pelletier, having been invited to dine with Queen Myaca sat down for dinner with her. A robot butler poured wine into tubular crystal glasses then left the room. Myaca began the conversation by saying, "I have something I must tell you. I've been keeping it a secret. Now I feel it is time to reveal to the world that Prince Sentius is alive and well. In fact, Hadrian my carrier pigeon has been bringing me messages from my husband."

"But how can you be sure that the messages are from your husband?" asked Murdock who reminded the Queen that communication with those held prisoner within the dark dimension was considered to be almost impossible.

"No it isn't" said Myaca.

"Atira has told me that Hal contacted Prince Sentius through time and space when they visited The Dark Tower. They never saw him in person. But when they tried to draw close to the sound of his voice, Prince Sentius warned them to come no nearer to him. They too might become imprisoned within the dark dimension."

"Perhaps Pelletier and I should have a look at that tower" said Murdock. "We might discover a clue that would enable us to successfully penetrate the tower without doing harm to ourselves." When his suggestion met with no response from either Myaca or Pelletier, Murdock picked up a glass containing the delicious sherry for which his farm was so famous, and drained it to the dregs.

Following the dinner meeting with Myaca, Murdock wearily led the way back to his hovercraft parked within the imperial gardens. He hesitated to admit it to Pelletier, to do so would be admitting something akin to disloyalty, but Murdock frankly was tired of all the meetings of late with Myaca over tea and dinner. "This is the second meeting I've had with the Queen. Earlier today she invited me for tea. Unlike her father, Myaca never heeds any of my advice."

Pelletier, who'd hesitated to say anything in reply to Murdock's frank admonition, could tell from the strained and tired look on his face, that the mole was at the end of his tether.

"Prince Sentius was an enormous help to Myaca in many ways. He was especially valuable in giving her the advice she needed so she could implement her duties."

Pelletier knew that Murdock was being overly polite regarding the Queen's lack of interest regarding matters of state. Both he and Murdock silently knew that in Prince Sentius' absence, the Queen simply couldn't make any major decisions one way or another regarding important issues. "It's a pity he's not here", said Pelletier as he and Murdock climbed into the hovercraft so that they could return to the Sun Temple. "I think it's of the utmost importance that we do everything to bring about Sentius' release as soon as possible."

"Then you no doubt would agree with me that you and I should attempt to penetrate the dark tower?" said Murdock.

"I've been weighing the pros and cons for doing so. I think we should give it a try. I've heard Vorelis say the tower has structural weaknesses. If his assessment regarding the tower's structure is correct then anyone who knows a little about where the tower's weaknesses are might be able to penetrate its very core."

Murdock's long whiskers twitched as he pondered the possibility.

Chapter Ten

▼

Jaime, who'd always been fascinated by horses, wild or tame, suggested that the chariot team be allowed to run freely within the pasture for a few days.

With Hal and Amelia standing on either side of her, Jaime held out her hand as Chamelon cantered toward the fence so he could accept the carrot treat she offered him. Soon the other horses moved with the same effortlessly grace toward the fence, so that they too could receive a treat. When the bag of carrots was empty, Hyacinth, whose endurance was matched by her sweet nature, tried to find another treat inside the empty bag. Jaime laughingly withdrew her hand from the bag, patted Hyacinth, then left Hal and Amelia standing alone with the horses.

"We must become friends", said Hal stroking Chamelon's beautiful black mane "You'll be the one leading us to the high heavens where we'll find the hidden dimension. Only you can do it, Chamelon", said Hal. Chamelon snorted in return and began running alongside the mare Aleria. They playfully nudged one another before they became involved in a game of tag with the other horses. From afar, Orbutus watched his horses move effortless across the pasture grass. Although Hal had made progress in getting to know the steeds, Orbutus secretly knew that the horses' loyalty would always be his alone.

"We'll begin training in earnest early tomorrow" said Orbutus sitting opposite Hal and Amelia at the luncheon table. Glancing quickly at Hal, Amelia could see a look of uncertainty cross Hal's face. "Only the most confident and brave should be able to guide the chariot team into the far reaches of the universe."

Hal placed his fork aside as he considered Orbutus' remark. "

"A momentous leap into the future awaits you." Hal wasn't sure if he was ready for such a leap. He was afraid of stumbling.

                    *   *   *   *

Murdock gazed at his time screen and smiled. He saw Aleria affectionately nudge Chamelon as Ariel and Hyacinth circled them. His attention from watching the horses at play though, was diverted when he received an urgent message from Whitfield.

"I have returned alone to the lost city. Beneath the faded and chipped design of a wall painting there is a map revealing more than one way to penetrate the dark tower. I dare tell you no more. It is of the utmost importance that I join you immediately so that we may further discuss the importance of the discovery."

Within seconds, Whitfield was standing before Murdock within the Sun Temple. The mole led him toward a study where they sat down opposite one another in carved Martian antique chairs. Having made himself comfortable, Whitfield drew from his pocket the letter he'd pilfered from the Martian library the night he and Hal had fled to Earth in his time machine.

"I'm returning this letter to you now because I no longer have any further use for it."

Murdock curiously opened the letter. He began studying its contents as Whifield continued talking to him."The letter you peruse contains a passage indicating that the map to the Dark Dimension's Tower may be found in the lost city. I've just returned from the lost city where I've examined such a map. The Dark Tower is more than just a tower. According to the map's specification, it has entrances and exits, which like tentacles, reach out in all directions and encompass a huge area outside the Dark Dimension."

Murdock quickly glanced up from studying the letter when Whitfield said,

"The letter was found in one of the math volumes you allowed me to examine on my last visit to the Sun Temple. I thought under the circumstances, that it would be the right and honorable thing for me to return it to you. I would advise you to keep the letter under lock and key. If Menelus discovers that we know about the letter telling where the map is located, our lives might be in danger."

Placing the letter in its envelope, Murdock set it down upon the desk in front of him. He then rose from his chair and said "Menelus will never find the letter."

"You may have thought that your escape from the Sun Temple was clever maneuvering on your part. Now that you've been honest enough to return the letter to me, I can now let you in on a little secret.

"Sarius and I observed your clever escape through time and space. We watched the whole episode from the time screen situated in a hall adjacent to this study where we now sit. To put it bluntly, you and Hal were meant to find the letter. You were meant to discover the time machine too. So you see, Professor, we both have our secrets. Now that we've both confessed them, I suppose we may in earnest begin our penetration of the Dark Tower."

Whitfield had always suspected that Murdock knew Hal had pilfered the letter. He was inwardly amused to think that the mole had almost been as clever in his maneuverings as he had been.

Murdock quickly crossed the room, opened a cabinet door and with a paw, reached into the cabinet. He removed a bottle of his favorite Martian brandy and poured the red and tangy liquid into two glasses. Then passing a glass to Whitfield, and keeping the other for himself, he raised his glass in a toast to the occasion. "We have reason to celebrate. We also have reason to depart for the Dark Dimension's tower as soon as possible."

"I don't understand," said Whitfield. "Why are we to depart for the Dark Tower if Hal is in training to make the ascent?"

"The answer is simple", replied Murdock setting his wine glass down. "If you've study the map closely, you'll see that some of the passages within the tower are accessible through flight. Other passages may be accessed on foot. Legend has it, that "he who will brings the light of day to the dark region must first free the prisoner trapped there."

"I suppose that means Myaca's husband, Prince Sentius?"

"Of course", replied Murdock. "That's the reason we must be included in such a momentous adventure."

Whitfield placed his glasses on his nose and stared at Murdock who continued talking to him. "Beneath this sun temple is a huge wormhole. Those who've entered it have never returned. However, with the practical application of the equation you appear to be in the process of solving, that may change."

"Where does the wormhole supposedly lead?" asked Whitfield.

"The wormhole extends in many different directions", said Murdock trying to appear more erudite and knowledgeable regarding the matter than he really was. "The skill required in maneuvering those passages within the wormhole is great. The mathematical proof you're working on may present us with a vast labyrinth of possibilities for structuring our approach to the Dark Tower."

"I'm not sure I want to go through with your plan to vanquish the evils of the Dark Tower. I'm really not young anymore. Perhaps you should look for someone more fit to undertake the strenuous task involving tower conquest. In fact, I'm more than doing my part in striving to solve the mathematical equation needed to provide a practical solution to the problem."

Both the professor and Murdock appeared a little smug in their knowledge. Both knew that Whitfield was struggling with the proof of an unsolved equation. Murdock also knew it would be no easy task to recruit volunteers to participate in the Dark Tower's planned conquest. He'd hoped that Whitfield's inclusion in the madcap adventure would add dignity and prestige to it.

Murdock appeared nonchalant when he said, "If you're unwilling to join me in the task, I quite understand you're reluctance to bow out from what might prove to be a dangerous undertaking."

Whitfield was feeling the pressure from Murdock. He didn't want to appear cowardly by rejecting Murdock's offer to assist him in tower conquest. "I'll have to think about it", he said.

"Very well", said the mole rising from the chair where he sat, "If you feel that way, I'll begin the search to find a replacement for you. Murdock then opened the door to his study. Followed by Whifield he began walking down the vast Sun Temple corridor until they stood before the time traveling screen. Whitfield stared at the screen and was shocked to see staring back at him an image of his younger self.

"How dare you do this to me!" he said. "I was ready to embark on the final stages of my career. Now you've sent me backward in time to when I was a struggling young man just graduated from university." The lines and wrinkles had entirely disappeared from his face. With his changed appearance Whitfield knew it would be difficult for him to face his colleagues at the Primary Institute for Study. "My friends will never understand", he said helplessly.

"When you return to the Institute looking like your young self again, you can just say that you took a little vacation through time and space", said Murdock seeming rather apologetic.

"To be perfectly honest", said Murdock sounding as if he were pleading with Whitfield, "I think neither Sarius nor I have the expertise to manipulate the currents within the wormhole without you guidance."

Whitfield knew he had no more experience in the skill required for maneuvering wormholes than Murdock did but he wasn't immune to flattery. He felt as if he'd already been sucked into time's current and was already standing on the edge of the wormhole.

"When do we leave?" he asked compliantly.

Sarius, the ubiquitous robot who'd been standing outside the study doorway eavesdropping on the conversation Murdock was having with Whitfield, finally made his presence known.

"Excuse me", he said entering Murdock's study with his usual flair for arriving unannounced. "I'm in charge of packing provisions. Now that you'll be accompanying us on our journey, I just wanted to know what special items you'd like me to include for you", he said speaking to Whitfield.

"We'll need to do a little planning in that regard", said Murdock interrupting Sarius. "We can discuss the matter over breakfast. I don't want to go anywhere until I've eaten a decent Martian breakfast—which means will leave tomorrow."

The following morning, Sarius took the opportunity to accomplish last minute details such as telling a few robot friends that he was going to be out of town. Later he and Whitfield met Murdock who unveiled his new time machine, based on Whitfield's design

"The machine isn't exactly like yours", said Murdock proudly turning to Whitfield. "Your design certainly inspired my own. For travel purposes, I've installed a mode making the machine both aquatic and amphibious. It's built for comfort as well. You won't have a problem taking a snooze in it, should you so desire. Now if you'll just follow me I'll show you the clothing and gear you'll be taking with you."

As Murdock and his companions prepared for their adventure, elsewhere in time and space others were making plans to launch one too.

*   *   *   *

Amelia held Chamelon's bridle as Orbutus steadied the rest of the team.

"Today we'll practice levitation and mimic the maneuvers of the flying chariots of old", said Orbutus who'd motioned for Amelia to step aside so that he and Hal could begin the practice session. Hal, hesitantly took the reins and felt the team's power as the four magnificent horses began cantering gracefully around the huge pastureland,

Bill and Lillie, who'd been watching the practice session from Bill's farm, looked on with amazement.

"What's Hal doing with a chariot team in the middle of Tom's cow pasture?" asked Bill turning to Lillie.

"Perhaps it has something to do with that circus he's working with," she said gazing in bewilderment as the chariot and horses clattered by in a dusty cloud.

"Hoo, hoo" hollered Hal who felt as if he were losing control of the team.

"Here, let me have the reins", said Orbutus taking them from Hal's hands as the chariot team soared over a fence and into Bill's cow pasture.

"Get out of the way" cried Hal as the horses and chariot rumbled past Bill's cows and narrowly missed hitting the chicken coop before coming to a halt in the front yard.

"Sorry" said Hal who apologized to Lillie for running through the turnip patch. "I hope we didn't damage your crop."

"Well, just a little," said Lillie trying not to seem too upset.

"Perhaps Orbutus and I can help you replant the crops", he said, stepping down from the chariot.

"We might have to take you up on the offer", said Bill glancing at the turnip patch. Then, having been distracted by what he saw in front of him, he asked. "What in heaven's name is that thing you're driving?" Hal felt ridiculous riding around in a chariot and wearing the charioteer's costume he'd donned for the occasion.

"I'm training as a charioteer for the Circus of Wonders. Since Amelia has taken herself and Natasha out of the ring for a while, the circus needs a replacement act, and I'm it", said Hal introducing Orbutus to them. "Orbutus was just giving me a few pointers on how to drive a chariot."

"Bill and I thought you'd gone back to New York", said Lillie who walked up to Chamelon and gently patted the horse's nose.

"Right now, I'm taking a little vacation from my duties with Worthy Enterprises". The circus managers thought they could use a little outside business advice, so I'm doing that too. Once Orbutus and I get the team to star level performance, and once the circus finances begin to improve, I'm going back to New York."

"I see", said Bill who said. "Let's see you roll again."

Hal took the reins of the chariot, once more and made sure that this time he was a safe distance from the turnip patch. Orbutus, who stood just behind him winced a little as Hal shouted giddy up to the horses who began cantering around Bill's cow pasture.

"Look out Lula Belle", shouted Bill in warning to one of his cows grazing alone in a corner of the field. Lula Belle turned her head and managed to blink slightly as the chariot raced by and missed her by only a few inches. She then moved over slightly and placidly continued to chew upon the corner field's long grass.

"If that team had grazed Lula Belle I don't think she'd have been able to give milk for a month," said Bill turning to Lillie.

No sooner had Bill gotten his words out, when with astonishment, he and Lillie watched as the chariot team sailed directly over the chicken coop and landed on the opposite side of the field.

Hal was still at the reins as the horses galloped full circle around the pasture, when the chariot suddenly became airborne again.

Ariel, the white mare, had taken over from Chamelon, and she was leading the other horses skyward. The chariot was now about 50 feet above the ground.

"Don't look down", said Orbutus who knew if Hal did, he might lose his nerve and they'd go plummeting to the ground. Hal could feel himself floating, and although the feeling was exhilarating, it was also frightening.

Bill grabbed Lillie's arm and said pointing, "I believe Hal's gotten a bit carried away. I know he's been trying to avoid hitting the chicken coop but this is ridiculous." Several of their best laying hens were now airborne and soaring alongside the chariot.

Hal quickly reined in Chamelon and noticed that Matilda was about to land on the stallion's head. Emma Mae, another hen was already sitting atop Aleria's head and was trying to lay an egg there.

"I think the chickens are trying to tell us something", said Hal who succeeded in slowing the horses down long enough to allow the law of gravity to encompass horses and chariot once more.

Hal, Orbutus and the horses were now on the ground, and right next to the chicken coop too. Emma Mae still clucked happily atop Aleria's head but had decided not to lay an egg there. Instead she flew down from her perch and began searching the grass for succulent bugs.

"I couldn't have done a better job if I'd tried" said Orbutus congratulating Hal on his momentous ride.

"I only wish things could have gone more smoothly" said Hal who hadn't expected to take on chickens as passengers. Clucking excitedly Matilda had flown down to the ground. She now was busy pecking at the chariot's wheels as if the chariot was some sort of strange bird. She then flew up into the air and landed on Hyacinth's back.

Lillie tried scattering chicken feed around the ground in an effort to entice the star layers back into the coop but to no avail.

"Come on now" said Lillie talking to the hens. "Natasha, that elephant who sometimes wanders over to the side of the fence to keep you company is retired from circus life. She'll tell you that performing in a circus isn't all that it's cracked up to be."

Emma Mae and Matilda often had watched from the pasture as Natasha went through her circus routine, and thought Natasha to be quite glamorous. On more than one occasion when Bill and Lillie had been busy in the house doing chores or watching TV, Natasha had taken her friends for a ride on her back as she went through her maneuvers. The hens would cluck with delight and fly above Natasha's ears then settle themselves behind her head as she maneuvered her way around the field. At the end of a performance, Natasha would stand on her hind legs and trumpet a bellow of triumph as her two friends cackled loudly in applause-- so loud it would seem as if they'd lain the golden egg.

Unfortunately, Hal seemed unable to stun an audience with the same charisma as Natasha. He knew his ride into the sky with the horses was only for show. Sure it was a heady experience, if only for a few minutes, but that genuine feeling of having been there, done it and succeeded just wasn't there.

Hal gazed at Natasha grazing by herself in a corner of the field. He knew she was a star—and one that he wasn't about to leave out of the performance. He wandered over to the elephant and patted her trunk. Then turning to Orbutus he said, "You take the horses and the chariot. I'll plod my way into the heavens in the same manner Hannibal conquered the Alps. Natasha and I are about to outshine and outdistance all previous records into the unknown. Phaeton's chariot ride may have failed because the guy didn't have an elephant.1

I believe we can begin training in earnest", he said hopping a fence and allowing Natasha to pick him up and place him behind her ears. For the first time, Amelia, who'd been watching them didn't try to join in. "Let Hal do this one alone" she thought. "This is his moment to succeed."

Natasha began skipping around the field as if her several tons of elephant weight were only ounces. She was doing the same stunt she'd learned to do and performed for the first time while crossing the Cloud Bridge.

Hal looked up and a butterfly that had been flying amidst the field came and settled between her ears. "How strange" he thought. The butterfly looks exactly like the messenger butterfly that had accompanied them across the Cloud Bridge. "We'll do this stunt again tomorrow", he whispered to Natasha as she trumpeted a wail of triumph.

$$*   *   *   *$$

Murdock, Sarius and Whitfield, having finished breakfast within the Sun Temple's great dining hall gathered up their gear and walked along the huge corridor toward the time machine.

Although flattered Whitfield was also annoyed to think that Murdock had the audacity to base his time machine's design upon his own. Taking a rear seat in the contraption. He bounced a couple of times on the seat before he decided it was comfortable. He then watched with amusement as Sarius tried to squeeze a few more of his and Murdock's personal belongings into the provision hold. The latest editions of ROBOT LIFE not programmed into his ipod were stashed into the hold along with several boxes of fruit nut cookies and a special blend of pomegranate tea.

Turning to Whitfield, Murdock said, "If there's anything you wish to bring along with you now you need to make sure that it gets packed—otherwise, you'll find yourself on the short end of those just like home comforts."

Whitfield stepped from the time machine and handed Sarius a stack of physics notebooks along with a personal diary.

"I believe the machine is getting a little weighed down", said Murdock placing a bottle of his favorite sherry within the cargo hold. Whitfield, who felt it inappropriate to have alcoholic beverages aboard the time machine turned his head and pretended he hadn't seen the mole slip the bottle into the hold. Seeing the look of disapproval on Whitfield's face, Murdock simply remarked, "I just thought I'd bring an extra bottle of sherry along in case we have to bribe our way out of any difficult situations."

Murdock's remark brought a snicker from Sarius but an air of distain from Whitfield, who settled himself within the time machine's cabin, fastened his seat belt and donned a crash helmet.

"It's time to begin the countdown", said Murdock climbing into the pilot's seat. Murdock then fastened his seat belt, placed a crash helmet on his furry head and began revving up the machine's engine.

"To what great destination are we first headed", asked Sarius who'd placed his hands over his ears and tried to block out the loud rhythmic pulsing of the time machine's engine. He then reached for his crash helmet and placed it on his head as Murdock, happily eluding any planned itinerary, said: "Only time will tell."

The time machine began to tremble and shake. "I hope you remembered to bring along your book of instructions in case we have a malfunction or mechanical breakdown," said Whitfield

Murdock ignored Whitfield's remark. He was concentrating on the soft pulsating rhythm of his machine's engine. The engine's rhythm began to grow weak and uneven. Murdock's whiskers nervously twitched. He knew the engine wasn't responding in the way it was supposed to respond. When he thrust the computerized throttle forward, nothing happened. "We seem to be momentarily grounded," he said to Whitfield, who was enjoying the prospect of going nowhere.

Murdock felt deeply humiliated. Perhaps he should have insisted that Pelletier accompany them. He would have made certain that the time machine was in proper working order before anyone set foot in it.

"If you'll allow me to make a suggestion", said Whitfield yawning. "Why don't we undertake this little adventure later after—"I've"---- he said coughing in feigned embarrassment, "checked out the engine thoroughly."

Whitfield knew that an essential ingredient needed to make the time machine operate efficiently had been removed. In fact, he had the part hidden inside his jacket pocket but he wasn't about to tell Murdock that he'd pilfered it. "Anyway" said Whitfield stepping out of the time machine, "Why don't we call it a day."

Murdock, who appeared visibly upset to think that his specially designed time machine might be flawed, reluctantly agreed. Removing his protective helmet, and alighting from the vehicle, he started to check the machine's interior controls as Whitfield watched with amused interest.

"Perhaps I can be of assistance", said Whitfield opening the compartment door containing luggage and personal belongings. After searching through a pile of food and clothing, he found the instruction manual. "I believe your machine's design is almost an exact replica of mine with only one difference. Your vehicle lacks the mode enabling the machine to adapt to carrying any number of passengers up to twenty. I must admit, I prefer my own design to yours. With a little applied knowledge to be lifted from my repair manual, I think I'll be able to discover your machine's mechanical failure. We should be underway through time within the next day or so."

Murdock was furious. He secretly felt that Whitfield had tampered with the machine's controls but refrained from making an accusation "I told Queen Myaca that we'd be underway this morning. Now I have to send her a message saying we've experienced a malfunction. Can you imagine what gloom that information may place upon an already gloomy situation? Myaca has put her trust in us. We've promised to penetrate the Dark Dimension and bring Prince Sentius home to her. Now she may feel we're not in earnest in wanting to rescue him. She may scrap the entire project altogether or find other candidates to undertake the job."

"Don't be absurd", replied Whitfield. "I don't think Myaca would want any of us replaced right now."

"Oh, I do hope so", said Sarius who was listening to the conversation his companions were having. "This is the first time a robot has ventured into far flung dimensions. The honor is mine. If I fail to carry out my mission, I might injure the reputation of the entire robot community."

"Relax", said Whitfield confidently. "I feel sure I'll have everything repaired, and the time machine ready for us to travel in before you know it."

Murdock began unloading the time machine's cargo hold. Then turning to Whitfield and handing him his books, diary and suitcase, he said. "These are yours in case you don't have everything up and running within record time."

"Here, here", said Sarius who was trying to act as mediator between the two rivals. "Perhaps we'd all feel better if we had a tea break. I'll have the butler bring us some of your favorite blend. I'll make sure too that he includes some of those delicious fruit nut cookies."

"I think you're right", said Murdock thanking the robot for his thoughtfulness. "A tea break might be just what we need right now."

Sarius hurried away to locate Murdock's butler, as Murdock kept a watchful eye on Whitfield. The mole hoped he didn't seem too apologetic when he said. "I know your time machine's design is a unique one, and an excellent one at that. I also know that your design has already been put to the test, so when I was so presumptuous as to include some of your ideas into my own design, I thought you wouldn't mind. It was all done for economy's sake, you know."

"If you'd only asked me for a little help", I would have been more than happy to draw up and implement another time machine design for you. In fact, had I done so we might now be departing."

Murdock was about to say something about his time machine's design being better than Whitfield's. It was too late. Sarius, having returned from the pantry, carried a tray he set down before the disgruntled time travelers. Turning to Murdock first he said pouring him a cup of tea, "Would you care for one or two lumps of sugar?" Murdock accepted the attention as his due.

"I hope it's not too warm", said Sarius who handed the scientist a cup of tea too. He knew that Whitfield had hurt the mole's feelings. He didn't bother to ask if he'd like any sugar with his tea. He then offered Murdock his favorite fruitnut cookies before pouring himself a cup of tea.

Whitfield pretended to toil all day on the time machine. The important missing machine part, hidden in his jacket pocket, wasn't installed in the time machine until he was sure Sarius and Murdock weren't around. If Whitfield thought he had the upper hand in guiding the journey into time and space, though, he was wrong. Unbeknown to him, while he pretended to toil away, Murdock and Sarius were meeting in Murdock's office.

"We both realize that Whitfield is a brilliant man", said Sarius. He also seems to have a very large ego. Fortunately we robots don't have any of those complicated human complexities. We're programmed to get along with as many beings as possible. We don't allow robot pride to stand in the way."

Murdock, who appeared a bit upset to think that Whitfield, someone he'd trusted enough to introduce to the Queen, was now trying to overshadow him. "I've tried to overlook Whitfield's rivalry, and to regard him as a friend. Right now I feel as if any friendship between us is quite impossible."

"I suppose I was trying too hard to prove to Whitfield that a mole was capable of constructing a brilliant design modeled upon the one he'd already devised. I just wanted Whitfield to understand that I was standing tall, and that I wasn't on a lower rung of the evolutionary scale."

"I have an idea", said Sarius. "I really don't think you or Whitfield are going to find getting along together to be an easy task. The journey into another dimension will require give and take. I'm not sure if Whitfield has that sort of resilience of spirit. Sarius didn't think that the mole had what it took either but he remained silent on that point. "I think we should include John Pelletier in our time traveling venture. He regards you as a friend."

"I know", said Murdock who felt ashamed that Pelletier, the friend he'd originally intended to accompany him on his great adventure, had been excluded from it. "I don't think Queen Myaca finds Pelletier indispensable enough to allow him to take part in an important expedition right now," said Murdock who tried to camouflage his thoughtlessness.

"You may be right. I believe the main reason the Queen wants Pelletier around right now is that in your absence, Pelletier is one of the few beings she can still trust. Vorelis is another. If he could be summoned from his duties in the lost city, he could temporarily serve as Myaca's loyal protector. Pelletier could come with us", said Sarius diplomatically.

"What a splendid idea", said Murdock. "I can't imagine anyone more valuable as a friend or participant in adventure than Pelletier. Obviously the queen recognizes Pelletier's strengths too. If ever she doubted his loyalty, she now must realize that Pelletier's assets outweigh his weaknesses. If only we can persuade Myaca to allow Vorelis to take Pelletier's place as her protecter. She must realize how important Pelletier's presence aboard the time machine would be to us as we embark into the unknown in search of the dark tower."

Soon Murdock and Sarius were aboard his hovercraft and circling the castle fortress where Myaca was in seclusion.

"What a pleasant surprise" she said, greeting Murdock and Sarius, before leading them to a spacious drawing room where splendid sculptures and mementos from the far reaches of the galaxy were displayed about the room. A portrait of Myaca's late father hung from a wall and stared down at them as Murdock and Sarius sat in chairs opposite the queen.

Myaca listened thoughtfully as first Sarius then Murdock explained the nature of their visit. "I am convinced madame that Pelletier's inclusion in our journey into the dark dimension is of paramount importance. Pelletier is a man of mysterious talents. His uncanny ability to assess a situation is unparalled in my opinion. To be perfectly honest I can't imagine embarking into the unknown without his presence."

Myaca rose from where she was seated opposite her friends. Turning to them, she said Pelletier could accompany them. "In fact, I was in touch with Vorelis this morning. He's planning to return here today."

"Thank you" said Murdock bowing before the Queen. "Your safety and welfare has always been my greatest priority. I shall summon John Pelletier to us immediately, and tell him that he is to embark with us on our journey into the Dark Dimension."

Myaca pulled aside a curtain revealing a time screen. With a sweep of her hand, she allowed Murdock to send a message first to Pelletier telling him that they were in urgent need of his presence and a second message to Vorelis telling him that Myaca was in immediate need of his presence as her protector.

Within seconds, both Pelletier and Vorelis materialized.

"I don't anticipate that you'll have to help us out of any dilemmas" said Murdock turning to Pelletier. "Should the occasion arise where diplomacy might be the solution to solving a problem, we'll consider your help. However, I've learned how important it is to remain cool in almost any situation however trying. I'm just hoping that the other members of the expedition team will learn from my example and do likewise."

Myaca, who'd been trying not to laugh at how pompous the mole was behaving, said. "Vorelis and I will be tracking your progress through time and space should your party require our assistance."

Murdock, who'd taken Myaca's remark to mean that she knew about the repairs his time machine was undergoing said, "Don't worry Madame. I've been supervising Whitfield's repairs to the machine."

Myaca smiled sympathetically. She knew the mole was under pressure to be proven worthy. She was relieved to know that he would have a loyal ally and friend in the person of Pelletier.

"I wish you all the best of luck", she said leading her guests to the great door of the Palace fortress then bidding them good-by.

Upon arrival at the Sun Temple, Whitfield met his traveling companions. He was surprised to learn that Pelletier would be joining them in their adventure.

"It was Queen Myaca's suggestion", said Murdock a little smugly. "She thought we might need an extra mediator should we run into any situations requiring skilled diplomacy"

Whitfield was no fool. He knew Murdock was trying to get back at him for taking apart his time machine and putting it back together again—and all in a day's work too. Nonetheless, he was pleased to learn that his friend Pelletier would be accompanying them on their momentous journey into the dark dimension.

"I'm afraid your repair manual has been of little use to me. I've had to substitute my own in order to do repairs to your machine."

Murdock's whiskers twitched in fury at the remark but he refrained from insulting Whitfield. With nose held high in the air, he simply replied, "As you wish" but he couldn't resist saying. "In case we discover that your repair manual appears to be of no further use to us, we always have mine. In fact, I'm never without it."

Whitfield was about to say something in reply to Murdock's remark but Pelletier, who'd just walked into the room, told the mole how much he liked the time machine's sleek design.

Proudly beaming, Murdock replied, "I've added a few extra features to the machine's original design. A computerized entertainment nook enables beings and robots to surf the galaxy and discover the best shows from current and past millenniums. The seats are also more comfortable than those of the original design".

"How convenient", said Pelletier sitting down in the machine then stretching his longs legs, and placing his hands behind his neck as he relaxed.

The following morning the time travelers prepared once more to make their way through time and space. Murdock, who'd always been religious and rarely ventured anywhere without offering up morning prayers to the sun, stood in front of a temple stained glass window and began to loquaciously chant in his molelike voice. His prayers permeating the Sun Temple's halls, continued to echo throughout the temple until Murdock felt sure the voyage was sufficiently blessed enough for them to depart.

The voyagers were nearly settled within the time machine's interior, when Murdock decided he needed to rearrange some of their "necessities". Even though John was bringing just a few personal belongings, Murdock insisted he needed to make more room for them. He started to throw aside Whitfield's repair manual and a few of his math books, when Sarius, whispered in his ear and reminded Murdock that by pressing a few buttons on the remote, the machine's cargohold could be enlarged.

"Sorry", said Murdock who reached for the remote hidden in a pocket of his imitation moleskin jacket. "I'm afraid I forgot about that hidden feature."

Whitfield said nothing in regard to the mole's petty action. He knew Murdock had already made himself appear inept by having to be reminded about the adjustment feature the very day they were to take off into the unknown. Since he didn't wish to add insult to injury, a smiling Whitfield again placed his math books and machine repair manual into the cargo hold before taking his seat.

Finally Murdock thrust the computerized throttle forward so the time machine could go careening off into time and space just as Whitfield asked him if he'd implemented a plan for penetrating the secrets of the Dark Dimension.

"Not yet" answered Murdock, who glanced down at the computerized time screen and realized they were headed toward disaster. A vortex was fast sucking them into another dimension. Flashes of lightning encompassed them. Turbulent interference buffeted the craft about as if it were a piece of paper caught in the wind. "I think we're going to crash", said Murdock losing control of the machine.

Chapter Eleven

▼

Hal and Amelia were having breakfast at the family farm when Vorelis decided to pay them a visit. He drove up their long driveway, pulled his late model purple coupe to a halt, and stepped from it. He caught a glimpse of Hal's son Nick, who threw the magician a fastball. Vorelis caught the ball with one hand, and quickly returned it to Nick, when he saw Hal step onto the porch.

"We saw your car pull up in the driveway. What brings you here so early?" asked Hal leading Vorelis toward the dining room where Jaime invited him for breakfast. Pouring Vorelis a cup of coffee, she then set a plate of scrambled eggs before him.

Vorelis took a sip of coffee, picked up a fork and began eating the eggs before he leaned across the table and whispered, "May we talk privately?"

Hal, who was busy enjoying his breakfast, said "Sure just as soon as we've finished eating."

"There's no need to wait, if you two want to talk privately", said Amelia getting up from the table. "I was just on my way to the barn so I could check on the animals", she said.

"I'll meet you there later", said Hal who could tell from the worried expression on the magician's face that something had gone awry with the conceived plan to invade the Dark Dimension.

Jaime, who'd just returned from the kitchen, looked at Vorelis and asked him if he was all right.

"I'm fine", he said, lying. Both Jaime and Hal knew something was terribly wrong.

"It seems", said Vorelis choking on his coffee that something unforeseen has happened. "Murdock's time machine has crashed somewhere in time and space, and I fear that either Narena or Menelus, may have had a hand in it."

"That's impossible", said Hal.

"The last message I had from Murdock indicated that the time machine had been swept into a time warp while Murdock tried unsuccessfully to maneuver his way through a wormhole. Murdock's whereabouts and that of his passengers; Whitfield, Sarius and Pelletier are unknown."

"Surely you must be mistaken" said Hal. "Murdock may be a mere mole but he always manages to pull himself out of impossible situations."

"The last message from Murdock was garbled but I know the worst has happened".

"If your last message from him was garbled, then you may not have heard everything clearly. From what you've told me about Murdock and from what I've observed as well, I can only say that it will be just a matter of time before you receive another message from him telling you that everything is fine. Give him a chance to make contact again."

"Perhaps you're right", said Vorelis a little uncertainly. "If you happen to be mistaken, we must begin making immediate plans for an organized rescue."

Hal took a gulp from the coffee he'd been sipping, nearly choking on it before saying: "Right now my presence here on the farm is necessary. I guess that lets me out as a member of the rescue team. I'd like to be able to pry myself away from work but duty calls."

"Duty calls elsewhere", said Vorelis solemnly gazing at Hal.

"I was hoping or rather expecting that this whole little planned conquest of the solar system could be put off until we'd taken care of business. I took a look at the ledger yesterday and the circus still appears to be operating in the red."

Jaime, who'd been listening to their conversation, wiped her hands on her apron and fixed her gaze on Hal.

"If it will make you feel any better, Orbutus has been working with the horses and Amelia has been helping me with Natasha. If the horses aren't used for mounting an assault upon the Dark Tower, we might use them instead to draw crowds of circus spectators."

"Absolutely not", said Vorelis, who having finished his eggs, reminded Hal that the secrets of levitation and time travel were not to be revealed to everyone. "The skills Orbutus taught you and your newly endowed gift for levitation were recently acquired only when you crossed the Cloud Bridge. But you didn't achieve that skill alone. Nyas, the monk who accompanied you, facilitated your journey across the bridge and made it seem easy. Practice makes perfect. Perhaps you need to see what else you and Natasha are capable of doing during the course of a practice session."

"Look" said Hal. "Amelia, Natasha and I are happy right here on the farm. Amanda is letting me have Mike for the summer and he loves being around the horses and the elephants. I don't want to take off for any fantasy ride into the unknown right now."

"Surely you jest", said Vorelis, who insisted that what might be regarded as fantasy on one level was reality on another. "Your friends may be in danger. They need your help."

"Very well" said Hal. "I'll continue to put Natasha through her routine but I don't think that she's going to want to go very far. Amelia is her surrogate mother, and she has also formed a family bond with Emily and Andy. As elephants, they may lack Natasha's performing talents but they provide her with friendship and stability."

"Please Mr. Worthy", said Vorelis putting his coffee cup aside and getting up from the breakfast table, "just show me your routine."

"Very well" said Hal who got up from the table and began leading Vorelis to the porch where Jaime was calling for her grandson to come inside for breakfast. Hal knew Nick was impatiently waiting so that they could play catch together.

"I'm not hungry, Grandmother. Besides, Dad said he was going to play ball with me this morning."

"We'll play ball later Nick. Right now Mr. Forbush and I are busy with something important."

Jaime knew Hal wouldn't want his son watching him and Natasha float over fences into adjoining pastureland. She was afraid that if Nick told his mother about the adventure, she might think that her former husband was nuts and try to seek full legal custody of the child.

"Destiny won't wait. Duty calls" said Vorelis, who along with Amelia watched as Hal mounted Natasha and the two began moving across the cow pasture. When they came to a fence, Natasha abruptly stopped in her tracks. Hal froze in fear. He was afraid the big pachyderm was going to trample the fence down and destroy Bill and Lillie's newly planted turnip patch.

"Come on, Natasha, you remember how it's done" he said trying to encourage the elephant to tread lightly and with ease and grace.

Natasha hadn't forgotten how to levitate. She was just feeling a little stubborn. She had no audience and Natasha hated to do any of her tricks without applause and bystanders.

"Come on Natasha. You can do it." called Amelia. Standing next to Amelia was now Nick, who having decided he wasn't going to eat any breakfast since he couldn't play ball, was watching his Dad take the elephant through her routine.

Knowing she now had an audience, Natasha raised her trunk and let out a trumpet call as she floated over the fence and turnip patch.

"Wow", said Nick who called out to his father. "Hey Dad, can I go for a ride too?"

Hal, who'd heard Nick calling him, and was unaware that he had been watching them, tried to tell him that he needed to go inside the house and do what his Grandmother had told him to do. It was too late. Nick was the audience Natasha needed. She could hear him applauding her and cheering her on as she floated a few feet higher into the air.

Hal knew he and Natasha needed to end their routine before someone else saw them and reported them as a UFO. Amelia quickly climbed over the fence and began running just beneath Natasha who continued to float gracefully over Bill's pasture. Fortunately, Bill and Lillie weren't home. It was only sheer luck that Natasha hadn't run any interference with the power lines.

Nick, who'd been running alongside Amelia decided to return to the house so he could fetch his phone camera and take a picture of the elephant's antics for his forth grade show and tell class.

Jaime, who was now standing on the porch and saw Hal atop the elephant floating along, called out to her grandson, "Your breakfast is getting cold. You should know by this time that when you're told to do something you do it."

"I just wanted to get a picture of Dad and the elephant", he said tearfully. "The kids at school will never believe me when I tell them about what I saw unless I show them a picture too."

"Never mind that now", said Jaime growing even more impatient with the child. "You need to eat a healthy breakfast first before you go chasing that elephant and your father all over the field."

Nick continued to sniffle and protest but finally sat down to eat his oatmeal as Jaime placed a little brown sugar and milk atop it.

"Now eat your oatmeal so you'll grow up healthy and strong. Then we'll find the phone camera and see if your father wants his picture taken."

Nick, who sat in his chair and sulked, finally decided to eat the cereal as quickly as possible so that he could record the image of his Dad and the elephant as they demonstrated their unusual antics.

Fortunately Jaime had time to hide Nick's phone camera so that when it was time to go outside again, he couldn't find it.

"Now the kids at school will never believe me", he said whining.

"Never mind dear", said his grandmother, "If you've lost that phone camera, we'll buy you another one."

Jaime knew it was a hopeless effort to keep the child from running into the yard so he could witness his father's strange antics atop the elephant. Nick ran toward Amelia who was standing directly beneath Hal and Natasha. The elephant loved being the center of attention. Now that Nick was part of her audience again, she was ready to show off even more.

"Come down at once Natasha" shouted Amelia. The big pachyderm had really grown attached to Hal. She loved being around him. For the first time she knew she had Hal all to herself. But Natasha wasn't stupid either. She knew it was Amelia who brought her all the good things in life like the bags of carrots and juicy watermelon treats. Hal was too wrapped up in his own little world to know what elephants really loved.

Within seconds, Natasha had turned around and was floating once more toward Bill and Lillie's turnip patch. Amelia held her breath as Natasha cleared first the fence and then the turnip patch. When the elephant's great hooves were once more firmly planted upon the ground, Hal alighted from behind Natasha's ears and the elephant set him down upon the ground.

Then turning to everyone, Hal said, "I'm teaching Natasha how to skip rope too."

"Wow" said Nick patting Natasha's trunk, "Can I help out with her training?"

"Sure" said Hal a little uneasily. "Let's try throwing a few fast balls back and forth first though."

"I must commend you on a job well done", said Orbutus who'd just walked up to Hal and said, "I was busy feeding my horses but I happened to look up and saw you floating over the pasture. I must say, I couldn't have done a better job myself but there is still much that you must learn regarding the art of levitation. However, the elephant seems to be quite proficient at it. Perhaps you can learn by watching her in motion. In fact, the sooner you fully master levitation the sooner we can begin undertaking the urgent mission lying ahead for us."

Vorelis, who'd been standing next to Hal, patted Orbutus on the shoulder, and said, "I have to leave. Perhaps you can inform Mr. Worthy of the details.'

"Vorelis tells me that Murdock and his passengers aboard the time machine have found themselves deposited in a rather restricted area, said Orbutus feeling terrible about being the bearer of bad news.

"I know all about that", said Hal. "Vorelis has already told me everything."

"Did Vorelis impress upon you the terrible urgency and tragedy of the situation?"

"Please" said Hal. "I don't want to hear any more."

"But Narena, may have blocked the plans of Murdock and his companions to penetrate The Dark Tower's dimension."

"I don't understand", said Hal. "Why wouldn't she want Murdock and his companions to free Prince Sentius?"

"The answer is quite simple", replied Orbutus. "Narena rules the underworld alone. She wants no interference from her neighbors. She's quite concerned that if Myaca and Menelus become embroiled in solar system war that her domain might be affected by the conflict."

"Doesn't Narena realize that she might be affected by Menelus's grasp for power if she doesn't join the alliance?" asked Hal

"Narena is no fool", said Orbutus. "She also realizes that she holds the key to unraveling the mystery surrounding the perfect equation. She has the grail. She won't easily give it up."

Hal gazed at Orbutus thoughtfully before saying, "If she has the grail and Menelus knows she has it, why isn't he making an assault upon her kingdom in an attempt to take it from her?"

"Narena is wise. Deadly devices surround the grail, and insure the grail's security from thieves and intruders. If one knows how to avoid the devices he'll win the grail but to my knowledge no one has ever been successful in that regard.

"There is a legend that within the lost city is a wall map giving the exact location of the grail's whereabouts. If one studies the map carefully, he'll also see where the devices have been placed.

"If Murdock and his passengers have reached Narena's domain, they may also have drawn too close to the grail—which means their journey may have ended."

"What's wrong?" asked Amelia who could see the look of concern on Hal's face. "I'm afraid your father and his companions have crashed aboard a time machine while trying to penetrate the Dark Dimension."

Amelia turned from Hal. She took a deep breath before turning back to him and saying, "Now I've heard it all. This whole idea of a Dark Dimension is really nothing more than a fantasy—another one of Dad's time traveling escapades he's concocted so he won't have to face the real world."

"Your father didn't concoct the idea of traveling through time so that he and Whitfield could confront the evils of the Dark Tower. They weren't alone when they went catapulting into the obscure reaches of time and space. The robot Sarius and the mole Murdock were with them."

"Look", said Amelia sounding slightly exasperated. "Father has never grown up. He's just playing another game of hide and seek, and expects us to come looking for him and Whitfield."

"I only wish your father was playing a game of hide and seek. He and his companions really are lost right now. They need to be rescued."

"I'm sorry", said Amelia beginning to cry. "It's just when life is getting better for me something happens with father and everything seems out of control again."

"I really think your father loves you Amelia. I think you're being too hard on him right now."

Amelia didn't believe what Hal had told her. With tears streaming down her cheeks, she turned away from him when he said, "Orbutus and I are in training for an assault upon the Dark Dimension. If your father and those with him are facing the consequences of having drawn too close to Narena's realm we must help them."

"Perhaps they should find their own way out of their predicament", said Amelia still sniffling. They were fools to launch a rescue of Prince Sentius. His life can't be worth so much that the lives of those seeking his rescue should be endangered or sacrificed."

*   *   *   *

Orbutus knew he had to proceed with caution. Hal wasn't ready to accompany him. Without Hal's support Orbutus was reluctant to attempt a rescue.

"I feel my horses and I are ready to scout the area surrounding the Tower to see if we can locate the place where the time machine may have gone down." Orbutus then whistled for his horses to come to him.

"It is time for us to explore the outer reaches of time's universe", he said patting Chamelon then caressing the heads of Hyacinth, Ariel and Aleria. Leading them toward a corner meadow where the chariot glistened in the early afternoon sun, Orbutus carefully harnessesd the horses to it. Within minutes the magnificent horses had lifted the chariot off the ground: They then pulled it into the high reaches of the atmosphere until it disappeared altogether. When Orbutus gazed downward, he saw neither earth houses nor any familiar landmarks. He knew they were floating effortlessly toward another time and dimension

"Outdistance the moment", he shouted as his valiant horses raced towards Narena's hidden domain. Chamelon pawed the atmosphere with his hooves. The other horses snorted and whinnied as with speed and grace, they drew closer to their destination. Within, seconds the flying horses and chariot gently hoovered above a hillside in close proximity to Narena's underground kingdom.

Trees, ferns and thick foliage covered the hillside where craggy rocks and broken sculptures of unknown deities lay hidden beneath them. Orbutus and his horses flew just above the rough landscape as he tried to determine where to set down the chariot. Finally, he selected a smooth grassy patch of turf situated near a primeval spring bubbling up from beneath the earth. Stepping from the chariot, Orbutus untied his horses then led them to the spring so they could drink.

After the horses had drunk their fill, Orbutus sank to his knees. He too drank from the spring. He then followed his horses as they grazed peacefully along a grassy hillside. As he moved with his horses he happened to glance downward and saw a small metallic fragment that had caught the sun's brillance. Retrieving the fragment from the ground and placing it in his pocket, Orbutus continued to look for other fragments but could find none.

He was about to lead his horses back to the chariot, when he heard a piercing noise. The noise's intensity was such that the horses whinnied in pain. Orbutus sank to his knees. He placed his hands over his ears until the noise slowly subsided and became nothing other than a low vibrating throb.

Reaching into his pocket, Orbutus found a device Vorelis had given him to aid in the contact of marooned time travelers. He knew Murdock and Pelletier carried similar devices with them. When he attempted to contact them, he thought he'd heard a garbled voice. The sound of the voice diminished replaced instead by the low vibrating throb.

Gazing around uneasily, Orbutus dared stay no longer. The forbidding aura of something unseen and terrible caused him to shiver. He also realized his horses were straying from him. They had wandered so far astray that they tripped and stumbled, trying to free themselves from the growth and entanglement of strange and exotic weeds. Chamelon, the beautiful black steed was the first to return. Whistling for him, Orbutus gratefully embraced him: He had led the other horses back through the frightening maze of entanglement.

Once more Orbutus harnessed his horses to the gold and silver chariot that shimmered in the late afternoon sun. Then mounting the chariot, he directed the horses to begin their ascent skyward.

"Chamelon, black steed of day, lead us forward", he shouted as the stallion with his great strength began drawing the chariot forward. Orbutus then focused his attention on Ariel and Aleria. Trusting them to draw the chariot beyond the pull of gravity, he called first to them and then to Hyacinth: "Bright Stars and Day Flower, overcome encroaching night."

Within seconds, the chariot team was flying over the hillside instead of down it. Orbutus breathed a great sigh of relief. Clouds enveloped them as they made their way toward an ethereal sunset. Time's current then drew the chariot into a vortex, placing it once more in the sky above the family homestead.

Within minutes, Orbutus gently set the chariot down on familiar turf as the horses slowed from a fast canter to a gentle stride around the circumference of the cow pasture.

Hal and Amelia, seated side by side on a pasture fence, watched as the chariot approached them. When Orbutus brought the chariot to a halt directly in front of them, they asked simultaneously, "Where did you go? We've been looking for you."

Acknowledging their greeting, Orbutus quickly stepped down from the chariot, and unharnessed the horses.

"Excuse me for disappearing so abruptly. I felt compelled to search out the area near the dark dimension where we believe our friends may have crashed."

"During your search did you encounter any sort of resistance to your visit?" asked Hal.

"Narena's army is an invisible one. Unseen but deadly devices defend her realm. Devastating vibrations emitted from beneath Narena's subterranean domain often elude detection.

Orbutus then reached into his pocket and produced a fragment he believed to belong to the ship Murdock had been piloting. "I've tried but failed to contact Murdock with my time traveling device. I'm not sure but I thought I heard a garbled voice. It faded quickly when interference blocked the voice's transmission."

Amelia burst into tears.

"I hope his machine still lies intact. There is no certainty our friends survived a catastrophic crash." Orbutus then handed the fragment to Hal who studied it carefully before he recognized that the fragment appeared to be made from material identical to material Whitfield had used to create his time machine.

"Murdock's ship must have been a near replica of Whitfield's design", said Hal returning the fragment to him. Then placing an arm around a weeping Amelia, he tried to comfort her.

It was clear to Hal that although Amelia had never been close to her father, the idea that Pelletier and his companions had perished aboard a time machine, was too painful for her to bear.

"I can't imagine father going to his death in such a manner. Surely he and his companions are still alive," she said sniffling. "At all costs we must set out in search for them."

Orbutus felt guilty for having been the bearer of bad news. "There is the possibility that they're alive. Vorelis has given me a microchip which when implanted into my time traveling device might enable me to replay what I heard. Even if the noises emitted are indecipherable, the device might help us pinpoint the exact location from where the noises originated."

Amelia stopped sniffling.

Orbutus glanced downward. His face was tired and drawn from the ordeal he'd been through. Hal and Amelia helped him with the horses.

"Every venture into a hidden dimension becomes increasingly stressful for the horses," said Orbutus covering Chamelon with a blanket. "They require proper food and rest in anticipation of a journey", he said following Hal into the barn where Amelia was already feeding Hyacinth, Ariel and Aleria.

"Our next venture into the Dark Dimension must be planned with care. If we draw too close to Narena's domain, we might end up like the unfortunate time travelers who've preceded us."

CHAPTER TWELVE

▼

When Myaca was told that Murdock had probably crashed his time machine within the Dark Dimension, she said,"I never should have allowed Murdock to undertake such a dangerous mission." She knew he was careless— to be more precise reckless. He was also loyal and courageous.

She'd remembered the time she'd received a report from Martian authorities telling her how Murdock had crashlanded his hovercraft in her favorite palace garden. She'd ignored the report. She'd told the authorities that she'd speak to Murdock. No major damage had been done to her garden. Murdock appeared to be truly sorry for his action. "Perhaps you shouldn't drive your hovercraft around at near warp speed", she'd suggested." Murdock had promised Myaca that the incident wouldn't happen again.

"Madame, you mustn't be so hard on Murdock", said Vorelis interrrrupting the Queen with the utmost sincerity. "I have every reason to believe that what happened to the time machine may have had nothing to do with the way Murdock manipulated his craft."

"I've been in contact with Orbutus, one of your loyal charioteers. When he learned about the unfortunate accident, he immediately investigated the circumstances surrounding the machine's disappearance. If our assumption is true and Orbutus is correct, Murdock crashed the time machine because it drew too close to Narena's realm. Deadly vibrations emitted to keep intruders from penetrating her realm, brought Murdock's craft down.

Myaca listened to Vorelis, before she interrupted him. "You needn't tell me anymore. I know my cousin Narena well enough. Her deceit is hard to equal. No doubt, she had something to do with the time machine's crash."

"Are you afraid of Narena?"

Myaca hesitated before answering him.

"The subterranean domain over which she rules isn't her only domain. Her rule extends into the land above and encompasses much of the territory surrounding the Dark Dimension. Yet her rule and the defense of her realm is one of intimidation rather than force. Since her rivals are unsure of her strength, they leave the sleeping tigress alone." Myaca then looked at Vorelis. "Yes, I suppose I am afraid of Narena." She then beckoned him to follow her. Walking toward a door, she began leading Vorelis toward the Forbidden Room.

"I feel closer to my husband here within these palace walls than almost anywhere else, she said as she and Vorelis gazed at the portraits of her ancestors. They then continued along the corridor together until they stood before the same door where first she'd heard the haunting voice of Prince Sentius.

"Narena may know where my husband is being held prisoner within the Dark Dimension. She may also know of the whereabouts of Murdock and his companions."

"Perhaps you're assuming too much", said Vorelis who stood behind Myaca as she gazed at the room's unopened door.

Myaca ignored his remark. "I've never fully explored this room. I was a child, when I first heard strange whispers coming from here. I was told never to open the room's door or to step inside the room.

"Not long ago I thought I heard a voice that sounded like my husband's coming from here. Myaca reached into her pocket and produced a key so that she might enter the mysterious room. With Vorelis standing behind her, she slowly placed the key in the lock. She bravely turned the doorknob, pushed the door open and stepped inside the room.

The elegantly furnished room represented the style of furnishings from many periods in history. Vorelis quickly stepped in front of Myaca. "Wait here", he said as he began further inspection of the room. After walking for nearly an hour and seeing nothing but beautiful furnishings and tapestries, Vorelis returned. Then taking her hand in his and leading her forward, he said, "I believe the room occupies an infinite amount of space and extends in every possible direction."

Myaca sighed in resignation as Vorelis suggested that they return to the corridor and lock the room's door behind them. She obediently started to walk alongside him but stopped suddenly when she saw a fragment lying upon the room's floor. She stooped to pick it up. Upon examination of it she handed the fragment to Vorelis. Immediately he recognized the fragment to be similar to the one Orbutus found when he was searching for Murdock, his companions and remnants of their time machine.

"My husband has visited this room since his imprisonment" she said. "Only he could have placed the fragment upon the room's floor for us to find."

Vorelis knew that Myaca's palace was surrounded by a force field making it impossible for intruders to penetrate palace walls. "I don't see how he managed it", he said contradicting her but Myaca interrupted him.

"My husband wears a ring I gave him that enables him to penetrate the forcefield". "Perhaps Narena gave Sentius the fragment in the hope that its discovery might discourage others from attempting his rescue or from obtaining the grail. Perhaps my husband remains where he is because he knew it was inevitable that Murdock's machine would crash. To know the future is forbidden within this domain but not within the Dark Dimension."

For the first time, Myaca felt her husband had knowingly betrayed her. "If my husband knows the future then he would have known that it was safe for him to return here now."

"Other lives are at stake", contradicted Vorelis. "Sentius remains where he is so that he may help rescue his friends. You mustn't doubt him."

"Perhaps you're right", said Myaca feeling ashamed for what she'd told Vorelis.

*   *   *   *

After their crash in an area near the Dark Dimension, Murdock and his companions lay amidst the time machine's wreckage. Murdock's protective helmet was dented, Pelletier was semi conscious, Whitfield mumbled incoherently and Sarius kept begging someone to please reboot him.

Still wearing his crash helmet, Murdock struggled from the tangled rubble that had been the time machine, and quickly found the electronic memory device that would reboot Sarius.

"Thank you" said Sarius wheezing a bit. "If you hadn't come to my rescue when you did my functional capacity for memory and performance might have been permanently damaged."

"We've no time to waste", said Murdock quickly unfastening his crash helmet. "We need to see what we can do to help Pelletier and Whitfield. They have cuts and bruises that need to be treated."

Murdock knew he had a few cuts and bruises too. For the moment, the usually well-groomed mole, ignoring his torn coat, rummaged through what was left of the time machine's storage cavity, and searched for the first aid kit. "Here it is", he said with all the cheerfulness he could muster in the face of near tragedy.

"I believe Pelletier is beginning to come around", said Sarius who kept patting his face and encouraging John to wake up. Murdock, who'd placed a pillow under Whitfield's head, knew the old scientist was in a state of temporary shock. If left alone, he too would come around on his own. Murdock then turned his attention to the ration chest. He was pleased to discover that most of the provisions were intact and unspoiled.

When John and Whitfield finally came around, Murdock and Sarius had already built a small fire and were busy making use of some of the emergency provisions they'd stashed away in the machine's cargo hold.

"Where are we?" groaned Whitfield blinking his eyes.

"I'm afraid we haven't quite figured out the answer to that question." Murdock handed the scientist a cup of warm pomegranate tea. "Drink this. You'll feel better."

Sarius, who'd been stirring a pot of meatlike stew and vegetables, removed the pot from the coals and handed bowlfuls of the substance to his marooned comrades. He then sat on a rock, made himself as comfortable as circumstances would allow, and commended himself on turning the dehydrated freeze dried concoction into something quite palatable.

Whitfield stared at the bowl of stew Sarius had offered him. He then took a few sips from the cup of warm pomegranate tea. "At least we've got something to eat", he said accepting the meal with pathetic, comforted relief.

Pelletier who'd said very little, gazed around at the unfamiliar landscape, and had a gut feeling that they were in big trouble. "Somehow we've got to retrace our progress through time and space. There should be a record within the craft's navigational system indicating where we've been, and where we currently are. At all costs, that record must be found for it might help us eventually get out of here."

"Never fear", said Murdock who'd placed his teacup aside, and was busy rummaging through rubble. "I think I've located the instrument containing the record." Charred but intact, it appeared to be in one piece even though several wires protruded from it. Murdock picked the instrument up, handed it to Sarius, and was grateful to John for his assistance in further salvage of the craft's vital instruments. "If we can just get everything put back together and in proper working order we might have a 50/50 chance of getting out of here".

"It looks like we've got company", said Sarius who glancing up from what he was doing saw someone approaching them.

"My name is Deanira", said a young woman elegantly attired in the manner of an Egyptian princess. "Narena, siren and guardian of the underworld, rules the land upon which you now stand as well as the land beneath you. As her special envoy, I welcome you to her domain" she said extending a hand in greeting.

"As you can see" said Sarius pointing to the shattered craft, "We've encountered an unfortunate accident during our quest for another dimension. Any assistance you might offer us in our effort to repair the machine would be appreciated."

Followed by her guards, who accompanied her, Deanira circled the shattered time machine and assessed the damage done to it. "Hmm" she said thoughtfully, "It looks as if you've gotten yourselves into a predicament—or if I may say it more appropriately, a heap of trouble."

"Heap?" said Murdock seeming offended by the word. "The time machine is not a heap. It's a magnificent, finely tuned specimen of advanced technology. Its pieces and fragments only need to be coached back into place so that we may be on our way again."

Embarrassed by Murdock's remarks, Sarius pretended to cough uncomfortably before he said, "Perhaps you'd be kind enough to tell us what may have happened to our craft. We encountered some rather peculiar atmospheric conditions just before we heard ear piercing noises prior to the craft's breakup."

"What may have happened to your craft may have everything to do with its faulty engineering", said Deanira who was determined that the visitors would get little or no information from her. Then turning to Pelletier whose reputation as a time traveler had preceded him she said. "If you can understand any of this conversation I'm having with your companions then you might also infer from it that unless you find the means to repair your time machine you are quite on your own. Surely as a time traveler of the highest order you must realize the necessity of self-reliance."

"Of course I do", said Pelletier. "My companions and I are doing everything in our power to repair our craft. Perhaps you could give us just a little assistance."

"I'm powerless to help you", said Deanira. "Until Narena decides to aid your journey through time and space, consider yourselves marooned."

"Are you holding us prisoners then?" Expecting Deanira to answer his question honestly, Pelletier gazed directly at her.

Deanira's answer was decisive. "If you can't find the means of escape from this domain then perhaps you are holding yourselves prisoners here", she said turning to leave.

"Wait" said Pelletier holding out an arm in desperate appeal to her. "Why are you doing this to us---why won't you help us?"

At first Deanira hesitated. She then turned, directly faced him, and decided to answer the question.

"Narena wants anonymity for her realm. She wishes to have no contact with the outside world. She's certain that your Golden Age is doomed— that you have neither the will nor the means to prevent catastrophe from happening."

"But that's not so" said Pelletier, who followed after her and tried to plead with her. Sarius, who ran alongside Pelletier was determined that his friend should not be left alone with Deanira, who surrounded by guards, continued to ignore Pelletier.

"May we meet with Narena?" asked Pelletier who was certain that he could bring the Siren Queen to her senses, and that she would supply them with the help they needed to repair the time machine.

Finally, Deanira hesitated. Turning to Pelletier she said, "Very well but I can't promise that such a meeting will accomplish anything." She then quickly turned away from him and surrounded by her guards, moved toward Narena's underground hillside fortress.

A huge iron gate opened for her so Deanira and her entourage could set foot inside the fortress. Pelletier rushed after them. Then, just as the fortress gate was about to lock behind him, Sarius, who'd trailed Pelletier shouted, "stop!" Rushing forward, he grabbed his friend's arm and pulled him to safety.

"Excuse me", said Sarius awkwardly. "We need to let our companions know where we're going. In fact, it would be inappropriate that Murdock, who acts as one of Queen Myaca's ministers, not to be present during such a rare visit to Narena's fabled realm."

"Very well" said Deanira who spoke from behind the fortress gateway. "Return to your companions. I'll lead you to Narena's realm when you and they are ready to follow me there."

Followed by her guards, Deanira disappeared into the hillside fortress leaving Sarius and Pelletier standing alone.

Sarius gazed at the closed gate. Sounding relieved, he said "Well that was rather rude of her just to leave us like that. What are we to do now?"

Pelletier realized the robot probably had prevented them from entering into what could have been a disastrous situation.

"Thank you", he said. "I think you've managed to stay one jump ahead of Deanira. Let's get out of here before she decides to open the door and extend an invitation to us that we can't refuse."

"I think it's becoming very clear that our escape from this strange domain is entirely in our own hands. The sooner we rejoin Murdock and Whitfield, and help them with the task of repairing the time machine, the better", said Sarius.

Whitfield, who saw his friends moving toward camp, got up from where he was so he could meet them. "Good heavens man", said the old physicist. "We went looking for you. Murdock and I were worried for fear that you might have been abducted. If you ask me, Narena's envoy didn't seem especially friendly."

"She invited us to accompany her into the hidden realm so we could meet with Narena. We declined the invitation", said Sarius.

"Yes", agreed Pelletier. "It didn't seem wisdom to accept such an invitation unless our esteemed friends were included."

"Well wasn't that considerate of you", said Murdock who was now standing alongside the professor. "We wouldn't want you to be abducted without us," he said laughing in his familiar molelike gurgle."

The rivalry between Whitfield and Murdock had been forgotten. In their desolate surroundings, the mole and physicist seemed almost appreciative of each other's company.

"Well, replied Whitfield, "I think I speak for Murdock when I say let's get out of here."

"But how are we to escape? We've repaired the machine's communication system, but the craft is still splintered and damaged. There's also interference being emitted from a source signal coming from the surrounding mountains." It might be risky as well as impractical to approach the signal's source to see if we could overcome the powerful vibes. Narena guards all entranceways to her most sensitive fortifications with sophisticated, deadly devices.

"There must be another way for us to block the signal", said Sarius. "There are caves within the surrounding mountainside. One may lead to the signal source."

"Look" he said pointing to a magnificent eagle descending in their direction. "There's the fabled golden eagle that penetrates the Dark Dimension and serves as messenger to other worlds."

The eagle, circling several times, flew toward the hillside and hovered above a cave opening there. Pelletier gazed at the bird through a pair of binoculars.

The sun's brightness was fast diminishing but the golden eagle seemed to outshine impending darkness. His magnificent image glowed like white fire outlined against the spectacle of a crimson sky, as he perched upon a craggy rock then swept down before the marooned time travelers.

"I believe the bird may have just shown us exactly where to find the signal's source," said Pelletier putting aside his binoculars. The bird returned to the craggy rock and remained perched upon it. Then with a lamenting cry he swept upward into the early evening sky and was seen no more.

"How can you believe a mere bird is capable of knowing where the signal source is?" asked Whitfield.

"Birds have uncanny instincts and are capable of traveling great distances to remote reaches within time and space. Is it said that the eagle will lead the lost traveler to safety. We should begin our ascent toward the cave as soon as daylight permits," answered Pelletier.

Darkness settled around the campsite where the incapacitated time machine reminded the travelers of their vulnerability to danger. The evening atmosphere grew still. The mountainside's dim outline gradually faded from view. Only the wind whispering between rock crevasses disturbed the silence surrounding them. Pelletier, who'd found himself unable to sleep, only hoped that the eagle had been pointing the way toward a path that would win their escape.

When dawn gradually invaded night's darkness, the first sight Pelletier gazed upon was the cave entrance half hidden by small trees.

"The cave looks different in the morning light", said Sarius who stood alongside his friend.

"If you ask me it looks like a tempting illusion", said Murdock who thought their present task of mountain conquest, might prove to be a waste of time.

"If we move at a steady pace, we should reach the cave entranceway within several hours", said Pelletier.

The sun grew high in the sky and Whitfield removed his hankerchief. Then mopping his forehead, he said. "We've been walking and climbing toward one landmark for several hours now. I don't believe we're any closer to it than when we first started climbing. Perhaps the object we're pursuing is an image in time so far away from us that it seems as though we're making no headway toward it at all."

Murdock removed his time traveling mirror that had been shattered when the time machine crashed. "I've been told that one way to repair a shattered device is to place the mirror in the sunlight at just the right time of day. The sun seems appropriately placed in the sky now for me to do so."

Murdock placed the mirror's shattered pieces upon the ground. Within seconds an unseen force brought the mirror's fragments together again. Quickly retrieving the mirror, Murdock held it up so that the mirror caught the sun's healing rays. Instantly a brilliant light encompassed the machine. Murdock knew the time traveling device had succeeded in cancelling the machine's historic confrontation with disaster. The machine now sat unflawed and whole upon the ground.

Pleased at his success, Murdock started to put the mirror in his pocket. He hesitated when he recognized a familiar image upon the mirror's surface. "Draw no nearer to the signal's source." The image and voice was that of Deanira.

"Your time machine broke apart because you wished to set foot in a place where battles never have been fought. Narena will be no part of a celestial struggle. If Menelus challenges Saturn's power, he'll be thrown to the dirt by Jove's thunderbolt. In the wake of his fall the warring planets' destruction by asteroids will follow. Myaca and her allies will then appear to be clear winners in the conflict but their victory will be a hollow one. The hatred that exists between the conqueror and vanquished will persist."

The image of Deanira then disappeared from the mirror's surface.

CHAPTER THIRTEEN

▼

Myaca sat upon her garden balcony and listened to melodious birdcalls. She then held out her hand so that Hadrian could perch upon her finger. "You who are so free must help me comfort one who isn't", she said folding up a message and giving it to the little bird so that he might carry it to Prince Sentius. Although Sentius had warned Myaca of the danger of contacting him, Myaca's loneliness had taken precedence over wisdom. Stretching out her arm, she watched as Hadrian flew from her hand, and soared into the heavens toward the Dark Dimension.

Being a devout sun worshipper, Sentius gave thanks for Hadrian's safe arrival. He then eagerly read Myaca's message. "The chariot of the sun will bear you from the Tower's darkness. Only then will we be reunited and the tear within time's peaceful fabric mended." Sentius first fed Hadrian with scraps from his own meal. He then placed the bird in a secure place so Hadrian could rest in a cage before beginning the arduous journey home to Myaca.

The following morning, Hadrian carried Sentius' message to Myaca. He soared into the sky until he'd left the dark dimension and was reunited with Myaca who read Sentius' message.

*   *   *   *

"Vorelis must be summoned at once", thought Myaca who walked down a long corridor until she stood before the time traveling mirror. Within minutes, Vorelis had been summoned and stood in her presence.

"Sentius has contacted me", she said showing Vorelis the message Hadrian had brought her. "Orbutus and Hal must at once prepare to rescue my husband and our friends from the Dark Dimension. If our friends penetrate Narena's palace, their fates may be sealed and they'll never return to us."

Vorelis was thoughtful. He wasn't sure if either Hal or Orbutus was ready to penetrate the Dark Dimension. "The Dimension has hidden barriers and hurdles", he said. Instinctively Vorelis knew his own expertise under such circumstances might be superior to that of Hal or Orbutus.

"I will penetrate the dark dimension and rescue our friends from danger. The journey under my protection is yours to participate in as well," he said. "There is no time to waste. We must leave as soon as possible."

Skeptical at the prospect of stepping into the unknown, Myaca hesitated. "I can't leave my domain. If Prince Sentius tries to contact me and discovers I'm not here, he might think that I'd again been abducted by Menelus. Bowing to Myaca's wishes Vorelis allowed her to accompany him along a corridor leading to the forbidden room. He watched as Myaca trembling reached into her pocket and removed the key unlocking the room's door. After entering the room, Vorelis walked to a window and opened it. Beneath the window was the spiral staircase. Vorelis knew the staircase was the one Sentius must have traversed. When Murdock's time machine crashed, a source within the Cloud Temple told Vorelis that Deanira had presented Sentius with a fragment from it. Sentius wanted Myaca to know about the disaster that had befallen Murdock and his companions. He had risked his life when he entered the forbidden room and left the fragment there for her to find. When Sentius was found missing from the Dark Tower, his progress was traced to the forbidden room. He was then heavily shackled and forced to return to the Dark Tower. Vorelis carried the burden of that knowledge with him as he began his grim journey

"Be careful dear friend" said Myaca bidding Vorelis good by. She watched as he fearlessly descended the staircase.

*   *   *   *

As Vorelis set out on his mission to rescue the stranded time travelers, Murdock seemed confident that he had matters under control. Certain that the time machine was as good as new, he was eager to return to it so he might inspect it. "Let's forget about that distant cave. It appears to be too far from us. The time machine is our only hope for a ticket out of here."

Although Pelletier agreed with Murdock, he refrained from mentioning why. Neither he nor Murdock's other companions, dared mention that one of the delicacies enjoyed most within Narena's realm was giant mole. Prepared with just the right sort of spicy sauce and cooked at the right temperature, mole was a tempting dish for the flesh hungry inhabitants of Narena's realm.

Hurry, he said urgently insisting that everyone follow him. Soon the travelers found themselves standing before the time machine.

"Look" said Whitfield who could hardly believe his eyes. "The machine appears to be as good as new."

"Thank heavens", said Murdock who'd insisted on revving up the engines to see if the machine was properly tuned and was in the same perfect condition it had been in just seconds before its breakup. "It seems everything is in proper working order", he said finishing the test and stepping from the vehicle.

"We must make haste. The Queen will be concerned for our welfare," said Pelletier.

Even though the travelers were famished nobody dared mention food until Murdock broached the delicate subject. As his comrades busily reloaded the machine's cargo hold, Murdock went about the task of handing out strictly vegetarian rations to everyone,

Then, after they'd quickly finished their meal and were ready to depart, Whitfield wiped his brow and said, "I've increased the time machine's low level vibrations. Let's hope that will block the negative vibrations Narena's forces might send out to block our escape."

"It looks like you've finished the job just in time too" said Pelletier who saw Narena's cohorts, her so-called defenders of the realm, fast approaching them.

"They don't look too friendly," said Whitfield.

"They aren't the same crowd we saw earlier", said Sarius who could see they all carried spears and were wearing moleskin uniforms.

"Let's get out of here", shouted Murdock.

Whitfield and Pelletier quickly took command of the time machine. Murdock and Sarius were relegated to the rear compartment. Sarius, nearly overcome by stress, desperately pretended to be calm, and asked Murdock to reboot him. Murdock had no sooner finished rebooting Sarius when a large hostile creature nearly succeeded in tearing poor Murdock from his seat. Only Sarius' valiant effort in holding onto his dear friend saved Murdock from being left behind in the dust where he was certain to become prey to the desperate creature lying prostate on the ground but with one hand still clinging to the time machine.

"Are you all right? shouted Whitfield, who dared turn his back only for a moment to see if Murdock was still with them. The time machine was experiencing terrific interference but as determined as Narena's cohorts were to bring the time machine down, Whitfield was just as determined that such a disaster wouldn't happen.

A sonic boom was heard followed by a radiant splash of light. When the glowing light grew less intense and the humming noise had decreased, Whitfield knew he'd saved the moment.

Murdock, who'd passed out during the traumatic ordeal, lay slumped over in his seat. Sarius patted the mole's face and tried to bring him around. "It's all right my friend. We're out of harm's way now."

"I've set a course for Myaca' domain", said Whitfield. Within minutes, the time machine bounced a couple of times, lurched forward then went sliding through grass, and toward a golden pear orchard before coming to a halt

Relieved by the quick escape from danger and for the safe landing, Murdock thanked Whitfield for a job well done. "I couldn't have done a better job if my life had depended on it" he said trying to ignore the fact that he'd nearly been abducted, filleted and made into mole stew.

"Come", said Pelletier leading the way. "We must find Queen Myaca at once and tell her of our near brush with disaster."

"I think the Queen already knows", said Sarius who'd recognized Myaca's envoys approaching them.

An envoy stepped forward greeting the arrivals and said, "The queen is very anxious about your recent brush with disaster. We've been told to escort you to her immediately."

Sarius, who was feeling rather heroic for having saved Murdock's life, felt a surge of robot pride swell within him. Turning to Pelletier he said, "You know for years I've submitted real life account articles to ROBOT LIFE. They've always been rejected. Perhaps this time when I write about our daring experiences within the Dark Dimension, they'll take my work more seriously."

Seeming subdued after all they'd been through, Pelletier smiled slightly. At last when he saw Amelia again and she'd heard of his recent adventure, she perhaps would look upon him more favorably. "Sometimes running away is the only option one has in life", he thought as he and his companions entered Myaca's palace.

"Thank goodness you are alive and well. I thought you were lost to us", said Myaca extending a hand in warm welcome to her visitors. I never should have allowed you to embark on such a dangerous journey. I never expected that Narena would greet you in such a cruel and callous manner. How dare she refrain from according my distinguished representatives the hospitality they're due."

Thoroughly humiliated by the entire episode, Murdock wanted to tell Myaca, that as her distinguished representative he'd nearly met his doom. Sarius did it for him.

"Murdock was nearly dragged from the time machine and left behind", said Sarius who didn't hesitate to tell the Queen that it was he who'd saved Murdock from the clutches of an enemy.

Myaca smiled sympathetically and commended Sarius on his bravery. She then took Murdock's furry elbow in her own, and escorted him and his companions toward a reception area where food and drink had been prepared for them.

With a worried expression on her face, she said turning to John, "Vorelis is on a mission to Narena's realm. It must be cancelled. I'll dispatch Hadrian with a message for him immediately".

"Hadrian, who's he?" asked Pelletier who wondered if Myaca had friends in high places that he didn't know about.

"I'll introduce him to you" said Myaca. "I always carry his picture with me." She then raised her hand and touched the shiny surface of a tea table as the bird's computerized image suddenly appeared on the table's surface. "I often call upon Hadrian for his help" she said calling the bird to her through cyberspace. Within seconds the little bird flew from his gold cage. He made his way along a palace corridor before landing upon Myaca's shoulder.

"This is Hadrian", she said. "His service is indispensable to me. He never fails to serve me with distinction." She then asked that a robot guard bring her a piece of royal stationery and a pen so she could write Vorelis a note; "Return immediately. Follow dear Hadrian. Further penetration of Narena's realm is unnecessary. The time travelers have returned safely." Signed Myaca.

A robot butler served her guests food and refreshment while Myaca prepared Hadrian for his mission. Then with the carrier pigeon perched upon her shoulder, Myaca walked along the corridor, past the portraits of her ancestors until she stood in front of the door leading to the dark dimension. Taking Hadrian from her shoulder, she opened the door's room, walked to the window within the room and opened it. Then giving him the message for Vorelis, she said,"Fly swiftly and deliver this urgent message to our friend Vorelis." Silver wings like flashes of light, moved above the winding staircase leading to the Dark Dimension. So swift was his travel through time and space that Hadrian's shadow could hardly keep up with his form. .

When he finally found the magician, it was none too soon. He flew around Vorelis until he'd gotten his attention. The bird then dropped Myaca's message in front of him: Hadrian watched as Vorelis bent, picked it up from the ground and read it.

Vorelis then reached into his pocket for his time traveling device, sure that it would instantly transport him into Myaca's presence. He was shocked to discover that it was useless. He now understood the full meaning of Myaca's message. "Follow dear Hadrian. He will lead you on the journey back to your friends."

Daylight was dwindling. The forest was now deep and overwhelming in its primeval darkness. Hadrian's bright and silver wings provided light for Vorelis. The bird first circled the magician then flew ahead of him only to return to him, encouraging him to follow him along a chosen path.

Since he was used to finding his way out of almost any impossible situation, Vorelis felt reluctant to follow the carrier pigeon. But Hadrian's insistence was such that he made sure the magician never strayed from the designated path. He circled Vorelis or grabbed his cloak with his beak until the magician saw a clearing. Finally Vorelis recognized the steep steps that connected the Dark Dimension with the secret window, and Myaca's palace.

With Hadrian still leading the way, Vorelis then ascended the spiral staircase that led to the open window and secret room. From there, he was led along a palace corridor to a reception area.

"I assume you know everyone present", said Myaca, who surrounded by her loyal friends, welcomed Vorelis into their midst. "Thank goodness Hadrian found you in time", she said as Hadrian fluttered about her.

Would you care for some refreshment?" she asked as the little bird settled upon her shoulder.

"Why thank you Madame. I must admit that I do feel rather thirsty after what has seemed to have been an incredibly long journey."

"Thank goodness you've safely returned to us, she said smiling then handing Vorelis a glass of iced pomegranate tea.

"I'm afraid my schedule won't permit me to stay long. There are friends elsewhere in time and space, who need my support and assistance right now."

Certain now that there was no interference from the Dark Dimension to block his passage, Vorelis reached into his pocket for his time traveling device. He raised the mirror to the light. With a slight bow he was gone.

CHAPTER FOURTEEN

▼

Amelia wept tears of relief when Vorelis unexpectedly popped in for lunch at the farm and told her the good news. "Your father and his companions found their way back through time and space. They and are now safe and secure within Myaca's palace."

"Does that mean the mission to mount an assault upon the Dark Tower and rescue Prince Sentius is scrubbed?" asked Hal.

"No" replied Vorelis. "Suffice it to say that we have learned from the mistakes of Murdock and his companions. We'll proceed as planned. The time machine crashed near the Dark Dimension because the sirens emitted from Narena's realm caused the craft to break up. The machine's delicate structure wasn't strong enough to withstand the waves of vibrations that buffeted the craft. Where machinery may have failed, man and beast may yet succeed. Orbutus has already probed the region surrounding Narena's realm. He is familiar with the dangers there. He has returned unscathed. The door to the underworld kingdom lies open to you and Orbutus. The opportunities for conquest await you."

"Are you serious?" asked Hal incredulously. With a look of horror upon his face, he nearly choked on the sandwich he was eating.

"I think the idea of rescuing somebody from a Dark Tower is preposterous," said Amelia. Whoever heard of an elephant and a team of horses taking part in an assault upon a dark dimension? Natasha may be good at what she does but she takes her time. She isn't known for any speed records. As for the horses, from what I've observed, they perform best when they're in a friendly circus environment. Loud noises make them skittish. If Narena's sirens are as powerful as you say they are, they might frighten Natasha and the horses too."

"Trust me my dear", said Vorelis taking a polite sip from his soupspoon. "Conquest is certain. The elephant and horses won't fail. The dark dimension will be penetrated. Prince Sentius will return to those who wait for him."

Hal quickly threw down his napkin, got up from the table and excused himself, leaving Amelia sitting alone with Vorelis.

"No" said Amelia. "We've gone along with your games of pretending long enough. I'm not sure what we're acting out here but these little delusions we've been drawn into have interrupted life's normal flow long enough. Hal and I want to get on with our lives. We have a future together", she said, bursting into tears.

"Future? What sort of future are we talking about if it isn't a future entirely held in consciousness", replied Vorelis. "You have the opportunity to reject evil both now and in the past. You must act now to insure what happiness you might have in the future. Don't let life or love slip away from you. Don't allow selfish pursuits to take priority. Live for today and tomorrow." Amelia started to get up from the table and leave but hesitated. She stared as Vorelis as he slowly uttered, "I can see I'm not welcome here today".

He knew it was no use trying to persuade Amelia that the ride into the unknown might bring Hal greatness. Amelia just shook her head and started to cry. Vorelis stared down at the bowl of soup he'd been enjoying. Amelia then left the room and hurried out to the pasture where she knew she'd find Hal. He was standing with Natasha and he spoke to her as if she understood him. He leaned across the fence, patted her great trunk and said, "Are you ready to cross the sky again?"

Hal loved Natasha. She'd brought him and Amelia together. She was part of his family. He knew he'd never forgive himself if something unforeseen happened to the elephant. What if the Dark Dimension's high frequency noises hurt her sensitive ears or destroyed her equilibrium, and sent her plummeting toward the ground and certain death? He hugged her great trunk. Natasha's life seemed almost more precious than his.

"We don't have to do this", he said. "You and I, have a good life here. Whatever happens though, we will be together. If we succeed in the mission we're about to undertake, it will be because we love and trust each other."

Hal continued to embrace Natasha's trunk until he noticed that Amelia was standing next to them.

"May I come too?" she asked. Natasha answered the question for Hal. In an answer "yes": She raised her trunk and trumpeted a wail of exultation.

The following morning, a slight mist hovered over the grass surrounding the farm sanctuary. Orbutus, who'd risen early had already fed his horses and was working on a new circus routine with them. In an opposite pasture, Hal and Amelia sitting atop Natasha watched as the elephant busily ate the flowers from a wild shrub she'd discovered growing just inside the pasture. Vorelis, who'd decided not to leave, had spent the previous evening with the Worthy family. He'd watched as Natasha took Hal and Amelia with her on her morning grazing ritual. Wearing in his lapel a flower he'd plucked from Jaime's garden, Vorelis seemed unusually cheerful. "I guess you aren't planning on helping us with the farm chores", said Hal.

"I wish I could stay and help out. I need to be getting back to my office at the Circus of Wonders. I just wanted to advise Orbutus regarding his latest circus routine. I've time to help you and the elephant work on a new act too."

"Natasha is retired from circus life now", said Hal. "We were just letting her take us on a leisurely ride around the farm. I don't think we want to go anywhere right now.

"I'm afraid the gods may have other plans for you today" replied Vorelis. "I've just been contacted by Jove. He says the solar system alliances are awaiting your departure for the Dark Dimension. The matter concerning the rescue of Prince Sentius will wait no longer. The matter's urgency is made even more apparent by the fact that Whitfield has already done his part. He's solved the mathematical formula that is prelude to your assault upon the Dark Tower. In fact, the problem's solution was so simple that Whitfield is quite embarrassed. He's been asking himself, 'Why didn't I think of that before?' In other words, Whitfield's professional reputation is on the chopping block. Before he departs in embarrassment from the Primary Institute for Advanced Study you must do something to pump up his reputation. You have to make a practical application of his proof."

"Now wait a minute", said Hal. "What sort of a fool do you think I am? I'm not about to go riding off into the sunset looking for a way to conquer the universe."

"We're talking about the solar system here Hal—just the solar system", replied Vorelis. "Besides you won't be alone. Orbutus is ready. He and his horses are waiting momentarily to soar into the beyond."

Vorelis bowed as if he were standing before a Circus of Wonders audience. He then reached into his pocket so he could remove his time traveling mirror. He began going through his magic and light routine. The landscape surrounding them seemed to slowly disintegrate as Hal and Natasha became the focus of the routine.

"Oh no" cried Hal. "We're not ready yet." Vorelis ignored the protest. Natasha stopped eating the flowers off a shrub. She began levitating above the dissipating landscape.

"Tell Natasha to stop levitating at once", said Hal who watched Orbutus with his horses and chariot, race just ahead of them.

"I can't" cried Amelia who was still aboard Natasha too. "When Natasha gets the notion into her head she's going to do something, there's no stopping her."

Hal gazed downward. The hazy outline of terrain appeared almost surreal.

"I should have told mother that we wouldn't be home for lunch." Hal knew they were embarking on the journey they'd planned and talked about but were afraid to take. In the distance, he could see Orbutus. The magnificent team of chariot horses made its way toward an enormous cloud bridge: It spanned the heavens surrounding them, and connected the gap between one dimension and another.

Orbutus reigned in his horses. He allowed Natasha, whose ancestors had preceded chariots in carrying the gods into the heavens to take the lead. The magnificent horses first reared then circled the elephant. Suddenly the clouds surrounding them formed a sort of stairway. Natasha raised her trunk. With a bellow of triumph, she stepped onto the bridge. The caravan then ascended toward the rising sun as pink clouds like cotton candy encompassed them.

Natasha crossed onto the pink sky bridge with the same dexterity she'd displayed while performing a circus stunt. She'd danced upon the clouds as if she were dancing in a circus arena.

Hal and Amelia gently patted the elephant's great head as she fearlessly continued to plod into the beyond. "Good job Natasha", said Amelia bending over and resting her head against Natasha's brow. Hal leaned forward and continued to encourage her as well. "We're all in this together", he said. "There's no turning back now".

Orbutus pulled his chariot team alongside them and he said, "Once we descend the bridge, we'll be in Narena's domain and exposed to destructive siren vibrations. There's no way to drown out that music."

Hal, who'd thought he already heard faint music replied. "Yes there is".

He reached into his pocket and produced an ipod Vorelis had given him as a parting gift. "This device contains the recorded music from all of Natasha's known circus routines. If we play our music loud enough, it will calm the animals, and drown out other vibes."

"Let's try it." No sooner had Orbutus gotten his words out than the strains of soft, soothing, intoxicating, harmony encompassed them. "We're nearing the end of the bridge said Orbutus who ahead, could see land looming.

"If those melodic chords are notes of welcome, I don't feel at all threatened" said Hal who felt progress so far hadn't been hindered.

"The music is sublime", agreed Amelia. She felt as if unseen angels were leading the way.

Even the animals responded to the music's sweetness. Natasha emitted low grunting noises usually reserved for communication only with other elephants. The horses whinnied and neighed as if they were laughing among themselves.

The musical comedy didn't last. The listeners soon heard discordant siren vibrations. The shrill super sonic siren emissions caused the horses to shy and Natasha to raise her trunk in anguish. She bellowed a trumpet protest. Hal, who was nearly overcome by the cacophony, experienced such pain to his ears that he was almost incapacitated. His trembling hands groped for the ipod so he could drown out the dreadful music. Then with his fingers struggling with the controls, he pressed a small button. Strains of circus music flooded the surrounding atmosphere.

Once Natasha heard strains of familiar accompaniment, she relaxed, skipped and even waltzed to the music as she made her way across the bridge followed by the prancing and dancing chariot horses.

"I guess it's all a matter of who plays the loudest tune", said Hal who knew he'd succeeded in blocking the dreaded siren noises.

The Cloud Bridge had dipped down to the ground. The travelers were within a hundred feet of land. "Look, said Amelia pointing ahead, "We may have thought we were making our way toward Narena's realm. The Cloud Bridge has led us elsewhere." The land before them was the continent of Mu.

"Everything looks different from the way I remember Mu to be", said Amelia dismounting and sliding down Natasha's truck. Hal now stood beside her, and waited for Orbutus to step from his chariot and to join them.

"What do you make of it?" asked Hal who knew they were standing on the plains of Mu just prior to its final destruction.

Orbutus stared in disbelief, unable to utter a word. Amelia answered for him.

"We may have jumped from the frying pan into the fire."

"Yes", agreed Hal. "Our journey has led us to the Dark Tower he said pointing to the strange monstrous looking architectural landmark that served to represent the darkest evils of the solar system. "The Tower is inaccessible. The land around us is sinking. If Mu sinks into the sea from the devastating effects of floods and earthquakes, the Tower may be one of the few remaining landmarks suggesting Mu ever existed", said Hal, his face grave and pale. Only Orbutus offered a solution to what now appeared to be grim reality.

"The clock must be turned back. The event must be erased from history. That's why we're here. I think we're too late to turn back the clock", said Hal, growing both impatient and frustrated. "We can only do what we've come here for. We must rescue Prince Sentius from the Dark Tower, find the grail and return it to its proper owner".

"If we succeed in achieving the tasks set before us. If we free Prince Sentius and discover the grail there is nothing to stop us from erasing the dread event of solar system destruction too" said Orbutus.

Hal wasn't so sure. "The task rests neither with us nor with the gods. We've found the path to annihilation for which the solar system is headed. We're powerless. The events of history may be changed only if men and beings implement their change."

Orbutus's expression was grave as he considered Hal's remark. "We all have a universe within us. Let's hope that universe of peace and good will toward our fellow beings will cancel devastation's image, and cancel the dread event. We've got to try even if it seems impossible.

"The door stands open. Let's make ready the conquest", said Orbutus mounting his chariot and beginning his ascent toward the tower.

"I can't let him do it alone. Orbutus needs our help" said Hal who signaled for Natasha to follow in the chariot's path

Natasha bravely hoisted Hal and Amelia aboard then fearlessly trumpeted their progress toward the Tower.

"Look" said Amelia pointing at the landscape beneath them. "The sea surrounding the tower is receding. It now appears to be on dry land."

"Time has receded", said Hal, "Sentius is still held prisoner within the tower's deadly time capsule. We have to move quickly before history's tide changes, and the Tower is inundated."

Hal dismounted from Natasha. "Don't try to follow me inside. If my attempt to rescue Sentius leads to my own imprisonment then you must find Vorelis and bring him to my rescue." In dread, Amelia watched Hal enter the tower. She knew, John Pelletier was reputed to be as great a time traveler as Vorelis. For the first time in her life Amelia wanted to reach out to her father and call him to her side. Why wasn't he standing with her now as Hal set out in search of Sentius? Unbeknown to her, Pelletier was already within the Tower.

John knew exactly where the grail was hidden. He'd successfully disarmed most of the booby trap devices surrounding it: Only one other booby trap device remained undisarmed. Pelletier knew that final device was connected to Sentius' rescue. The device was programmed to go off and explode killing Sentius if he ever left the tower. Pelletier also knew, since he didn't have time to warn Hal before he reached Sentius, he would somehow have to find the device and disarm it before Hal tried to free the Prince. Pelletier's hands shook as he wiped the nervous perspiration from his brow, and groped forward through the darkness.

Hal continued to move up the stairs toward the place where he'd heard the voice of Sentius so many months earlier. Sentius had been moved to another tower location. After he'd visited the Forbidden Room and left the fragments from Murdock's time machine for Myaca to find, he'd been moved. He was now heavily shackled. Pelletier tried to call to Hal and warn him to stop. His voice echoed within Tower walls so many times that it was unintelligible. Hal continued on his way and with every step, drew closer to his own doom.

At least 30 tower stories separated the two men. Pelletier now stood in front of the heavy iron layered enclosure that encased the gold box containing the grail. Pelletier knew there were only two ways to get at the grail. One was to pry open the iron enclosure containing the grail. The other offered a less resistant method. Fortunately, Pelletier had discovered within the lost city's library, a secret combination that would unlock the box's layered enclosure and reveal its treasured contents. Within minutes he had successfully disarmed the deadly device surrounding the grail. He then leaned over and picked up the gold box containing the sacred grail. His hands trembled as he gazed at what he'd found. He dared not examine the grail. Pelletier knew Hal and Sentius were in danger. He had to warn Hal that Mars was present within the Tower ready to block the rescue of Sentius.

Thirty stories still separated Pelletier from Hal. Being the consummate time traveler that John was, he would bridge the gap between them.

John was aware that contained within the Tower were wormholes that if manipulated properly, could grant immediate access from one story to another. His first attempt to scale the Tower's heights ended in failure. In the fifth and final attempt, he found himself standing in the same room with Hal and Prince Sentius.

"Let's get out of here now" said Pelletier who saw that Hal had done nothing to free Sentius from the room where he was being held prisoner. Gold shackles, preventing him from moving freely, were attached to the Prince's legs. "I don't dare remove the shackles", said Hal. "The Prince has told me that if I do, a device will activate. There will be an explosion killing us all."

"The device has been deactivated. There's nothing now to prevent us from getting out of here as quickly as possible" said Pelletier. Then using a hammer he'd found lying on the floor in another room, he quickly broke apart the shackles and set Sentius free.

"Follow me", he said. "There's a wormhole exit leading from the left that will have us on the ground momentarily." Little did John realize that when he and his comrades found themselves once more outside the Dark Tower, more trouble stood in the way.

Amelia, who still sat atop Natasha, screamed as two of Menelus' guards with spears in hand lunged toward her and Natasha. She knew they had every intention of bringing Natasha down. Natasha reared and bellowed a wail of terror as they approached them and tried to force Amelia to dismount. Just as one of the men was about to plunge an object resembling a spear into her hide, Natasha's great trunk sent him tumbling about thirty feet away. She then turned and began to flee in terror as Amelia pleaded with her to stop.

"We've got to find Hal and rescue him. We can't leave without him". Natasha understood what she meant. The elephant also understood the law of the jungle better than Amelia. Their lives were at stake. They had to find an alternative way to rescue Hal. Two other men tried to pursue her but Natasha moved away from them until another assailant rushed toward her and tried to pull Amelia down from behind her back. Natasha then sent him hurtling into the air before he finally landed in a pile of seething igneous, volcanic rock.

Amelia held tightly to Natasha as the elephant drew away from the conflict unfolding before their eyes. Prince Sentius had finally confronted Menelus. They fought in combat. Orbutus, Hal and John Pelletier were engaged in another contest. They were succeeding in overthrowing Menelus' cohorts when Pelletier, with his time traveling device sent the enemy hurtling off into another dimension.

When Orbutus realized that Prince Sentius must be rescued from the life and death struggle with Menelus, he ran toward the chariot where his tethered horses reared and pawed the ground in terror. Quickly untying his horses, Orbutus mounted the chariot, and began driving it toward Sentius and Menelus. "Run for it", he shouted as Sentius ran for the chariot and Menelus, who pursued him, tried to block his attempt to board it.

Fortunately Chamelon, the team's stallion, had other ideas. He swiftly kicked Menelus aside, and allowed Orbutus to pull Sentius aboard. The team then drove off leaving a stunned Menelus stretched upon the ground.

Amelia watched the chariot team hurtle across land before levitating into the sky. She then realized that she and Natasha had to rescue Hal and her father just as Orbutus and his chariot team had rescued Sentius

"Hurry Natasha" she said prodding her onwards. "We've no time to lose." Within minutes, Hal and John were safely hoisted aboard Natasha and she moved steadily over land.

Quickly glancing over his shoulder, John said, I think we're being pursued. Menelus and what remained of the men who'd fought with him were following them. They had mounted swift horses and were trying to overtake them.

"What shall we do now father?" asked Amelia who saw the men were closing in on them.

"Hal answered for him, "I fear the greatest threat we're now facing may not be from Menelus and his cronies. Mu is beginning to subcumb to its final destruction.

"What are you talking about?" asked Amelia. "Jove said Mu's destruction wouldn't take place if we solved the perfect equation."

"Apparently we've failed in the equation's practical application" said Hal who gazed down at the gold box containing the grail. "Jove has struck the Earth with his thunderbolt.

Amelia knew she'd been ignoring disaster. She and her father both knew that Mu's total destruction was eminent. "A peaceful solution to the problems that face the solar system has failed", said Pelletier. "The only hope now is that some of Earth's other continents where pockets of colonization have taken hold will continue to prevail on the road toward a better civilization. If we can reach the Cloud Bridge, we might be able to make our way to one of Earth's more habitable continents.

"The earth is beginning to cave in", said Amelia gazing downward and seeing Natasha nearly stumble into a fissure formed by the earth's separation.

John reached into his pocket for his time traveling device. "The device is useless to us right now. The vortex leading to other dimensions has been blocked by war and conflict within the solar system. Only the grail may help us during this crisis time.

Turning the box over and raising its shattered mirror to the sun, John called upon the Divine Source to shield them from their enemies. Just as a brilliant light touched the shattered mirror and mended its pieces, herds of wild animals converged together and raced toward the Cloud Bridge. Animals of all kinds, intermingled with human survivors of the cataclysm. They moved in an orderly progression toward what appeared to be deliverance from a hellish scenario. The teeming herds of animals and people now stood between Natasha, her passengers and what remained of Menelus' approaching forces.

"Look" said Hal pointing ahead in the distance. "The chariot bearing Orbutus and Prince Sentius has made it onto the Cloud Bridge. "We must make it onto the Bridge too or we may disintegrate before we reach it."

Within minutes, Natasha who'd been levitating above the scorching earth, set foot on the great Cloud Bridge: It spanned the entire sky and offered passengers the only hope left for salvation. Swiftly Natasha moved forward and led herds of animals as well as throngs of people. Among some of the last species to move on to the bridge were several hippopotamus families. Frightened and exhausted their short legs and enormous weight had prevented them from keeping up with everyone else. Just behind the lumbering hippo stragglers followed Menelus and his cruel entourage. They'd been busy picking off any animals that might pose a threat to them as they crossed the Bridge. Now the hippos offered one more target opportunity for the cruel game hunters.

One of the hippos let out a squeal of anguish as a cruel dart meant to prod him forward burned his sensitive hide. Menelus, who grew even more impatient with the slow moving hippos, finally reached into his pocket and removed a ray gun so he could immediately liquidate the beasts. Before he could pull the trigger, the portion of the Cloud Bridge on which he and his cohorts traveled gave way beneath them. Menelus and his cronies fell hundreds of feet below into the fiery craters as floodwaters were beginning to engulf what was left of the continent of Mu. The slow moving hippos, oblivious to the fact that they'd just escaped annihilation, continued to lumber across the Cloud Bridge

Days seemed to pass. The Bridge's passengers were hungry and exhausted. There was no chance to stop and rest. Natasha was growing weak from the trauma and ordeal of the adventure. With words of encouragement from Amelia she bravely continued. Then when it seemed as though the passengers moving across the Cloud Bridge could move no more a land bridge was sighted. The Cloud Bridge gradually descended toward ground. A narrow land oasis provided food and water for the exhausted passengers en route to a new continent and a new home.

After Natasha helped her passengers dismount. Hal raised his hand and pointed to a welcome sight. On the distant horizon, was something resembling a green haze. "Land", he whispered. "I believe that must be the coast of Africa. The continent of Mu may have perished but Earth's other lands have survived the cataclysm. Animals and humans alike may start life anew," said Pelletier

"Thank heavens" said Amelia who rested her head on Hal's shoulder as he embraced her. Pelletier then turned to his daughter and Hal and congratulated them for their stalwart leadership in leading them all—animals and humans alike across the Cloud Bridge to safety.

"Amelia embraced her father. For the first time, father and daughter seemed united in a family bond. Then turning to Hal, Pelletier said, "You saved the moment. Thank you for helping to rescue Prince Sentius."

I think we have Natasha to thank too" said Hal reaching forward and embracing her trunk. The elephant emitted a low grunting sound as she acknowledged the sincere attention she was enjoying from those gathered around her. Then under Amelia's watchful eye, she began grazing alongside other wild animals on long green grass and foliage.

"Let's not waste time", said John, "As soon as Natasha has grazed and taken water from the oasis, we need to move forward. This land bridge could give way and send us plummeting into the sea if we don't reach the continent of Africa soon."

Hal agreed. Even the animals and small bands of human travelers who'd crossed the Cloud Bridge with them were eager to reach the vast continent which lay ahead on the smoke enshrouded horizon.

Once more Natasha hoisted her passengers aboard. As they rocked from side to side behind her great ears, she swung her tail and trunk back and forth with the satisfaction of knowing that she'd succeeded in doing her job well.

Within less than a week, the tired survivors of a catclysm stepped onto the continent of Africa and began their search for new homes and habitat.

"We may have been unable to save Mu from destruction but perhaps something positive has emerged from the tragic event we've just witnessed," said Hal.

"What do you mean?" asked Amelia whose eyes filled with tears at the thought of the destructive scene they'd left behind.

"Perhaps men will learn that they shouldn't take this planet or any planet within the solar system for granted. We have a responsibility to ourselves and other living beings to care for the environment. When we humans make war upon each other or destroy the natural habitat of other beings we eventually find ourselves without any place to live."

After Hal finished speaking, Natasha reached up with her trunk and helped her passengers dismount. Amelia was the first to set foot on terra firma. Kneeling down, she kissed the pristine African shoreline. Then standing upright, she gazed behind them.

Huge arks bearing humans and animals alike were headed toward the African coast. "Thank goodness those who care about their fellow man and fellow beings weren't left behind", said Amelia who watched as the arks pulled ashore and unloaded their cargo full of eager passengers.

Antelope, deer, lions, leopards, cheetahs, wild dogs, hyenas even snakes, alligators and lizards, with the help of the human passengers who'd accompanied them, had made it safely ashore. Within hours most of the animals had disappeared over the sand dunes.

When Natasha saw a herd of elephants that had crossed the Cloud Bridge behind her, she bellowed a triumphant welcome. Seeing Natasha's eager acknowledgement of them caused Amelia to turn and take hold of Natasha's trunk.

"Freedom awaits you". Go with them if you wish, dear friend. Just remember that I love you. I will never forget your friendship."

For a moment Natasha hesitated. She watched longingly as the herd crossed beach and dune. She started to follow the herd: She was just a few feet away from disappearing into it, when she drew back and returned to Amelia. The two friends stood reunited with one another. As she hugged Natasha's trunk again, Amelia wept tears of relief and joy to realize that her dear friend wished to be part of her human family once more.

"While I guess that settles that. It looks like you're staying with us," said Hal.

"Natasha may be staying with us but I think we'd better get moving", said Pelletier who'd noticed that water was fast retreating from the shoreline.

"Move to higher ground", he shouted in warning to other nearby human survivors. The recent cataclysm on the other side of the world had produced tidal waves.

Fortunately, most of the animals, as if sensing danger, had already disappeared over the sand dunes and were already on higher ground.

The human occupants who'd beached the arks and unloaded as many supplies as possible left them behind, and began running too.

Natasha, once again hoisted Hal, Amelia and Pelletier aboard before she quickly made a run from impending doom. She crossed beach and sand dune and was steadily making her way toward higher ground when the great tidal surge began to close in on them. Encouraged by Hal, Natasha raised her trunk bellowed one time, and began levitating above the water that now was sweeping ashore in a turbulent torrent.

"I think we're probably among the last to reach higher ground said Amelia who watched as human survivors looked up in surprise as Natasha levitated above them.

"Let's keep moving inland", advised Pelletier. "The surge may have receded but another might follow in its wake."

Within less than an hour, Natasha descended into a protective valley surrounded by high land.

"Dear Natasha, whatever would we do without you?" said Amelia who knew without the elephant's great levitating skills none of them would have made it to the mountain's opposite side.

"I guess we can call this place home", said Amelia dismounting Natasha then bursting into tears.

"We've made it. Let's not look behind", said Hal putting a comforting arm around Amelia as they slowly walked along together. They stopped and watched Natasha eat the heads off flowers that grew wild within the verdant valley. Seeming peaceful but bewildered by the terror they'd left behind, the image of Mu's final destruction was with them-- all even Natasha.

John hung his head in despair. Amelia gazed after her father then turned to Hal. "We've failed. We've even managed to lose Orbutus and Prince Sentius. We're lost. Goodness knows how or when we'll find our way out of this distant time and back to our own era in history."

"We may have failed to save Mu", said Hal "but we've got the grail. Somehow I feel certain that Orbutus is going to be able to find us. He wouldn't leave us alone with the grail when he knows how important it is to the future of the solar system.

Besides, there are always time traveling options for future solar system salvation. History can be replayed."

"What do you mean 'replayed'?" Amelia knew she never wanted to return again to Mu, not even under the most favorable circumstances.

"The gold box we have in our possession not only contains the grail; it's a guide for the living he said examining the outside cara maya inscriptions engraved upon the box. If we precisely follow the instructions upon the gold box, we will be guided in the right direction toward peaceful solutions to all problems regardless of the era."

Amelia didn't want to hear anything more about peaceful solutions. She shook her head and said."We're marooned!" She began to cry again. "Fate has abandoned us."

"No it hasn't". Orbutus startled everyone when he drew his chariot and horses alongside them. "The gods intervened. Who do you suppose sent Menelus and his cronies plummeting to their deaths when they were ready to annihilate the hippo population?"

"So it was you who caused the Bridge to sag and break off", said Amelia who looked at Orbutus wide eyed.

Orbutus stepped down from the chariot. He then introduced Prince Sentius who having stepped from the chariot too, stood before his friends.

"I'll never be able to thank you enough for your brave rescue of me."

"I think we have John Pelletier to thank more than anyone else", said Hal. His genius and quick thinking helped the rest of us get you out of the Tower. Our total mission was accomplished when he found you and retrieved the grail."

Sentius bowed slightly to Pelletier. "Your valor will be recognized."

John smiled offering Sentius the grail who took it from his hands. Sentius then removed the back panel from the grail and revealed a device enabling them to be transported through time and space."

In seconds they stood in the presence of Queen Myaca, who was standing in her royal garden.

At last Sentius embraced his wife who could only say, "I knew you'd come home."

The chariot horses reared. Natasha trumpeted the Prince's victorious return with a wail of victory. Everyone else applauded his joyeous return.

A short time later, when the friends gathered together in celebration of Sentius' victorious return, Murdock burst in upon the scene. He produced a bottle of his own vineyard champagne and ordered a robot butler to bring them some glasses so he could propose a toast to the time travelers' safe arrival.

Following the toast, Myaca, turned to everyone and said, "Come, we have unexpected visitors."

Both Jove and Saturn had been watching the time travelers' progress. As Sentius, and his rescuers, presented Myaca with the coveted grail, the gods congratulated them on a job well done.

"But we failed" said Hal seeming happy to be alive but despondent over a botched attempt to salvage sinking empires.

"Mu hasn't been devastated", contradicted Jove. "The great continent and all the planets that appear to have undergo irreparable damage, will someday rise from the ashes and begin life anew."

"I don't see how that's possible". We watched from the Cloud Bridge, and saw missiles and asteroids tear the continent of Mu apart."

"You also captured the coveted grail that contains within its gold encasement the secret of the future."

"We never opened the box containing the secret", said Hal.

"You didn't need to. The courage you displayed in the face of resistance to your effort to save the grail from those who would destroy it hasn't gone unnoticed. Only those with the heart of a lion and the meekness of a dove could have successfully undertaken such a task and won."

Myaca then crossed the room, and placed the grail upon a table. Taking a key from her pocket, she unlocked the sealed box. It was empty.

"We've failed", said Hal.

"No we haven't. There is hope", said John. "Whitfield has discovered a proof for the perfect equation. He should be part of this celebration. The equation for a better world has been discovered. Its enactment is up to individuals to implement".

Myaca was silent. She didn't answer John. Instead she gazed across the room where the Martian evening was beginning to close in upon the light of day. She walked toward curtains made from a 17th C tapestry, and drew them as far apart as she could. "The light still envelopes us" she said a little sadly. Then turning toward her guests, she said smiling, "Won't you join us for dinner."

Myaca led her guests toward the state dining room where a lavish meal of Martian fruits and vegetables had been prepared for her guests. A robot butler pulled out a chair for Amelia so that she could sit down between Hal and her father.

"The meal you've prepared for us looks marvelous. The fruits and vegetables are some of the largest I've ever seen. Would it be possible for our friend Natasha and the horses to partake of some of this bounty too?" asked Amelia

"I've forgotten neither Natasha nor Orbutus' fine horses. They're partaking of a meal of equal abundance", said Myaca.

During the meal, Myaca asked her guests how she might reward them for the service they'd just performed for her and Sentius.

Amelia gazed down at the gold plate in front of her. Then, picking up her gold fork and eating a delicious chunk of red melon, she said. "I think we'd like to go home."

Myaca gazed across the table at Orbutus, who appeared grave and silent.

"I shall miss my friends" he said, "My loyalty remains here with you", he replied solemnly.

"You needn't be separated from your friends nor end your contract with the Circus of Wonders. You are free to travel back and forth through time to visit you friends here as well."

Orbutus smiled broadly. "I am always at your service should duty ever call, Your Majesty."

Myaca again smiled before saying, "It's encouraging to know that one has such loyal friends." Then picking up the magnificent gold box, she handed it to Pelletier. "Your heroism saved my husband."

Politely bowing in gratitude. Pelletier passed the box to Hal and Amelia. "This box is one that should be passed from one generation to the next. Perhaps someday you can give the grail to Nick.

Turning to her guests, Myaca led them toward an open palace door. "It's time for you to leave us. The horses and elephant are in the royal gardens patiently awaiting your return. Within a few minutes you should find yourselves in familiar surroundings. She and Prince Sentius then made their way up palace steps and along a magnificent corridor. Everyone else remained behind in the garden except John Pelletier. He accompanied Murdock as he followed Queen Myaca and Prince Sentius into the palace.

"Aren't you coming home with us?" cried Amelia who'd expected her father to remain with them. She was disappointed to realize he had other plans.

John turned. In a voice loud enough for everyone to be sure of the message, he replied, "Don't worry, I'll be in touch."

Amelia started to follow her father but Hal caught her arm. "Let him go. He's a time traveler. He's got to live his life the only way he knows how."

They then stood together and watched as Pelletier disappeared into the palace.

"Are you sure our friends are of no further use to Your Majesty?" asked Murdock who hated to see them go. She didn't answer him. Myaca glanced at Murdock then at Pelletier whose face appeared drawn and sad. Drawing aside a curtain revealing a time traveling screen, she touched it. Immediately her friends found themselves home, and standing in the center of the cow pasture.

With Hal and Amelia still on board, Natasha began meandering in a familiar pasture corner. The horses, now unhitched from the chariot gently cantered over to a nearby fence and interacted with the friendly hens in an adjoining pasture. Having now dismounted from Natasha, Hal placed his arm around Amelia's shoulder. Accompanied by Orbutus who walked behind them, they began walking toward the house. Nick, who'd been playing ball in front of the house, ran toward his father and hugged him. "Where've you been, dad?

"Sorry we missed lunch" said Hal.

"Lunch! You've missed days, Dad. Grandmother's been worried about you."

"Here", said Hal who held out the gold box so that Nick could have a look at it. "We brought you home a present. Someday when you're old enough to understand, we'll let you have it."

Nick inspected the gold box then said to his father. "You visited that far-away place again didn't you, Dad?"

"We took a small detour through history", said Hal who knew his son was beginning to understand something about time travel.

"Did you go to the place Grandma visited when she was young?" asked Nick who couldn't take his eyes off the beautiful box with it curious inscriptions.

"You visited Mu didn't you?" Hal gently ruffled the little boy's hair. Taking the child's hand in his he said, "You'll visit that place someday. Right now you need to grow up so you'll be ready for the journey."

Jaime, who'd been standing on the front porch watching her son's approach walked toward him and embraced both Hal and Amelia before saying, "Welcome home."

She didn't bother to ask them where they'd been. Intuitively she knew they'd taken the journey into time and returned with the coveted prize.

Nick handed his grandmother the gold box. "Dad brought this home with him. He says someday I can have it." Jaime took the box from Nick's hands. She then walked onto the porch where she sat down on the porch swing. She gazed at the cara maya inscriptions etched into the box as Nick standing next to her said, "It's a special prize"

"Place the gold box next to the sundisk in your grandfather's study", she said to Nick. "He and my father will want to examine it."

Jaime then left her family and their friend Orbutus who'd now gathered in the living room of her home. She left the house and began walking through the field toward the place where she'd found a strange sundisk so many years earlier. The late afternoon air was still. Only the chirping of crickets or the somber lament of morning doves hiding in the tall grass surrounding her could be heard. Jaime knew the sundisk had opened doors. She also knew, once she'd learned to decipher the sundisk's strange writing how easy it had been to become lost in a labyrinth leading to distant times and places. Now her son had found a second prize. He too had become a time traveler. Another piece of the puzzle had been solved and put in its proper place", she thought. "The serpent coils in the sun where mother earth opens to the sea" she said aloud then smiled faintly. Jaime relished her moment alone with her memories. She felt something tug at her. She turned to see if someone was standing behind her but no one was there.

She walked back toward the house where she knew the reality of the present awaited her and where the future awaited her children and grandchildren.

Endnotes

Chapter One

1. Chucara means "House of the Sun". Based on documents of Garcilasco de la Vega. Robert Charroux, ONE HUNDRED THOUSAND YEARS OF MAN'S UNKNOWN HISTORY (NEW YORK, 1970), pp. 41, 50 and 61

2. The circle was one of the first three symbols used in man's religious teachings. It was looked upon as the most sacred of all symbols. It was a picture of the sun called Ra and was the monotheistic or collective symbol of all the attributes of the deity . . . The sun is found depicted on the stones of Polynesian ruins, on the walls of the Temple of Sacred Mysteries in Egypt, Babylonia, Peru and all the ancient lands and countries. . . It was a universal symbol. James Churchward, THE LOST CONTINENT OF MU (New York, 1968), p 114.

Chapter Two

1. Ovid refers to a Golden Age and its fall. Ovid's METAMORPHOSES, Vol. I , Bk. I, trans. Frank Justus Miller, ed. T.E. Page, E.Capps, W.H.D. Rouse (Cambridge, Ma, 1916), pp. 128-131.

2. James Churchwards, THE CHILDREN OF MU (NEW YORK, 1968), pp. 136-137

3. Ibid, p.112

4. Ibid, p. 110-114

Chapter Three

1. Harlow Shapley, OF STARS AND MEN (Boston, 1958) pp. 47-48.

2. Edmund Harold, FOCUS ON CRYSTALS (New York, 1986) pp. 9-13.

3. Ovid's Metamorphoses, trans. Rolfe Humphries, Bloomington, Indiana, p.368.

4. James Churchward, THE LOST CONTINENT OF MU, (New York, 1968) p.114

5. She (Queen Moo) visited the Maya Nile colony in Egypt during the first century of its existence, 16,000 years ago as related in the Troano manuscript. Ibid p. 232.

6. Mu sank about 10,000 B.C. James Churchward, THE CHILDREN OF MU (New York, 1968), p 54.

7. Ibid. p. 84

Chapter Five

1. Birds are messenger symbols from a lost land. Francis Maziere, MYSTERIES OF EASTER ISLAND (New York, 1968), p.65. Birds as symbols of Creation involve law and order and are found in ancient Mexico, the lore of the American Indian and in ancient Egypt. James Churchward, THE CHILDREN OF MU (New York, 1968), pp.61-62

Chapter Six

1. The equilateral triangle came out of the geographical make-up of the Motherland consisting of three separate areas of land, which were geographically called the Lands of the West. Jame Churchward, THE LOST CONTINENT OF MU (New York, 1968), p.118

2. The tau was a universal symbol. It is found in the writings of the Hindus, Chinese, Chaldeans, Incas, Quiches, Egyptians and other ancient peoples. Ibid, p. 122.

Chapter Seven

1. James Churchward, THE CHILDREN OF MU, (New York, 1968), pp. 222

2. James Churchward, THE LOST CONTINENT OF MU, (NEW YORK, 1968), p. 147

Chapter 8

1. WORKS OF LACTANTIUS, Vol. I, trans. W. Fletcher, (Edinburgh, 1899). p.39.

Chapter 9

1. Ovid's METAMORPHOSES, Bk II, trans. Rolfe Humphries, (Bloomington), pp. 28-49

Bibliography

Berlitz, Charles. ATLANTIS. New York, 1984.

_____. THE BERMUDA TRIANGLE. New York, 1974.

Charroux, Robert. ONE HUNDRED THOUSAND YEARS OF MAN'S UNKNOWN HISTORY. New York, 1970.

Chatelaine, Maurice. OUR ANCESTORS CAME FROM OUTER SPACE. Garden City, 1978.

Churchward, James. COSMIC FORCES AS THEY WERE TAUGHT IN MU. New YORK, 1968

_____. CHILDREN OF MU. New York, 1968.

_____. THE SACRED SYMBOLS OF MU. New York, 1968.

_____. THE LOST CONTINENT OF MU, MOTHERLAND OF MAN, NEW YORK, 1968.

Goodman, Jeffrey. AMERICAN GENESIS. New York, 1981.

Greene, Brian. THE ELEGANT UNIVERSE. New York, 1999.

Harold, Edmund. FOCUS ON CRYSTALS. New York, 1986.

Johnson, Donald. THE PHANTOM ISLANDS OF THE ATLANTIC. New York, 1996.

Maziere, Frances. MYSTERIES OF EASTER ISLAND. New York, 1968.

Ovid. METAMORPHOSES. Trans. Rolfe Humphries. Bloomington, 1964.

_____. METAMORPHOSES. Trans. Frank Justus Miller, ed., T.E. Page et alii. 2 vols.Cambridge, Ma, 1916.

Santesson, Hans Stefan. UNDERSTANDING MU. New York, 1970.

Savoy, Gene. ANTISUYO: THE SEARCH FOR THE LOST CITIES OF THE AMAZON. New York, 1969.

Shapley, Harlow. OF STARS AND MEN. BOSTON, 1958.

Stemman, Roy. ATLANTIS AND THE LOST LANDS. London, 1976.

Tompkins, Peter. MYSTERIES OF THE MEXICAN PYRAMIDS. New York, 1976.

THE WORKS OF LACTANTIUS: ANTE-NICENE CHRISTIAN LIBRARY. Trans. William Fletcher, Ed. Rev. Alexander Roberts and James Donaldson, Vol I. Edinburgh, 1899.